Water Wishes

Bound By Tides

Book I

By
Freya Aguiar

Cover design by Freya Aguiar.

ISBN 979-8-9990602-0-4 (Hardcover)
        979-8-9990602-1-1 (Paperback)
        979-8-9990602-2-8 (Ebook)

Printed in the United States of America.
First Edition.

Dedication

Aliyah & Kora, my twins who aren't twins, my very wishes come true, your bond inspired this story. Your laughs encouraged its continuance. I hope you see yourselves in the best parts of Atlantis Bay.

The Weighted Oath

Inscribed in the Hall of Tides

The crown is not a circlet fair,
But grief wrapped tight in salted air.
It binds the brow, it seals the fate,
It weighs the heart beneath its weight.
I chose the sea. I chose the throne.
I chose the realm above my own.
No love is held without a cost—
For what I keep, I know I've lost.
The tide takes all, both blood and breath.
It favors law. It honors death.
So judge me not, if I must drown
The voice that cries beneath this crown.

Prologue

The Queen stood at the helm, statuesque and unmoving, while the world around her thrashed in fury. The storm was unlike anything she had conjured or weathered. She guided the illustrious wooden ship as it tore through towering waves, carving a relentless path forward. The sky and stars were gone, swallowed by an unearthly storm. She stood as the only beacon in the darkness, power churning through her veins and glowing beneath her skin in ripples of emerald light. Rain poured in sheets, cascading off her chiseled form. She did not flinch. Below, the sea raged toward something long buried, a girl not yet awakened but already at the center of its storm.

Lines clanked and snapped against the mast, entangled in winds that warred with themselves. Along the hull, the ornate carvings writhed like they were alive, shadows twisting them into monstrous forms. The crew reefed the sails with frantic precision, not to save themselves, but to preserve the kingdom's most sacred vessel. Even now, they feared disappointing her more than drowning. They'd seen what her sorrow could summon.

From the corner of her eye, the Queen saw the Commander stagger up from the lower deck, drenched and pale, her hand sliding along the slick guardrail as though she were a child clinging for balance, not the decorated officer she was. Her eyes betrayed the message before her lips opened.

"They're gone," the Commander said, her voice slicing through the wind like a blade.

The Queen turned, slow and deliberate in her movement. "What do you mean, 'they're gone'?"

"We cannot find them anywhere, Your Majesty." The woman kept her voice steady, but her gaze faltered.

"You are certain the entire ship has been searched? Not an inch overlooked?"

"Yes, Your Majesty. Positive."

The Queen stepped closer. "Then tell me, Commander: how did they vanish without a trace? Without help?"

The Commander's face drained of color. The Queen saw it, the truth forming behind the fear. Still, she did not press. She had no time for confessions. She swept past her, storm-blind and resolute, striding toward the control room as the sea raged louder. Behind her, boots pounded. A shout rang out, and then came a splash.

The Queen did not turn. She did not need to. The Commander had flung herself into the sea.

One ship had been missing from her armada that afternoon. She had noticed, but ignored it. She had been distracted, consumed by the mission, and worn thin by the constant strain of cloaking the truth. Hiding the child, and what her birth meant, from both allies and enemies had taken a toll. The magic required to keep the secret had begun to falter, and with it, her focus. He had known. He had watched the heartbreak spread like rot beneath the surface, slowly eating away at her resolve. Then, swift as a seabird taking flight, he escaped.

The storm mirrored her grief, rising up around her. The sea didn't crash. It howled, like it remembered something it was never meant to. A voice threaded through the wind, low and wordless, not quite human. It fed on her pain, her fury, and her unraveling restraint. The line between her power and the weather blurred until she could no longer tell which force responded to the other.

She startled the young operating attendant when she opened the carved wooden doors of the control room.

"Connect me to the *Rivermaiden*," she said.

The attendant's blue eyes widened for a moment before she quickly turned the dials, fingers flying in practiced motion. When the connection clicked into place, she held the receiver out awkwardly, her posture stiff with uncertainty. The Queen reached out, calm and precise, and took it without a glance.

"I want Captain Ondina," she said, her voice sharp and clear.

"It's me," a deep voice crackled back.

"How did you get on the *Rivermaiden*?" she demanded. A rare quiver slipped into her tone.

"I can't say," he replied softly.

The Queen dismissed the attendant with a tight nod. The girl turned and hurried out, her footsteps quick and uneven as the door thudded shut behind her. For a moment, the Queen stood in silence, brushing her hand across her bare neck where the necklace had once rested. Her fingers lingered. She turned back to the radio.

"And the baby?" the Queen asked, her voice barely above a breath.

"She's with me," came the reply.

"Bring. Her. Back," the Queen commanded, with each word sharp as a blade.

"I can't do that. I won't."

"How could you do this?"

A long silence followed.

Then, softly, "She's our baby."

The Queen bowed her head. Her jaw tightened. The wind outside screamed against the glass. "I will find you. Both of you."

She placed the receiver down with precision, though her knuckles were white. One hand braced against the counter; she bowed her head. The storm roared louder, as if it had heard her vow.

He had betrayed her. Made her swear that awful promise. Bound her to it. Forced her to drag out the pain, refusing to let her end it. She could feel the promise burning against her skin, carved into her soul like salt in a wound.

But if she was bound, so was he.

Her face hardened. Determination surged. She reached inward and offered up the sacred bond, the thread that once tethered her to him, sealing the ancient spell. It splintered with a pain that echoed through her bones. She knew he felt it too. No matter how much time might pass, the spell would hold. And the promise would be fulfilled.

She would ensure that fate by calling upon all the might of the sea, all the power she had to give. The sound of static filled the room as ancient words spilled from her lips, carried on silver-blue wisps. The mist swam around her before escaping through the cracks in the hull, racing out into the open sea. It traveled fast and far, searching.

As the spell left the Queen, it consumed the last of the storm's energy. The wind, once howling, softened to stillness. The waves that battered the ship grew calm. The sails fell slack, and the ship no longer groaned under pressure. Outside the control room, the sea leveled, quiet and reverent, as if the tempest had never been. The silence that followed was thick with power. The storm had not broken. It had bowed.

She stood tall once more.

CHAPTER ONE

The Long Road

Bay woke up burning hot.

Her forehead had been pressed against the car window, and now the sun was slowly roasting her. She peeled her cheek from the warm glass, squinting at the triangle of light pouring in. With a groan, she rolled away, grabbed the sweater tied around her waist, and wadded it into a pillow against the pile of luggage in the middle seat. Stretching out across the worn leather, she tried to fall back asleep.

But the oldies playing up front made it impossible. Her wireless headphones had died hours ago, and of course, she'd forgotten the charger. Izzy had warned her. "My parents love the radio. Commercials and all," she'd said, rolling her eyes with the weariness of someone who had suffered through decades of dad jokes and '80s tunes.

They were just crossing into northern Oregon now, and the trip was everything Bay imagined a normal family vacation would be: cheesy pit stops, terrible music, annoying siblings, and a station wagon packed to bursting. Honestly, she loved it.

Bay adored the Plowmans. She often imagined what it would be like to be part of their family. In her mind, she fit in. Even though she didn't look like them at all. She had sunlit blonde hair and golden skin, with deep charcoal-black eyes that didn't match anyone else's in the car. At fifteen, she was petite and wiry, almost elfin next to Izzy, who was nearly a head taller despite being four months younger.

Izzy and her brother James looked just like their dad, with chestnut curls and warm brown eyes. Kelly, their college-aged sister, had inherited their mother's sleek black hair and angular features. The whole Plowman gene pool was blessed with good looks.

And lately, Bay had started noticing just how attractive James was, though she'd never admit it out loud. Definitely not to Izzy. She knew her best friend was tired of classmates and tagalong girls crushing on her brother. Some had even faked friendship just to get close to him. It was a sensitive topic, and betting their friendship on it wasn't just risky. It was reckless.

Luckily, Kelly was away at college this spring break, and that left a coveted open seat on the Plowmans' annual road trip. Izzy had acted fast. Really fast. To fill it.

"Please, Mom? Bay has no plans. What, you want her to sit home alone?" she had asked, dramatically clutching Bay's shoulder and shaking her head in mock pity. Bay, mortified, had stared hard at her shoes.

Mrs. Plowman raised a brow. "Izzy, let's chat in the living room, shall we? Bay, will you excuse us for just a moment?"

Izzy returned minutes later, grinning like a goblin who'd just gotten away with a prank.

Bay groaned. "Izzy, you totally put her on the spot!"

"She gave me The Look," Izzy replied with a finger wag and theatrical scolding voice, "'Please don't do that again!' But, hey—it worked. You're coming." Then, with a wink,

"Besides, I think she didn't want James to ask first. Ben creeps her out."

Every inch of the faded red station wagon was packed to the gills. Camping gear filled the trunk, groceries and blankets were stacked like Jenga pieces, and a bike rack crammed four bikes onto a rack meant for three. Somehow, Mr. Plowman had also managed to strap two coolers and a collapsible canopy to the roof.

Bay had the middle row mostly to herself if you didn't count the luggage mountain beside her. Izzy and James were wedged in the back row like reluctant sardines.

For over two hours, Bay had tried and failed to nap, mostly to escape hearing "Brown Eyed Girl" for the hundredth time. But then she heard the magic words.

"Well, it looks like this construction's going to hold us up for at least an hour," said Mrs. Plowman, sounding weary. "I'm hot and tired. What if we take a detour and stop at Cannon Beach for a picnic?"

Bay froze. Her heart slammed against her ribs. She gripped the seatbelt strap without thinking, her pulse roaring louder than the radio. The air shifted. Just slightly. A strange warmth rolled through the car, carrying the scent of salt and something older. It reminded her of rain on stone. No one else seemed to notice. But Bay did. Her fingers tingled against the nylon strap. The word beach rang in her ears. It felt heavier than it should, like it meant something more.

"Hmm..." Mr. Plowman considered. "Might actually save us time. We could take the 101 the rest of the way. Nice coastal views. And yeah, a break sounds pretty good."

Bay held her breath. Cannon Beach. The actual ocean. She had never been to the beach. Ever. To be more accurate, she was strictly, absolutely, and unequivocally forbidden from going to the beach. Growing up, her dad had tried to make up for it with malls, camping trips, and baseball games—all of them landlocked activities. But his rule about the ocean had always felt absurd. Worse, it had no explanation.

She wasn't allowed near lakes or pools. Didn't know how to swim. Couldn't even eat seafood. Watching *Finding Nemo*? Forget it. Ocean documentaries? Off-limits. One time, when she was six, she had to explain to an entire sleepover why they couldn't watch *SpongeBob SquarePants*. The shame still haunted her.

When she was thirteen, he refused to let her go to the class bonfire on the California coast. That was the last straw.

"Why, Dad?" she had asked in desperation. "Why can't I go to the beach?"

He had said nothing at first, just stood and walked into his room, but returned shortly after. He had pulled the faded photograph from his dresser, which was a picture Bay knew well—her mother's face. Heart-shaped and glowing, nearly identical to Bay's own, except for the eyes. Her mom's were ocean blue; Bay's were pitch black.

"Atlantis—" he began, before correcting himself. "I mean, Bay…"

Her full name was Atlantis Bay. When she was little, he'd called her Atlantis, but she had banned that name in grade school. It never felt like her. Bay was her. Bay was simple. Real.

"You can't go to the beach because your mother was lost to the sea," he said, his voice cracking. "And I can't lose you too."

"Lost to the sea? What does that even mean?" Bay had demanded. "Did she drown? What happened? Why won't you tell me?"

"I... I can't," he said, his voice fraying. He sat down heavily on the edge of the bed, elbows on his knees, burying his face in his hands. "You just can't go, Bay. Please. Don't ask again."

She had never seen her father like that, so hollow and undone. So, she hugged him and said nothing more. And she never asked again. But the questions never stopped gnawing at her.

A month ago, when Izzy invited her on this trip to central Washington, Bay's dad had insisted on calling the Plowmans to confirm their route. Bay knew what he was really doing, checking to make sure there were no beach stops.

And there weren't. The plan had been to take Highway 5 straight up. Until now. And this time, she wasn't going to let it slip away. Her fingers still tingled, and the salty aroma still hung in the air. She pressed her forehead to the glass, and for just a second, she thought she heard the faint call of her name. She blinked and brushed it off, but the sound clung to her like a thread she couldn't quite pull free.

CHAPTER TWO

The Ocean

Bay's heart pounded in her ears as they took the off-ramp. Trembling, she slowly inched her way up in her seat and looked out from the edge of the car window so that only her big, black eyes peeked out. Izzy and James were still sound asleep in the back seat, and their parents were chatting idly about directions while the car wound through twisting forest roads. Meanwhile, Bay was actively willing the water to come into view.

She feared that if she breathed too quickly or moved too fast, her chance to see the ocean would vanish again. Something inside her knew the ocean held a missing piece of her past, something more than what her father had told her. She needed to see the water. She needed to know about her mother. Somewhere in the tide, in the hush between waves, she hoped to hear the truth she was never told. She needed to understand the pull in her chest, the ache in her head every time she thought of the sea. No matter how it might hurt her dad, Bay had to know.

Finally, after a long tree-lined curve, the ocean revealed itself, shimmering like sparkling diamonds beneath a pale blue sky that stretched out forever. She watched, wide-eyed, mesmerized, drawn in. The sea called to her, sang to her, as if whispering her name. Her whole body yearned to run straight to its edge.

Something deep inside of her snapped taut, a thread she hadn't known was there, straining against her skin as if it might tear her open.

A strange pulse shot through her chest. Her skin prickled. For a fleeting second, she thought she felt something inside stir awake.

Ding. Her phone buzzed. The spell broke. Bay sighed and glanced at the screen. A text from her dad. Then another, and another. Then the phone started to ring.

Frantically, she switched it to silent mode. She ignored the call and tucked the phone under her leg, hoping no one had heard. Luckily, the Plowmans' music and conversation drowned out the noise. They still thought she was asleep.

A moment later, Mrs. Plowman's phone rang in the front seat. Bay froze.

"Hello, Trent... We... Oh, I see... Um, well, we were just going for a quick picnic. We can ask Bay not to go into the wa— Oh. Okay."

Mrs. Plowman paused, listening. Bay could hear her dad's frantic voice on the other end.

"No, no, it isn't any trouble. We didn't have this on our agenda anyway. No, none of the kids are even awake. We were going to surprise them with the picnic. We can just keep going. Uh-huh. We'll be staying at the Oasis Lodge in Vancouver just like we planned. No, we won't stop at the ocean... Okay, she's asleep, but I'll have her call you when we get to the hotel. Goodbye."

"What's going on?" Mr. Plowman asked.

"We need to turn around," Mrs. Plowman replied. She turned to glance at the back seat, checking to see if any of the kids had heard. Seeing all their eyes closed, she lowered her voice. "Bay's father still has a big problem with the ocean. You remember Izzy saying his wife died at sea? I bet that's why he wanted to check the itinerary. He was making sure we weren't stopping anywhere near the coast."

"His wife passed years ago, though. You'd think... Wait, how did he even know we were going to the beach?"

"He must be tracking her phone with parental controls."

Of course, Bay thought. How could she be so stupid? She should've turned her phone off.

"Well... what should we do?" Mr. Plowman asked.

"Greg, let's just turn the car around and head to the hotel."

"She's fifteen, Jill! Don't you think this is odd?"

"Yes, but she's his only child. Remember how we were with Kelly before James came along?" she added with a soft chuckle.

"True..." Mr. Plowman said as he turned the car around. "Remember when she fell off the couch and we took her to the emergency room?"

Bay's attention snapped from the Plowmans' conversation as a familiar cold tingling started to rise in her, pulling tight across her skin. She clamped her hands together, trying to calm herself. Trying to push away the hollow ache gnawing at her chest.

It had been just Bay and her father for as long as she could remember. No mother, no grandparents, no other extended family. Her father, Trent, had been the only child of elderly parents. Bay had never known his mother, who passed away

15

before she was born. Her grandfather was a quiet, distant man who either disliked children—or simply disliked Bay; she had never been sure. He died when she was six and had hardly been present before that.

On her mother's side, there was only silence. The only thing Bay knew was her first name: Allura. She didn't know her mother's last name, where she had lived, or what she had loved. Whenever Bay asked, her father would shrug as if he didn't know, or didn't want to remember.

It felt deeply unfair. How could she grow up with half of herself missing? How could her father look at her, love her, and still keep her past locked away?

Bay knew he loved her. He was sensitive, kind, and thoughtful. And yet, there was always a sadness in his eyes when he looked at her, an ache that mirrored her own. But beneath that sadness, something else lingered. Something he would never speak of.

For years, Bay had lived with a gnawing sense of isolation, as if she carried a heavy, frozen darkness inside her. Sometimes, without warning, the cold would rise, an icy grip wrapping around her ribs, squeezing until she could barely breathe.

When she was young, she would wake up shivering, crying out for her dad. He would come running, wrap her in blankets, and rock her back to sleep. He took her to doctors who always said the same thing: *Nothing is wrong.*

But the older Bay grew, the worse the episodes became. Eventually, she learned to hide them. She stopped calling out, stopped asking for help. Instead, she wrapped herself in blankets and waited for the freezing nights to pass.

Until one night, in the darkest corners of her mind, Bay found something else. A flicker of warmth. A pulse of light. It curled beside her fear like a sleeping ember. At first, she thought she imagined it, but the warmth stayed, whispering to her, You are not alone. I am here for you.

Night after night, when the cold crept in and the silence grew too heavy, that quiet spark spoke again. It had no name, so Bay gave it one: Light-Voice. It didn't just offer comfort. It argued with the dark. It hummed when Bay needed courage. It told stories Bay didn't remember learning and sometimes muttered sharp little remarks when she got too moody.

Bay never told anyone about her Light-Voice. When she was little, she feared someone might take it away, and with it, her fragile lifeline. As she grew older, she clung to it, fiercely, even if it wasn't real. Even if it was only something her mind had stitched together in desperation, it was hers.

And when the darker feelings came, so did the aching, hungry thing that lived somewhere just beneath her ribs. She named that feeling too, fittingly: Darkness. She felt like a yin-yang sometimes, held between two worlds, light and dark. And whenever Darkness curled too tight, Light-Voice always responded in the same way: *You are not alone. Not ever.*

Now, sitting in the back of the Plowmans' car, Bay felt the cold return. Stronger. Sharper than before. Burning tears slid down her cheeks. She squeezed her eyes shut, as if that might stop the ocean and the connection she had yearned for from slipping away again.

The pull toward the water was unbearable. Loneliness surged like a rising tide, fierce and primal, leaving her gasping for air. It felt like a grief she hadn't deserved but couldn't escape. She took long, steady breaths, concentrating her entire will on the tiny warmth still pulsing inside her.

You are not alone.

You are not alone.

You are not alone.

CHAPTER THREE

Of Light and Cold

I didn't know, Dad. For the hundredth time!" Bay's voice was exasperated as she spoke into the phone. "I was asleep in the back seat with my phone on 'Do not disturb'. No, Dad, please! I had no idea we were going to the beach!" Realizing it was pointless to keep arguing, even with lies, she sighed. "Okay." She set the phone down on the bedside table with a soft click.

Bay walked past the two queen beds and knocked gently on the connecting door to the Plowmans' room. The family had booked adjoining hotel rooms so the kids could pop in and out easily. Izzy and James had gone to their parents' room to give Bay some privacy for the call. Earlier, when they'd checked in, Mrs. Plowman had explained what happened at the beach and apologized for putting Bay in this awkward situation. She'd also said Bay's father wanted to speak with her right away.

"I'm sure it'll be okay," Mrs. Plowman had said kindly. "He's probably just worried and wants to make sure you're alright."

Bay had sat on the edge of the bed for a long time, staring at her phone. She knew it wouldn't be okay. The Plowmans didn't understand the depth of her father's aversion to the ocean. Every time she even mentioned it, he looked like he might blow a fuse, so hearing they'd gone near it had sent him completely over the edge.

When Mr. Plowman opened the door, the whole family looked up at her with concern. Bay lowered her gaze, fingers fidgeting with the chain around her neck. She hated attention, even on good days, and this was definitely not a good day.

"Um... my dad wants to talk to you," she said quietly, then added, "I'm sorry."

"Okay, kiddo. Don't worry. It's just a little mix-up—we'll get it taken care of." Mr. Plowman gave her a warm smile and stepped into the room, picking up her phone with an air of calm confidence.

Bay joined the others and sat beside Izzy at the desk, resting her head on her folded arms.

"I don't get it," James said, his voice sharp. "What's the big deal? It's just the beach. He's acting like she's a baby."

Bay's head sank deeper into her arms, the tension in her chest growing.

"James, don't be rude," Mrs. Plowman said sharply. Then she turned to Bay with gentler concern. "What did he say?"

Bay raised her head slightly, meeting her gaze. "He said he's on his way."

All three of them spoke at once, stunned.

"Here?" Izzy asked, eyes wide, clearly surprised.

"What the heck?" James blurted out.

"Now?" Mrs. Plowman added, her voice tense with disbelief. "What do you mean, 'on his way'?" The last words were slow and deliberate, as though she couldn't quite process the idea.

"He said I have to go home with him tomorrow."

"I'm sure you won't, sweetheart. Greg will calm him down," she said soothingly, but it didn't sound convincing.

"See, Mom? You should've let me bring Ben!" James groaned. "This is nuts. So now what? We just sit around in this hotel all day tomor—"

"Shut up, James!" Izzy yelled, hurling a pillow at him.

They launched into a full-on wrestling match as Mrs. Plowman tried to restore order. "These walls are paper thin!" she hissed, looking flustered.

Bay remained still, her head once again on her arms. She was humiliated, angry, and trying not to cry. The image of the ocean still filled her mind. The pull had faded, but not completely. A quiet throb vibrated behind her eyes, dull and rhythmic like distant waves crashing in her mind. Her fingertips tingled again, faintly but enough to know the ocean hadn't let go.

Mr. Plowman returned just as James had Izzy in a headlock, and Mrs. Plowman was mid-scolding.

"Ahem," Mr. Plowman said, clearing his throat.

Everyone froze. Bay lifted her head again.

"Bay, I'm sorry," he said gently. "Your father is already on his way to pick you up. He said... it's not safe for you here. That's all he'd tell me."

She nodded without speaking, afraid her voice might crack.

"He said he'll be here by eleven tomorrow morning, so we don't miss check-out."

"That's not fair," Izzy protested. "She didn't even do anything. Can't you tell him—"

"That's enough, Izzy," Mr. Plowman cut in, his voice firm.

"I'm sure Bay's father has his reasons," Mrs. Plowman said. "Why don't we all get some dinner?"

After fifteen minutes of bickering over where to go to dinner, the Plowmans finally decided to pick up some food and bring it back to the hotel. Izzy stayed behind with Bay. "I don't get it," she said again, lying next to her on one of the queen beds. They stared at the ceiling. "I still can't believe he's coming just because we almost went to the beach."

Bay stayed silent, her thoughts circling back to the ocean, how she'd felt a chill wash over her when the car had turned around.

"Do you think he's really coming?" Izzy asked hopefully. "Maybe he's bluffing. My parents always threaten stuff like that, but they never follow through."

Bay could feel the silent wish behind the words, almost hear Izzy hoping she wouldn't have to leave. Light-Voice gently nudged her out of her spiral: You should talk to her. She really wanted this time with you.

Bay turned to look at Izzy, who had always been a good friend—maybe a little hyper, a little much sometimes—but always loyal. Always caring. Bay loved the way her eyes lit up when something excited her. The freckles across her nose made her look younger, like a storybook character. But right now, her cheeks were pink with frustration.

She really is upset that you're leaving, Light-Voice whispered. *And it's okay to tell her the truth.*

"He really is on his way," Bay said softly. It hurt to say it, but it felt worse to pretend.

"I didn't think you were serious," Izzy admitted. "I thought you were exaggerating—like when I say my mom's gonna kill me over something."

"Nope. Not exaggerating." Bay sighed. "I'm really sorry, Izzy. You talked your mom into letting me come. I ruined your vacation."

"You didn't even know—" Izzy began.

"Yes, I did," Bay interrupted. She confessed about pretending to sleep in the car, ignoring the calls and texts. But she didn't mention how the ocean had called to her or how it still hadn't fully let go.

Izzy wrapped an arm around her. "You didn't ruin my vacation, Bay. I just... I wanted you to stay and hang out with us. Your dad is nuts." She grinned. "And, hey, at least we didn't have to bring weirdo Ben."

Bay laughed, finally. So did Izzy.

Her laughter faded into quiet, and for a moment, Bay stared at the ceiling, her heart still aching.

You haven't lost all of her, not yet, Light-Voice whispered gently.

And for the first time since the detour, Bay let herself believe it might be true.

CHAPTER FOUR

The First Crack

Bay woke up when she heard the knock and listened to the muffled conversation. Her dad must have been driving like a maniac, because he knocked on the Plowmans' door at 8:30 a.m. She sat up and slipped on her jacket as she heard Mr. Plowman welcome her dad into the room. While the two men exchanged awkward pleasantries, Mrs. Plowman excused herself to go into the kids' room and get Bay.

A thin crack of light seeped into the room as Mrs. Plowman entered. Izzy and James were still asleep, and Bay reached in the dark for her necklace on the nightstand. Her fingers found the small gold starfish, with an intertwined shield and sea serpent stamped on the back. It had once belonged to her mother. Her fingers curled around the warm metal, and a calmness rippled through her as she clasped the chain around her neck.

Bay got out of bed, scooped up the rest of her things, and headed out the door.

"Do you want me to wake Izzy up so you can say goodbye?" Mrs. Plowman asked in a whisper.

Bay shook her head no, unable to speak through the tightness in her throat. She didn't want to cause any more dramatics.

And with Izzy, goodbyes were always dramatic. She hated them.

When they were little, Izzy gave a long, mournful goodbye to her goldfish before a week-long camping trip. She cried the whole drive, swearing the fish had looked sad. When they returned, it was belly-up in the tank. A few months later, it happened again with her hamster. After that, Izzy decided goodbyes were bad luck. She said they made things disappear.

Since then, she avoided them like they carried curses.

Bay didn't mind. They'd had their moment the night before, and that was enough.

Mrs. Plowman gave her a small, pity-filled smile that made Bay instantly uncomfortable. It wasn't the sympathy she hated. It was the reminder of the way people looked at her when they thought they understood her situation.

Nobody understood.

As Bay's father carried her luggage to the car, she gave both Plowmans a hug and thanked them. She tried to apologize for the inconvenience, but they both shushed her and told her it was no trouble at all. There was no space in their kindness for the real tension that filled the air.

Bay, teary-eyed, followed her dad to his car in the parking lot, the burden of her frustration making it hard to breathe.

"Look, Bay, I know this seems…" her father started, as he got into the driver's seat, his voice tight with the exhaustion of a long drive.

"Crazy!" Bay finished angrily, slamming the passenger-side door as she sat down beside him. "I'm so embarrassed. Dad, how could you?"

"Bay," he paused and sighed. "You know the rules."

"I didn't break the rules! I was sleeping, Dad, and the next thing I know I'm at this hotel getting chewed out by you on the phone!"

He was quiet, his hands gripping the steering wheel like it might help steady him. "I shouldn't have taken a chance. I was worried something like this might happen."

"Something like what? A picnic at the beach? Dad, this is out of control!"

Her dad sagged in his seat, but she wasn't finished. Anger flared inside her, hot and wild.

You shouldn't be so hard on him, Light-Voice said, trying to soothe her rage. But Bay wasn't ready to listen. Not this time.

"This is ridiculous, Dad. I am not Mom. I'm sorry that you're scared of the ocean, but I'm not. I lost her, too, you know!" The bitterness in her voice rang sharper than she intended.

"You don't understand," her father said firmly, fatigue dragging at every word.

"Then make me understand!" she snapped. Her throat tightened; her eyes stung. She was unraveling.

Her dad turned in his seat to look at her. Something shifted in his gaze.

"You look just like her," he said. There was a distant look in his eyes, one that made Bay's stomach knot. The grief she had tiptoed around for years filled the car like seawater, heavy and unrelenting.

Take it easy on him, Light-Voice pleaded again, softer this time.

But Bay couldn't stop. The grief wasn't his alone to carry. She had her own. "That isn't going to work on me this time," she said, her voice trembling. "This is unfair, Dad. I'm not your little girl anymore."

"Yes, you are!" he snapped, startling her. His voice cracked with emotion, and, for a moment, his eyes flashed—not just with sadness, but with fear and anger.

She flinched. "Why are you mad at me?" she whispered. It slipped out before she could stop it.

Her father closed his eyes. Silence filled the car, thick and unmoving. Then, slowly, he reached into his shirt pocket and pulled something out. His movements were hesitant, almost reluctant.

He held out a photo toward her. She looked at it, annoyed, ready to dismiss it as just another picture of Mom, she thought bitterly. Another guilt trip. "I already know what you're going to say," she muttered. "That's a picture of Mom, and I know you're still so upset she died, but I—"

"You haven't seen this picture, Bay," he said, cutting her off. His hand trembled as he thrust it toward her. Then, with a sharp breath, he let it fall into her lap.

Bay stared down at the photo in her lap. It was a picture, but not one she recognized.

And then her father's voice, low and certain, shattered everything. "Your mom is not dead."

CHAPTER FIVE

The Story Beneath the Waves

ay held the picture as if it might catch on fire. Her breath trapped somewhere between her lungs and her throat. The car started, and her dad began the drive. Bay's hands trembled. When she finally dared to look at the photo once again, it made no more sense than it had the first time.

It was a snapshot of a sandy beach, warm and golden. A group of women were smiling, radiant and serene. Around them sprawled what Bay at first assumed were seals—sleek, colorful blurs in the background. But the longer she stared, the more her heart skipped.

They were not seals.

Mermaids? Light-Voice gasped, stunned.

The scales did not stop at the women's waists like in the movies. These rippling patterns spiraled upward, coiling across hips, ribs, and arms. Her mother sat at the center of the group, bronzed and beautiful, with long, sun-kissed blonde hair and a breathtaking salmon-pink tail. The scales shimmered far past her waist, curling over her shoulders like an elegant skating costume. Iridescent and dazzling, they glowed in oil-slick hues of sea-glass green and rose gold. Around her neck gleamed Bay's starfish necklace, with its ocean-blue gem at the center.

Bay's world tilted. "I... I don't understand. What does this mean?" she said, her voice thin, the photo trembling in her grip.

"Your mother is a mermaid," her father said quietly.

She is alive, Light-Voice whispered, awestruck.

Bay wanted to believe it. She wanted it more than anything. But she wasn't a little girl anymore. She was almost sixteen. Old enough to know when something sounded insane. Still, the way the ocean called to her. That pull in her chest. The ache of it. Could this be why?

It's true. I know it's true. Where is she? Light-Voice cried.

"Where is she?" Bay echoed aloud, without meaning to.

"Allura lives in a mer-city in the Pacific Ocean," her father replied, eyes steady.

"A mer-city?" Bay blinked.

"Enchanted villages," he explained, "where mermaids and their families live."

"Underwater?"

"Some, yes. Others are part land and part sea. A few are entirely above the waves but always close to the ocean."

"Have you ever been to one?"

"Yes."

"How do they stay hidden?"

"The entrances are enchanted. Invisible to humans. You can only enter if you've been invited or if you're merfolk. They don't appear on any map. To find one, you need a *siren stone*."

Bay tilted her head. "A what?"

"A *siren stone*. They glow green, like sea glass. They light a path for any mermaid in need. There's always one within a few miles of a mer-village, either on land or in the water."

Bay ran her thumb along the edge of the photo. "This feels... impossible."

"Mer-magic," her dad said, with a soft, sad smile.

She looked up, startled by the warmth in his expression. His eyes sparkled with something like relief, as though he'd been waiting for years to tell this story and finally could.

Bay's questions tumbled over each other, but he held up his hand gently, his eyes glinting with memory. He began to explain.

Mermaids were always born female, and each was gifted only one chance to bear a child. While they could give birth to sons, such births were rare and often shrouded in superstition. Many believed sons were not truly merfolk at all, but human. Even the most magical among them could not transform; that gift belonged to the daughters. Most females grew their tails easily, though a few struggled, caught between worlds. Adult mermaids could glide effortlessly between sea and shore, but the young had less control. Until around age ten, they could not survive fully submerged for long.

Bay was spellbound.

He told her how some mer-cities welcomed humans. Others stayed hidden. Some mermaids shunned humans entirely, seeking them out only to have children before returning to the waves. Others, like Allura, wanted more. A real connection. A family.

She traced the edge of the image with her thumb. "Did Mom enchant you? Is that why you loved her? Did she leave us?"

He laughed gently. "No. She didn't enchant me with a spell, if that's what you mean. Although it felt like it. I saw her once on a beach, in her human form. Just once, and I couldn't stay away." He'd been hiking alone, searching for a good climbing spot, when he stumbled onto a small crescent of sand lined with gigantic rocks. And there she was. No beach bag. No shoes. Just a red swimsuit and the wind in her hair.

"She looked like she had stepped out of a dream," he said, his voice thick with memory. "But when she smiled at me... I forgot every question I meant to ask."

He returned to the same beach, day after day, bringing her little things—carved shells, sea grapes, and polished stones. They talked for hours. He never pressed her, never asked where she came from. He didn't want to scare her away. Slowly, she trusted him. Bit by bit, she told him the truth.

"It's sacred," he said, looking at Bay, "for a mermaid to share her secret with a human. It means she loves you."

Bay's heart ached. She had never known how her parents met. That simple, beautiful beginning had been hidden from her. But now she could see it. The longing in her father's eyes. The sincerity. Whether it was true or not, he believed it. All of it.

"Why didn't we live in a mer-city with Mom?" she asked.

"We did. For a while. In the biggest one," he said. "But when you were little, we had to leave."

"Why couldn't she come with us? Why can't we go back and find her?"

His face darkened. "I had to make some hard choices. One day, maybe you'll understand."

Bay's throat burned. "What's more important than family?" she whispered. She begged him to let her visit, call, write. Anything. But his answer never wavered.

"No one can know where you are. Or what you are. Not even your mother." He leaned in, eyes fierce. "It's a matter of life or death, Bay. There are forces that would do anything to find you. Things even your mother couldn't stop."

No matter how hard she pressed him, her father refused to share any further details. Bay's life was in danger. Real and grave. So, she turned away and looked out the window. The sea shimmered in the distance, calling to her. Her heart pounded like a war drum. She had to go back. She had to see the water again. She had to find her mother.

Her father thought the truth would scare her away, but it only sharpened her desire. Fueled her. The ache in her chest surged. The ocean pulled harder, stirring something inside her. Something old and knowing and wild.

She believed him. Not just because of the photograph. Not even because she wanted to believe. She believed because… she already knew. Her mother was alive. And she, Bay, was a mermaid.

All these years she had carried a hollow space in her heart, a wound she couldn't name. Now, at last, she had answers. Not just answers. A second chance at belonging. She could feel her mother's love again.

No matter the risk.

CHAPTER SIX

The Runaway

er dad had wanted to drive straight through to Sacramento, but after everything that had happened and having already driven through the night, they were both exhausted. They took an off-ramp into Eugene, Oregon. As they exited, Bay spotted a sign for the Valley River Center, a shopping mall with big windows and people streaming in and out.

They found a hotel nearby, just a day's drive from home. Over room service, Bay peppered her dad with more questions about her mom and the mer-villages. By seven that evening, her dad was out cold, crashing the moment his head hit the pillow, while Bay lay awake staring into the dark.

You don't even know how to get to the beach. It's seven p.m.! You can't just run away to the ocean in the middle of the night, Light-Voice warned.

But Bay knew this was her only chance. Once they got home, her dad would never let her near the ocean again.

You can't leave him. He'll be all alone, Light-Voice insisted, stronger now.

That's his choice, Bay thought back. *And what about Mom? She lost her entire family.*

What about the dangers Dad warned you about?

It's been fifteen years, Bay countered. *Maybe they're gone. He hasn't spoken to Mom in all that time. Who knows if the threats are even real anymore?*

35

You should try talking to him again. Convince him to explain more. To come with you.

I've tried for as long as I can remember. I'm not waiting another minute to meet my mom. Her jaw clenched. *She's out there.* Bay knew what she had to do.

The pull was too strong. The ocean called her like a whisper she could not ignore. She had to see the water again, to touch it, feel it. She needed to understand her whole self as both the daughter of a human and the daughter of a mermaid. So many pieces were still missing.

Quietly, she sat up and slid off the bed. The sound of her suitcase zipper slicing through the silence made her wince. It was hard to know what to bring. She didn't know how long she'd be gone or where this path would lead. Her hands trembled as she packed a backpack with clothes, toiletries, her phone, and her purse.

She tiptoed to her dad's nightstand. Reached for his wallet. Froze.

You can't leave him, Light-Voice whispered again.

Bay's hand dropped. She looked at him, the man who had raised her. His curly dark brown hair, his strong jawline. In her mind, she saw his honey-colored eyes giving her the look, the one that said he knew she was up to something.

A memory floated to the surface. She had been six. They were hiking one of the hills behind their old town home, the trail rocky and sunlit. She had wanted to reach the top so badly, too fast for her little legs. He told her to slow down. She didn't. She slipped on the gravel and scraped her knee, sobbing not from the pain, but because she thought the climb was over.

36

But he hadn't turned back.

He lifted her onto his shoulders and carried her the rest of the way. At the summit, they stood together. She remembered how the wind felt on her face, how small the trees looked from above. He had said, "Next time, we go slower. But we always finish."

She blinked back tears.

She wanted to hug him goodbye. To say she loved him. To say she was sorry. But she knew he wouldn't understand. He'd try to stop her.

There's no other way, she told Light-Voice softly. And this time, it didn't argue. It understood.

She picked up his wallet and slipped out two bank cards. Tears blurred her vision. This would change everything. He had always been a good dad. It had always been the two of them.

Bay gave the hotel room one last look, then eased open the heavy door and stepped into the hallway.

Now what?

She needed to move fast, just in case he woke up early. Her thoughts turned to the mall she'd seen earlier. It was only a few blocks away, and there would be people around. That seemed safe enough.

She slipped out of the hotel and turned down a quiet residential street. The summer light still lingered, soft and golden, calming her nerves as she passed tidy homes filled with laughter and glowing TVs. She jumped more than once—at a barking dog and at kids leaping from behind a bush.

Soon, she reached the mall parking lot and lingered out front, blending in with the crowd of teens waiting for rides.

Pulling out her phone, she searched for a beachside hotel and mapped a route. It was an hour and a half away. Too far to ride-share the whole way without raising suspicion. So, she took the next bus and headed south, for nearly an hour before getting off at a roadside diner near a gas station. From there, she booked a ride. When the car arrived, a young woman in her early twenties leaned out the window. "You Bay?"

Bay nodded.

The driver didn't seem fazed by her age. She just smiled, started talking, and didn't stop.

Bay was relieved. The woman launched into a story about how she'd moved to the Pacific Northwest with her no-good (now ex) boyfriend, how he'd left her stranded, and how she'd fallen in love with Oregon and stayed. She talked about her job, how much she liked driving people around and meeting new friends, and about the occasional sketchy passenger she never wanted to see again.

Bay listened silently, grateful not to have to talk. She didn't know what she'd say, even if she had to. As they neared the beach hotel, Bay glanced at her phone—and froze. Her dad could track her. He could see exactly where she'd gone. At first she had considered asking the driver to drop her right at the water's edge, but now, better not to be so obvious.

"Can we stop at that Shell station up ahead?" she asked. "I need to grab a few things."

"Sure," the driver said, easing off the road. "I could wait and take you the rest of the way. It's getting late."

"No, that's okay. It's not far—I'll walk. Thanks."

"Alright. Hope you enjoyed the ride!" she chirped, already tapping her app for the next passenger.

She processed the payment to the driver, silenced her phone, then wedged it deep between the backseat cushions. With any luck, that would throw him off her trail.

Bay stepped out of the car; her hands were trembling—not from the cold, but from everything she was about to leave behind, including her phone. It felt more real now. Bigger. Unstoppable.

She took a deep breath. The air was different here, cooler, moister, with the faintest salty edge. The call of the ocean surged again.

No turning back now, Light-Voice said.

Bay nodded. At least she wasn't alone. Light-Voice glowed brighter now.

CHAPTER SEVEN

Whispers in the Van

Bay crossed the gas station lot and walked into the small convenience store. The automatic doors slid open for her, and she stepped inside. A teenage girl with blonde hair pulled into a high ponytail sat on a stool, reading a magazine and chewing gum.

"Welcome to Quick Rick's," she said in a monotone, without looking up.

"Er—thanks," Bay muttered, her eyes scanning the store for the ATM. She found it in the back, next to a slushy machine. Reaching into her bag, she pulled out one of her dad's bank cards. She stood there, staring at the glowing screen. Her fingers hovered over the keypad.

What are you doing? Light-Voice asked.

Bay didn't answer. Her heart thudded loudly.

You're stealing from him?

He gave me his PIN number for emergencies.

That's not what this is, and you know it

"I don't have a choice," Bay muttered under her breath.

Yes, you do. You always do.

"No, I don't!" Bay yelled aloud, startling herself.

"Did you need something?" asked the girl behind the counter in the same bored tone of voice and still not looking up.

41

"Oh, never mind," She called back, forcing her voice to stay casual.

Bay turned back to the machine and moved her hand toward the keypad. Or tried to. It stopped midair, suspended like it had hit invisible glass.

You are not going to steal from Dad, Light-Voice said firmly.

Bay stared at her hand. "Are you doing this? Let go!" She mumbled.

No.

"I'm going to go see a counselor when I get home if you don't quit it!" Bay snapped through gritted teeth.

Good. Maybe you'll stop acting irrationally.

Bay strained, trying to move. Her hand slowly began to retreat instead. She stumbled back and bumped into a shelf, knocking a stack of granola bars to the floor.

"What are you doing?" The girl behind the counter had walked over, her voice now laced with curiosity.

"Sorry. Couldn't decide what snack I wanted," Bay said quickly, forcing a sheepish smile as she knelt to gather the mess. "I'll pick it all up."

The teen rolled her eyes and walked back to the register.

Bay exhaled and returned to the ATM. "Look, if there are dangers out there, I need to be prepared," she whispered. "There might not be another chance to get money."

Light-Voice didn't respond. But Bay could feel it there, quiet and disapproving, still listening. Bay took a breath, withdrew the maximum allowed, then slid in her own card and emptied her savings. She stuffed all of the cash into her purse, her nerves rattling from the weight of it as she headed back out of the shop.

She scanned the gas station lot and then the main street. It was a small beach town, and most of the shops had already closed. In the distance, she could barely make out the line of the ocean about a mile away. The urge to get to the water was overwhelming.

While Bay lost herself in thought, staring at the distant horizon, an old van full of teenagers pulled into the gas station. Two young guys climbed out, the driver with dark-brown curly hair and the other tall and thin with blonde hair.

"I invited Sara to join us at the beach. Think she'll come?" the blonde one asked.

The curly-haired boy shrugged and loaded two bundles of wood into the van as a gas attendant asked if they needed anything. "Yeah, full tank please, and I grabbed two piles of wood."

The van door slid open, and three girls slipped out. Two of them walked into the store, while the third leaned against the back of the van, texting rapidly. They were dressed in beach attire: swimsuits, flip-flops, sweatshirts, and cutoff shorts. It was getting dark, but they seemed ready for the night ahead.

Bay walked up to the girl leaning against the van. She looked about seventeen, with short light-brown hair and hazel eyes, almost hidden as she stared down at her screen. She didn't notice Bay standing in front of her.

"Hey," Bay said awkwardly.

"Hi," the girl said, looking up and squinting at Bay, trying to place her.

"Are you all headed to the beach?"

"Yeah, Florence Beach," the girl replied kindly.

"I got split up from my friends, and my phone died," Bay lied. "I'm meeting them down there. Would you mind if I caught a ride?"

"Umm, it's not my ride, but let me ask Tony," the girl said, then walked over to the boy pumping gas. Bay held her breath as the girl whispered something to him.

Tony peeked around the car and caught Bay's eye. "Sure, but she'll have to pay twenty bucks for gas!" he shouted, and the group laughed.

Bay reached into her purse, but the girl called out, "He's kidding."

Bay zipped her purse shut, glancing at Tony, who was grinning. She gave him a shy smile "Don't trust their kindness too easily," the Light-Voice murmured, and Bay hesitated at the van door for just a second before climbing in.

CHAPTER EIGHT

A Silent Wish

The others were loud and carefree, laughing about summer plans. Bay sat stiffly beside them, her insides knotted with everything she wasn't saying — her father, her escape, the journey ahead. She gave one-word answers, trying to smile, but mostly just stared out the window. The group didn't seem to notice, lost in their own chatter.

I wish he would look at me, just notice me...

Bay turned sharply. The thought sounded almost as if it had come from within, but it wasn't Light-Voice, and it wasn't her own. She scanned the van's occupants. The two boys were in the front, talking. Bay sat next to the sliding door, while the girl with the short black hair and brown eyes—who had been in the convenience store—sat behind the driver. She seemed to be the only one not involved in the conversation, and she kept turning her gaze toward the blonde boy in the front seat.

Then came another voice. *You could give her that.*

The thought slid into her mind like cold water under the skin. A faint metallic taste crept onto her tongue, like copper dipped in saltwater.

Bay blinked, startled. The voice wasn't hers. At least... she didn't think it was.

What's wrong? Light-Voice asked in alarm.

Did you hear those voices? Bay asked, confused.

What voices?

Bay didn't know what to think. Had she really heard that girl's voice in her mind? Had someone else responded? She was still uncertain. The girl seemed unaware of her and was now engrossed in conversation with her friends, though she kept sneaking glances at the boy in the front seat.

Bay turned back to the window, shaken. The ocean was closer now, its call tugging at her like a magnetic force.

What a beautiful sight, Light-Voice murmured in awe.

The sun was setting behind the rocks as crowds gathered on the beach to enjoy the warm evening. Bay couldn't wait any longer to reach the water.

"Stop!" she cried out, desperate. The van skidded to a sudden halt, sending everyone jerking forward. A car following too closely swerved to avoid rear-ending them, its tires screeching. The sound of screeching tires died away. Everyone in the van fell silent. Tony, who had been driving, turned to her.

"Please, I see my friends..." Bay added quickly, pointing toward a group of teens on the beach. Her cheeks burned as she realized how abrupt she had been.

Tony pulled over. "Sorry," Bay said, unbuckling her seatbelt and throwing open the van's sliding door. She grabbed her purse and slung her backpack over her shoulder. "Thanks," she mumbled, then stepped out awkwardly, feeling the tension in the air. The van's door slammed behind her, and the sound of their laughter died away as they drove off.

Bay stood still for a moment, watching them go. Her body was tense with embarrassment, but she took a deep breath and brushed it off. Turning back to the beach, she walked away from the group she had pointed to, giving them a wide berth. The colors of the sunset danced across the waves, and she couldn't tear her eyes away from the breathtaking view.

As she approached the water, she realized her tennis shoes weren't suited for the beach as sand quickly filled them. She sat on a small rock to peel them off and stood, feeling the warmth of the sand beneath her feet. She wanted to run to the waves, but she sought solitude instead. Heading toward some cliffs, she found a secluded spot, tucked out of sight, before heading to the water's edge.

Out of breath, Bay stood there, hesitant to step into the water. She wanted to believe what her father had told her, but a part of her doubted it. He had been so certain, but maybe the story had all been a fantasy.

What do mermaids do? Light-Voice asked softly.

Bay thought for a moment. *Transform, I guess.*

Then it hit her. She couldn't swim. She didn't have her phone. Fear gripped her.

I am here, her inner voice reassured her, and her determination returned.

She stood, her feet in the water, feeling the waves' pull. Though it was cold, it wasn't the freezing chill she had expected. The water was soft, silky against her skin. Surprised, she moved further in until the water reached her knees. Still, nothing happened. She lifted her left foot to examine it, no scales, no webbing, nothing. Maybe she had to be naked?

Try it, Light-Voice suggested.

Reluctantly, Bay returned to the beach, stripped down, and ran back into the water, this time fully exposed. A wave lifted her toes, gently pulling her into the ocean. Fear crept up her spine as she backed away, remembering her father's warnings. What could be lurking in the dark water? Still, nothing changed.

Maybe your whole body needs to be in the water. Head too? Light-Voice offered.

Bay took a deep breath and sat down fully immersed in the water until she ran out of air. Nothing happened. Frustrated, she stood, pulling her head back above the surface and taking a deep breath.

Nothing. Alone in the water, she felt foolish. She had come all this way only to find that everything her dad said was a lie. Had she been chasing shadows this whole time?

Stomping out of the water, Bay's anger flared as she grabbed her clothes and started working them over her wet skin.

She sat next to the ocean, staring at the black waves, mist pouring in over the tide. She was all alone with no phone. Darkness and cold swelled inside of her again. The feeling of being alone more present than ever.

You're not alone, Light-Voice said, but Bay wasn't in the mood to cheer up.

She also wasn't ready to make her way back to her dad. She wasn't ready to acknowledge that he must have concocted this whole stupid story to avoid facing the reality that her mother had abandoned them.

She grabbed a rock and hurled it. Then another. And another. Reaching for one more, her hand closed around a small green pebble. It glowed. Bay froze.

CHAPTER NINE

The Siren Stone

ay turned the glowing rock over and over in her palm, barely trusting what she saw. The stone sang faintly, a quiet hum rising from within as though it were alive. She cupped it in both hands and lifted it to her face, eyes wide with wonder.

A *siren stone*. Just as her father had described. The rocks that lit the way to Mer-cities.

A sharp stab of guilt pierced through her. For doubting him but also for running away. Suddenly, there he was in her mind: sleeping in the hotel bed, even the furrow in his brow at rest, the weight of his worry pressing down on her chest. She felt awful. But she couldn't stop now. Not when the next stone could be close.

Bay whirled around and scanned the shoreline. There, about ten feet to her left, another emerald pebble glowed like a beacon in the dark. Her heart skipped. She sprinted to it, in fear that it might vanish before she got there. But just as her fingers wrapped around the second stone, she spotted a third, this one flickering just beneath the surface of the waves.

Without hesitation, she charged into the ocean. The cold slapped her skin. Her clothes clung to her legs and arms, but she didn't care. She plunged her hand into the water and pulled out the stone. It was slick and smooth, its glow even more vibrant underwater.

Then she saw another.

And another.

The stones led her like breadcrumbs as she weaved through surf and tide, climbing over sea rocks and darting around tide pools. Her breath came fast, her muscles burning from the sprint. She paused only briefly, just long enough to pull on her shoes, as the sand gave way to uneven dirt paths and jagged boulders that tore at her feet.

The mist grew thicker with every step. The moon was high, but its light struggled to cut through the haze. Still, the stones shone through, their glow unyielding.

Then—she stopped. The next pebble lay ahead, resting atop the first step of an old wooden bridge. It stretched out across the sea, vanishing into the fog. Suspended by thick, knotted rope, the planks beneath it looked heavy and worn, water-darkened with age. Each one was nearly two feet long. A line of them disappeared into shadow.

Bay swallowed. The mist curled around the bridge like a living creature, and even with the moonlight overhead, she couldn't see where it led. Still, the stone was there. Waiting.

CHAPTER TEN

The Voice inside

I am not supposed to be this awake. Not like this.

Most days, I hover quietly in the background, a flicker at the edge of thought. A whisper. A warmth. Something soft enough to be mistaken for instinct or memory. Something gentle, present only when needed.

But not tonight. Tonight, the ocean breeze seeps into every corner of me. It pulses through Bay's skin, and something inside me pulses back, something forgotten.

Since Bay first saw the ocean, I've been increasingly able to experience the world as she does. The fog I used to drift in has thinned. I can see her thoughts as they form. I can feel the sand beneath her feet. I can hear her breath, fast and shallow. I can almost remember the feel of it for myself.

I've always been the quiet thought. The guide. The spark that steadies her in the dark. I never questioned that before. Never wanted more. But now, something in me is shifting. Waking.

There's a memory—I think. it comes in flashes, vague and unsteady. Water. Not just the ocean. A pool. A backyard. A plastic ball with stars on it. Sunlight dancing on her—my?—skin. Laughter. Was that hers or mine?

She was small then. So was I. Back when things were different. Before the cold nights came. Before the ache. Before I became the voice in her head. Before I was needed.

Now, watching her run barefoot across the sand, chasing green fire through the mist, I feel it too—the call. The longing. It tugs at something deep inside me. Like I'm part of it. Like I belong to it.

Maybe we both do.

She thinks she's alone in this. She always has. Carries guilt like armor, buries her questions under silence. She doesn't speak of the Darkness she feels, the way it creeps in when no one's looking. She doesn't speak of me either.

But I see her. I know her. And whatever this is—magic or memory, destiny or delusion—she doesn't have to carry it by herself. Even if I can't remember who I am or what I'm meant to be, I can still be here.

For her.

A whisper.

A warmth.

A light.

I am here, Bay. I'm still here.

CHAPTER ELEVEN

The Crossing

Bay stared at the bridge, her body trembling. It stretched into the mist like something out of a nightmare: thick rope lines, aged planks, and the endless, echoing crash of waves below. The green glow of the siren stone had led her here, but now... now the path forward looked like a trap laid out just for her.

You're going to cross that rickety thing, aren't you? Light-Voice asked.

"Yes," Bay answered, trying to sound braver than she felt.

Just... don't look down. And if we die, I'm blaming you.

She stared at the bridge, shaking slightly from the muscle fatigue in her legs and the fear tightening in her chest. Then, resolved, she adjusted her backpack straps and pressed forward. The wood groaned beneath her feet. The rope creaked in the wind.

Step by step, she crossed, gripping the rope so tightly her knuckles were white. She could see the turbulent ocean through the gaps in each step. She tried not to think about the bridge breaking and crashing into the sea, or herself drowning and never being seen again.

Then, suddenly, the rope went taut. Someone else had stepped onto the bridge.

She froze.

The wind carried voices across the water.

"She's close. I can feel it," a husky female voice whispered.

Bay's breath caught. Her heart thundered. Was that voice talking about her?

No, no, no, no—

R*un*! Light-Voice urged.

Bay launched forward, sprinting. The bridge bucked beneath her with every step. Footsteps pounded behind her. The bridge swayed, twisted. She nearly slipped when her hand skid off the rope, but she caught herself.

"She must not vanish again. Not this time," the voice growled behind her.

Bay's panic surged. Her lungs burned. Her muscles screamed. *I wish they couldn't see me*, she thought wildly.

The wind shifted. A sudden chill brushed her skin. A sharp tang bloomed in her mouth, like copper dipped in salt. The taste surged fast, metallic and cold.

The ropes vibrated. A sharp ache knifed through her—not her chest exactly, but something inside her.

Bay—no—! Light-Voice gasped, like wind knocked from lungs it didn't have. There was panic, raw and real.

Bay collapsed to her knees on the far side of the bridge. The pain vanished. So did the footsteps. Silence wrapped around her. The copper taste still clung to her tongue.

She scrambled up, stumbling off the bridge and into the brush. Branches scratched her arms, but she didn't care. She dove behind a cluster of thick ferns and held her breath. Moments passed. Then she heard them, two sets of feet hit the dirt trail behind her. But their steps never slowed. They ran right past her.

It worked, Bay thought, astonished.

Inside, Light-Voice whimpered. *What did you do?*

Bay didn't answer. She didn't know. All she knew was that for the first time, she had made a wish—and it had come true.

And something inside of her had paid for it.

CHAPTER TWELVE

The Village on the Sea

The mist was thick now, so thick Bay could barely see her own hands. It clung to her skin like breath held too long. Every step felt heavier, like the air itself had turned to water.

Still, she moved forward.

Panic pressed at her chest like a weight, but she buried it. She had to keep going. Her eyes strained, searching for the soft green glow of the stones that guided her. She ignored the fear creeping along her spine and focused solely on the rocks.

Her steps were slow and deliberate, each one a careful whisper in the thickening fog. Her feet caught on low brush just as a hidden wave crashed against the shore nearby, splashing cold water up her calves and sending a shiver through her. She pressed on, teeth clenched, trying to maintain control, and heard nothing but the echo of her own breath.

The trail of green rocks veered away from the ocean, climbing upward. Bay's heart stuttered. She almost hesitated, the familiar tug of the sea threatening to stop her. But she couldn't give in. She had to follow the rocks. She had to get out of this fog.

She caught her toe on a root and stumbled, barely catching herself on a slick boulder. Her breath hitched. The world around her was muffled and muted, as though she had stepped outside of time. She couldn't hear the ocean or even the sound of her own steps anymore. The silence was suffocating. A tremor ran through her at the thought of screaming just to break the oppressive quiet. But she didn't.

She stopped. She couldn't see another stone. The night and mist combined, making it almost black around her. She shivered, unsure what to do.

But then she heard it—a note of music, just a few measures long. Faint and sweet, like wind chimes in a dream. Her heart stumbled as she followed the sound.

The mist began to thin. The silence was broken. The world unfolded before her. A warm breeze brushed her cheek. The air shifted. Then, suddenly, she stood at the top of a hill, gazing down into a sun-drenched village that shouldn't have been there.

It shimmered like a dream.

Buildings curled upward in impossible spirals, their rooftops painted in brilliant fuchsia, seafoam, and goldenrod. Tiled paths twisted through the town like ribbons of coral. The smell of salt and citrus filled her nose. Bells rang in laughter from somewhere below.

Bay blinked. Once. Twice. It didn't vanish.

The fog was gone, replaced with light and music and motion. The village pulsed with energy, so alive it made her chest tighten. Her body trembled from exhaustion, but her eyes were wide. It was beautiful. Impossible. Like a secret someone had kept just for her.

The road down was steep and winding. She took it slowly, legs shaky beneath her. Her shoes squished with damp sand, and her clothes clung to her skin like ivy. But none of it mattered. She moved like someone dreaming.

She saw it then: a fountain at the heart of the town. It stood tall and radiant, with water cascading from its center in swirling colors: turquoise, lavender, and emerald. Perched above it, carved in brilliant green stone, was the figure of a mermaid.

Bay caught her breath and she stepped forward. Her eyes traced the curve of the cheekbones, the long hair frozen in mid-swirl, the knowing expression etched into marble lips.

The statue's eyes were familiar.

Bay's pulse quickened. Her throat tightened. That face, with its shape, its grace, its strength, was one she had seen before in her dreams, in the photograph, in the ache that never left her.

Her mother.

CHAPTER THIRTEEN

Serpentine

The likeness was unmistakable: the heart-shaped face, the almond eyes, the same necklace Bay wore. Dropping her backpack, she stared up at the fountain in amazement.

Her mother. Her actual face, etched in stone and captured in marble splendor. Why was her mother here, carved in stone at all?

A cloud of doubt crept in. Why hadn't she reached out? Why let Bay grow up alone? Rage and confusion tangled inside her, sharp and rising. Her emotions reached for something they had never been allowed to hold. Her fingers tightened around her own necklace as she traced the familiar emblem of the sea serpent and trident etched on the back. A gentle pulse came from the pendant, followed by a warmth that settled against her skin.

"It's serpentine," said a boy's voice behind her.

Bay spun around at the unexpected sound.

"The stone, it's serpentine," he said, pointing at the statue.

Bay stared at him, confused for a second before her focus returned to the fountain. "Thanks?" she muttered.

"I just thought you were trying to figure that out. A lot of new people ask about it when they first see it," the boy said.

She didn't look back at him, feeling a strange tension in her chest.

"My name's Cyrus," he said, leaning a little closer.

Bay hesitated; she turned from the fountain, eyeing him warily. He was tall, taller than he needed to be, with brown skin, a strong jaw, and a mess of wind-tossed curls the color of driftwood. His grey-blue eyes held a flicker of warmth, but they were far too steady, like he was watching more than just her movements. Something about the way he stood, relaxed and amused, just off-center, made her uneasy. He looked only a little older than she was, but there was a sharpness in him. She squinted her coal-black eyes up at him. His eyebrow rose, just slightly, in a way that made her feel like she was being sized up.

Why don't you tell him your name or say something? Light-Voice said.

Bay, still suspicious, did not respond; She had no intention of letting her guard down so easily.

"What's your name?" Cyrus pressed lightly, amusement in his voice.

64

He seems good, Light-Voice offered.

Good, really, you can sense that? Bay thought back.

Good-looking anyway…

Not helping! Bay chided back impatiently.

"And this is the part where you tell me what your name is," Cyrus offered playfully, his shoulders rising in a lighthearted shrug.

Bay shook her head when she realized she had been staring at him intently the whole time.

After a pause, he added, "Or aren't you allowed to talk to strangers?" A teasing smile played on his lips as he leaned in close, too close.

"Yes, I am!" Bay shot back.

"Well, then, what is your name?" His face was inches from hers.

Before Bay could stop herself, her hand reached out, her fingers brushing his cheek. He blinked, surprised, but didn't move away.

She yanked her hand back, stunned.

What was that?! she demanded internally.

Sorry! Light-Voice replied, a little too brightly. *You were taking too long.*

Bay stared at her hand like it had betrayed her. "My name? My name is Ba—Brittany."

"Okay, Ba-Brittany, what are you doing here?" he said with a laugh.

"It's Brittany, just Brittany," Bay snapped.

"Are you sure?" Cyrus asked, his smile widening.

"Yes, and it's none of your business why I am here," Bay answered sharply. She was exhausted and not in the mood to joke with this boy.

Cyrus blinked at the edge in her voice. "Okay, fair enough." There was a flicker of something gentler in his expression, but it passed as quickly as it came.

"Wait, how did you know I was new here?" Bay demanded.

"Well, for one thing, this is a small town, and I know most everyone here." He turned towards her once again. "Also, people who live here don't stand around gawking at me for thirty minutes."

"I was not gawking!" Bay insisted.

You totally were. Light-Voice laughed.

"Shut up!" Bay spluttered.

"I didn't say anything..." Cyrus said, giving Bay a puzzled look. Her cheeks turned red in embarrassment for having said that last bit out loud.

"Argh... Never mind." Bay knew she should apologize, but he irritated her, so she ruled out that option. "Look, do you know where a good hotel is around here?"

"Yes," Cyrus said, still smiling.

"Well?" Bay demanded when he didn't say more. She didn't know why he bothered her so much.

"Well, what, Ba-Brittany?"

"Where is a good hotel?" she said, exasperated.

"None of your business, newb!" Cyrus said smugly, with a crooked grin. Then he turned and walked off.

"Argh!" Bay huffed, grabbing her bag and stomping off in the opposite direction.

CHAPTER FOURTEEN

The Red Sea Inn

wo buildings sat straight ahead of her: a store painted in iridescent light blue that glowed like the moon and a lively green restaurant that was still crowded, even at this hour of the night. Though she was hungry, Bay decided the less crowded option might be better and headed toward the light-blue general store.

A tinkling bell sounded as Bay opened the door, and was greeted by the smell of orange and jasmine. Behind the counter, a lovely woman with long silver hair, loosely braided, looked up from her book and welcomed Bay with a warm smile. She had laugh lines that gave away a cheery disposition and large navy-blue eyes that sparkled.

The shop sold soap and personal care products, all packaged in glass, wood, or twine-wrapped bundles, no plastic, Bay noticed. It all looked handmade. She spotted a sign for shampoo bars and walked toward the display, as she suddenly felt the need to wash away the sea and sand. She picked up a few and sniffed them, settling on a burnt orange bar that smelled of bright, citrusy flowers.

At the register, she made her purchase and asked for directions to an affordable hotel. The pleasant shopkeeper obliged, and Bay tucked the bar into her purse before heading up the block toward the Red Sea Inn.

Bay's palms felt sweaty at the thought of checking in. Would they give her a room if she wasn't an adult? Would they ask for ID? Or call her parents? She had no choice. She couldn't sleep on the street.

Nevertheless, the streets were a delightful blend of old-world charm and inventive mechanics. Cobblestone paths twisted in winding turns. Iron-wrought lampposts lit her way, each unique: one shaped like seaweed, with glowing bulbs nestled among its leaves; another appeared as a giant seahorse clutching a luminous pearl. The buildings glowed softly, and none of the roads were made for cars. Everywhere she looked, rooftops brimmed with vegetable gardens.

She stopped in front of a big, bright red building. Smooth and rounded, it twisted three stories high like a licorice tower. A painted wooden sign read: RED SEA INN.

Bay froze. She was so close, but suddenly, her feet refused to move. What if she was turned away? What if they found out who she was? She was almost sixteen, but short and thin for her age. Most people thought she was younger. Her body screamed for sleep, but she stood paralyzed by doubt.

You can do this. I am here with you. Just breathe, Light-Voice encouraged.

Bay nodded and stepped forward. She pushed her weight into the heavy wooden door. "Thank you," she whispered.

Inside, the hotel looked much different than its bright exterior. Dim candlelight lined the walls. Dark polished wood covered the floors and furniture, like the inside of a ship. The walls were deep red, and a single chandelier hung from the ceiling, surrounded by old leather couches and a crackling fire in a stone fireplace. Nautical artwork adorned the space: giant sailboats, pirate ships. The front desk was a massive oak counter, sturdy and ancient. A small bar was situated to the left. Winding staircases spiraled into the upper floors.

"Good evening, Miss," a female voice called from behind the counter.

"Hello," Bay said nervously as she approached.

The woman was tall, her hair wrapped into a neat bun. Her green dress matched her polished demeanor, her bright-red nails shining like the furniture in the room. "How can I help you?" she said with a smile as her light-blue eyes looked Bay over.

"I—I'd like a room," Bay stammered. "Please," she added.

"For how many nights?"

"Uh..."

"You can pay each morning, if you prefer."

Bay nodded, relieved. "Yes, please."

"That will be $85 for tonight."

Bay handed over the cash, hands trembling, and received a heavy iron room key.

"Do you need help with your things?"

"No, I've got it," Bay said, slipping her purse into her backpack.

"Top of the staircase to the right. Room twenty-seven."

"Thank you."

Bay climbed the staircase, each step squeaking underfoot. She passed the second landing and continued up to the third. The hallway walls were dark green, the same polished wood floors and doors as below. She passed room twenty-three, then twenty-five, and then she stopped at twenty-seven.

She unlocked the door with effort, stepped inside, and shut it behind her. She locked it, then let herself collapse onto the floor and wrapped her arms around herself, just sitting. She'd made it.

Eventually, she stood upright. She left her backpack by the door and took in the space. Dim, but clean. The same dark green walls. A wooden dresser with a mirror. A bed. A nightstand with a golden seashell clock and a wooden telephone. Everything felt old and solid. The décor, nautical.

A painting showed a large wooden ship in the middle of a heavy sea storm with a mermaid carved on its bow, face lifted in defiance as waves crashed against her. The mermaid looked brave, cutting through the ocean waters, carrying the vessel through the storm.

She crossed to the window, hidden by its navy curtains, and slid them open on brass rings to let moonlight spill across the floor. From here, she could see the fountain—and just barely, the general store.

She sat on the firm mattress, unclasped her necklace, and placed it on the nightstand. The golden clock on the bedside table was shaped like an open seashell with a pearl inside. Blue, fluorescent numbers ran across the golden pearl and read 12:15 a.m. Five hours since she left her dad.

She was exhausted. Sore. But her thoughts were spinning too fast for sleep.

Bay pulled the shampoo bar and nightgown from her backpack and entered the bathroom. The fixtures were a mix of bronze and polished wood. There was no shower, but the tub was enormous, too big for the small bathroom, and it was also bronze-coated. She supposed its size was made to accommodate a mermaid's tail.

She undressed, shaking sand from her damp clothes, and stepped into the oversized tub. The warm water embraced her like silk pouring over her sore body. She lowered her head beneath the surface, then rose again, steam curling from her skin. Her hair floated like blonde seaweed around her. She scrubbed her hair and body with the shampoo bar, finally washing away the grime of the day. Her skin had never felt so soft.

Thoughts spun like whirlpools. Izzy. Her dad. The ocean's call. The siren stones. The chase on the bridge, the way she disappeared.

Her mother.

She must live here, Light-Voice said, full of hope.

I think so too, Bay replied. *Why else would there be a statue of her?*

She imagined meeting her. Being held. Telling her everything. Hearing her mother's voice. Tears welled up and spilled hot over her cheeks into the bathwater. She cried—out of fear, out of joy, out of guilt. When she was empty, she pulled herself from the water. Dried off. Dressed. Hung her wet clothes over the tub.

She crawled into bed, curled under the thick comforter, and closed her eyes. The room was still, but her heart was loud with hope, worry, and a flood of wishes.

CHAPTER FIFTEEN

The Breakfast

Bay opened her eyes as light beamed onto her face. "Dad, close the curtain," she muttered, turning and pulling the blanket over her head. Nothing but silence greeted her in response.

"Right... Dad isn't here," she said to the empty room, the memories of the previous day came crashing back in waves. It had been her who left the window curtain open, not her dad.

Her stomach growled loudly as she sat up, back pressed against the tan quilted headboard. When was the last time I had anything to eat? Or anything to drink? Images flickered through her mind. She imagined her father waking to an empty bed, calling her name, checking his phone... Searching. Panicking. Agonizing.

He must have found the driver from the app by now. Maybe even tracked her phone. He was probably tearing through the little beach town, desperate to find her.

He must be so furious. He must hate me, she thought, bowing her head as her long blonde hair tumbled down, shielding her face from the morning rays.

He is worried and upset, but he doesn't hate you.

The guilt hit hard. The lying, the stealing. Running away. Putting him through whatever nightmare a parent experiences when their child disappears. Moisture welled in her eyes.

Maybe it's time to reach out to him?

He'll want me to go home, Bay thought.

You could talk him into meeting you here.

"He'll insist I leave with him and forget all of this. I can't do that." Bay said out loud, sitting up straighter and wiping away her tears. "I need to know more. I need to find her. And..."

Myself, she almost said.

She would be cautious. Be careful not to draw attention. But she would not leave, not without seeing her mother.

The room was still cool, and she shivered slightly as she pushed the comforter off of her body. Her legs ached as she stood, still sore from the day before. She undressed quickly, folding her pajamas neatly at the end of the bed.

From her backpack, she pulled out clean clothes and her purse. She slid on jean shorts, a purple tank top, and a hoodie— casual, light. Hopefully the sun would chase away the morning chill. She reached for her flip-flops. Blisters had formed on her heels, just as she'd expected. Closed shoes weren't an option.

At the nightstand, she picked up her delicate starfish necklace and brushed her fingertips across the gold etching on the back: a coiled sea serpent wrapped around a trident. The only thing she had ever owned of her mother's. She felt the warming calmness once more radiating from the necklace. She closed her hand around the medallion, as if willing it to find her mother. Then she fastened it around her neck.

Downstairs, Bay paid for another night. The same woman from the evening before was behind the counter—still poised and polished, but with a strangely knowing stare. Without being asked, she recommended a breakfast spot across the street. It was as though she could sense Bay's hunger.

Bay pulled her hoodie tighter around her shoulders as the chill outside whipped across her bare legs. The cold air bit at her skin, but she was thankful to be out in the morning sunshine.

Across the cobblestone street stood a midnight blue building: The Lighthouse. A cozy coffee shop with golden yellow walls, wood cabinetry, and a small food menu posted on hand-painted chalkboards. Inside, the warmth wrapped around her. The air smelled like roasted coffee beans, citrus zest, and the sea.

She noticed something unusual. Every customer held a ceramic mug. As they approached the barista, they handed over their mugs with their orders. The barista filled them and returned them. No to-go cups. No plastic stir sticks. No disposable anything.

Bay looked around nervously, unsure whether she would be turned away for arriving empty-handed.

When it was her turn, she stepped forward, feeling a little smaller under the gaze of the barista. Who was yet another tall, blue-eyed woman. Her expression was patient, but the line behind Bay grew longer.

"I don't have a cup...sorry," Bay mumbled.

"You can borrow one if you're dining in or purchase a mug to go," the barista replied without missing a beat, her hands moving swiftly as she assembled orders.

"Thanks. I'll stay. Can I get a hot chocolate and a toasted bagel with cream cheese and salmon on top?"

The barista smiled. "Would you like the salmon raw or cooked?"

Bay blinked. "Raw. With extra salmon on the side, please." The moment the words left her mouth, her stomach clenched with anticipation.

Her order came on a small wooden tray laden with neatly-placed blue ceramic dishware, metal cutlery, and a cloth napkin. She felt her stomach rumbling as the smell of the salmon hit her rich, salty, and fresh. Her teeth tingled as she slid her tongue across them. *Are they...sharper?* she asked herself with slight concern.

She devoured the bagel in quick bites and moved on to the extra salmon, forgetting her fork. She scooped the raw pieces up with her hands, shoveling them into her mouth. The taste exploded, briny, smooth, and perfect. She lifted the plate, drinking the juice straight from the ceramic edge. It trailed down her chin. She licked it clean.

Why are you eating like that?

Bay froze, a finger still in her mouth. She looked up. A middle-aged woman stared at her, dark blue eyes narrowed in disgust. Bay could see the judgment in her expression. A flash of heat shot through her chest as she met the woman's gaze, held it, and smiled wickedly. Then she winked and slid another finger into her mouth with exaggerated grace. The woman turned away, but not before looking down her nose at Bay with indignation.

Bay blinked. The heat faded. Embarrassment rushed in to replace it. She pulled her fingers from her mouth and wiped them quickly on her napkin.

Not exactly the low profile I was hoping for, she thought, face burning. She stood, cleaned her table, and exited in a flash.

The cold morning air felt like a balm to her cheeks still hot with shame. Once she was out of sight of the lighthouse, she slowed a bit. Her breath fogged in the air.

Why did I do that? In normal circumstances, Bay would never have behaved so rudely. Not around strangers. And the way she ate... She felt sick. Ashamed. Confused.

Well, it's not an excuse, but you are a teenager. You were starving. And the fish was incredibly tasty. That lady didn't have to look at you like that.

Thanks, Bay thought, her face finally beginning to cool.

The wink and smile, though? Perfectly timed.

Bay laughed softly to herself, remembering the woman's outrage. And, just for a moment, she felt a little lighter.

NOW *the dancing sunbeams play*
On the green and glassy sea;
Come, and I will lead the way,
Where the pearly treasures be.
Come with me, and we will go
Where the rocks of coral grow;
Follow, follow, follow me.
Come, behold what treasures lie
Deep below the rolling waves,
Riches hid from human eye
Dimly shine in ocean's caves;
Stormy winds are far away,
Ebbing tides brook no delay;
Follow, follow, [1]follow me.

—Anne Hunter

1   Often titled "Mermaid's Song," this poem was written by Anne Hunter (1742–1821), a Scottish poet whose lyrics were frequently set to music by Joseph Haydn.

CHAPTER SIXTEEN

The Glass Shop

ay wandered through the cobblestone streets, unable to return to her room just yet. Morning light shimmered from every surface. She didn't know where she was going, but she felt pulled in a direction, and she let herself drift.

For a time, she indulged in window-shopping through coastal boutiques and shell-inlaid galleries. Having been forbidden the ocean all of her life, Bay wished she could spend the whole summer here, just to take it all in. She adored the beachwear and swimsuits as well as the food, the music, and the many works of art made from driftwood, shells, and sand. Her heart filled with the sight of so many treasures.

Almost as exciting was how the salty sea air expanded her lungs more deeply than she had ever felt before. There was a strange vibration to this little island village. It awakened something inside her. Maybe it was the briny air. The spirited music. The seagulls calling overhead. Or the lingering magic of the siren stones that had led her here. Whatever it was, it felt like she had found a tiny piece of the puzzle she'd been searching for.

At the further end of the village, buildings became sparse. The pier drew near. She realized where she was being led. The ocean called to her. She kept moving forward. Only one shop now stood between her and the harbor. It was the village's only worn façade, with gray tired walls pitted from age and neglect. The cobbles here were smooth and faded. Bay might have passed it by, but a flicker of gold light called her nearer.

She peeked through the window. Under dim glass shelves, hundreds of blown-glass figures glowed from within: dogs and cats, fish and mermaids, all frozen in twisted, uncanny expressions. There were no overhead lights; Yet somehow each piece of glass held its own ember of color.

The shop's walls were misty gray and empty. A perfect blank canvas for the rows of intricate pieces. The glass door reflected the harbor's ripples behind her, water dancing across the shop's treasures.

I don't think you should go in there. Something feels...off, Light-Voice cautioned.

Bay hesitated, torn between the promise of the sea and the lure of this strange, glowing shop. Then a soft spotlight at the back wall caught her eye. She stepped into the shop and past racks of gleaming glass, drawn to a single illuminated poster.

On it, Allura stood in her human form, as beautiful as ever, long blonde hair braided loosely, aquamarine eyes twinkling. She stood on an island of pearl and white, a platform that jutted into the sea. Behind her, pristine buildings shimmered in the sunlight with a golden banner along the top that read *The Pacific Palace*. In her hands, she held a flag, light blue bearing a golden trident and a coiled serpent. The same design that graced Bay's necklace.

The blue of the flag matched her mother's eyes. It even matched the gem on the necklace Bay wore around her neck. Those eyes were the only thing that contrasted Bay's, hers were round and black. Allura wore the necklace in the poster, just as she had in the fountain.

For a moment, Bay seemed unable to breathe. Her mother... here? Flames of longing and confusion tangled in her chest. She barely registered the soft creak of floorboards behind her.

"Can I help you?" whispered an aged voice.

Bay jumped.

An old woman stood beside her. Bay hadn't heard anyone approach and saw no door nearby from which a shopkeeper might have emerged. Still, here she was, sudden and silent. Though being startled left Bay uneasy, she couldn't deny there was something quietly enchanting about the woman. Her eyes were the clearest blue Bay had ever seen, almost as transparent as the glass glinting on the shelves around them. And while her skin revealed the soft wear of many years, she wore it with elegance. Her shoulders were held high, her posture composed, and her slender arms seemed capable of more strength than expected.

Behind her, Bay spotted a large iron furnace and a wooden stool. The furnace had a grated door and a lock. It was not lit now, but iron tools, glass rods, and unfinished pieces were scattered along the back wall.

This woman was obviously the artist. She had shaped every piece in this eerie shop.

"Is the Pacific Palace a town near here?" Bay asked, pointing up at the poster. She hadn't meant to ask, but the words seemed to form and rise on their own.

"Is that what you see, child?" the woman said in a honeyed voice. "Yes. It's a bit larger than a town. The largest trading village in the territory, actually."

"Is it far from here?" Bay asked quietly, turning to face her.

"It's about a two-week trip by boat from Avalon," the shopkeeper replied, her pleasant voice sending a shiver up Bay's back.

Avalon must be the name of this little town, Bay thought.

I think you should leave. Something isn't right, Light-Voice whispered again.

"Do you know if Allura is there?" Bay asked. Again, she seemed unable to follow the wise advice of her internal companion.

"Allura..." The woman's lips turned down. Her pleasant tone cracked. She studied Bay closely. "Curious. You see her as well?"

"Yes. Is she there?" Bay said softly, unsure how much she should reveal.

You need to leave. Now! Light-Voice urged.

If she has information on my mom...then maybe she can help. I should trust her, Bay thought.

No! Light-Voice shot back, firmer now.

Bay swallowed the urge to share more. Something felt too open, too exposed.

"That is where she lives, yes," the old woman said. "Why do you want to find her, child? Why go to the Pacific Palace?" Her blue eyes locked on Bay, and she moved closer.

"Oh...I...just want to see her," she managed.

"There are a few ships that take passengers from Avalon to the Pacific Palace," the shopkeeper said. "The transportation dock is just a couple of blocks down the road. But not many will take *humans*."

Bay flinched. *Why did the woman assume she was human?* And more importantly, why was Bay suddenly too afraid to correct her? She glanced toward the door, thinking to inch her way out. But her legs simply would not move.

"I could take you there myself," the woman said smoothly. "It would be such a nice little adventure for us." She stepped closer. Her smile widened, revealing pearly teeth that glittered in the dim light.

Bay stepped back, or tried to—but the woman reached out and gently touched her cheek.

"Would you like to go with me?" she whispered. "All you must do is tell me why you want to go, child. What are you holding back? It can be quite helpful to know the source of every creature's light…"

Run! Light-Voice screamed.

But Bay could not. She was frozen. Secrets tugged at her lips, begging to be spoken. She felt them forming, truths she had no intention of sharing. *I'm a mermaid. Allura is my mother. I ran away. I'm all alone.*

"Oh…well…I," Bay stammered, with sweat beading on her forehead. She tried to fight the compulsion. She had already revealed too much. But it was too late, because the shopkeeper knew everything.

"Say now, will you look at that," the woman said, cocking her head. "You look very much like Allura."

Bay's stomach dropped. "I think I should g-go," she said, her voice shaking. Still her feet would not move. She felt

83

Light-Voice warming inside her, a soft glow trying to pull her out of the trance.

"Oh, I think you should come with me. Your ship awaits," the woman said, pointing to a door behind her. Except that door hadn't been there before. That door had only just appeared and was now where the furnace had been. And beyond it, water glimmered. A false sea. A lie wrapped in heat.

Bay felt her feet begin to move forward. *I wish she would let me go*, she thought desperately. A chill spread from her toes— icy Darkness, surging up her calves. Her fear was feeding it. The taste of old coins filled her mouth. Light-Voice cried out in pain, fighting to hold it back.

And then—Bay stopped. Her body snapped free of its invisible bindings. Her wish had worked.

The old woman blinked, suddenly confused. She seemed to be fighting against something inside herself.

Bay did not wait to see who would win. She turned and ran, her heart thundering in her chest. Her flip-flops slapped the cobblestones, slipping from her feet more than once. She stubbed her toes hard but didn't care. She ran all the way to the Red Sea Inn, not looking back once.

When she finally felt safe enough to pause and catch her breath, she whispered a prayer of thanks to the universe, to anyone who might hear. She had escaped. And despite the horror of it all, despite the nightmare she'd just fled, she couldn't help but smile through the tears. Because now she knew.

Allura was only two weeks away.

CHAPTER SEVENTEEN

The Contessa

She reached the bright red building and finally felt safe enough to pause and catch her breath. Leaning one hand against the rough-textured plaster of the familiar bright red building, Bay waited until her heartbeat slowed and her body settled. In that moment, she wanted only to run upstairs and hide under the thick blankets in her room. She couldn't stop thinking about the feeling of her body being pulled forward, toward the furnace. Her feet had betrayed her. Her thoughts had not been her own.

What she wanted more than anything was to find her dad, to fall into one of his warm, bear hugs, and let everything else melt away. But she had learned something, something glorious. Something she couldn't turn back from. So, instead of running, Bay pushed open the heavy wooden doors of the Red Sea Inn and forced herself to walk to the innkeeper's desk.

She braced herself with the pride of someone who had survived something terrifying and was still moving forward. "Hello," Bay said, trying to sound relaxed.

"Good afternoon," the innkeeper replied with a smile that warmed even her sharp, hawk-like blue eyes.

"Do you know of a ship that takes travelers to other... villages?" Bay asked, her voice wobbling slightly. "An affordable one maybe?"

The innkeeper raised one perfectly manicured eyebrow as she studied Bay's appearance: flushed cheeks, tousled blonde hair, and clothes still messy from her sprint away from the glass shop. Without looking down, the lady opened a drawer and pulled out a small green card and then held it out with a hand tipped in pale-pink polish.

"That should be what you're looking for. Very reasonably priced. And the crew is discreet," she added with a knowing smile.

"Thank you," Bay said, managing a small smile in return as she accepted the card. The innkeeper tilted her head thoughtfully before returning to her work. Bay turned and made her way up the stairs, her legs still a little unsteady from the fear, exhaustion, or whatever strange power had gripped her inside that shop.

Was that witchcraft? Or mer-magic? She shivered. *Please don't let that be mer-magic. I don't want something so evil to be part of me.*

At the top of the stairs, she entered room number twenty-seven and made her way to the nightstand. Beside the golden seashell clock sat a wooden rotary phone. She studied the card. On one side, a golden sailboat glittered beneath the elegant letters: *The Contessa.* On the back, a phone number and a message that read: "Sail away with us on your next adventure!"

Bay dialed the number. "Hello...?" she said, unsure if she was calling the right place.

"Hi," came a young woman's voice. Confident. Warm.

"I—I was hoping to get a ride on the *Contessa*. Is this the right number?"

"Yes," the woman replied easily. "I'm Catalina. I'm the captain of the *Contessa*. Where are you trying to go?"

"I need transportation to the Pacific Palace. I was told you could help."

"We do offer that destination," Catalina said. "We have a couple of trips scheduled next month. When are you looking to leave?"

"Today."

"Today?" A small pause. "We won't be able to leave that soon."

Bay's heart sank. "Oh. Do you know of anyone else leaving tonight?"

"Hmm...no, not that I'm aware of."

"Okay," Bay said, defeated.

"I'm guessing you're in a hurry?" Catalina asked gently.

"A big one," Bay admitted. Her voice cracked with desperation. She was in a hurry to find her mother. And to avoid whoever had chased her across that bridge. If she stayed in Avalon too long, someone was going to find her.

"Well," Catalina said considerately, "why don't we meet up and talk through the details? We might be able to come to a mutual agreement for an earlier departure."

"Okay," Bay replied, nerves tightening in her chest. What kind of agreement? Money, probably. What if Catalina found out she wasn't an adult?

"How about the Sweet Cream Bakery?"

Bay blinked. "Okay," she said, even though she had no idea where that was. She'd figure it out later.

"Want to meet around four?"

"Sure."

"And what's your name?"

Bay hesitated. "Oh…I'm…Jo," she said at last, silently cursing herself for not being prepared again.

"Okay, Jo. See you then."

"Bye," Bay said, and hung up. She exhaled hard. Her legs still trembled, but she couldn't let herself spiral. If she kept moving, she wouldn't have to think.

She went back downstairs and asked the innkeeper about the Sweet Cream Bakery. The woman handed her a visitor's map and circled the location. Bay studied it and sighed in relief when she saw the bakery was nowhere near the glass shop. Across the top of the map were the words: Avalon Cove, as she had correctly guessed at the glass shop.

It was only noon. Even though the morning had been overwhelming, Bay decided to find lunch. She stuck to the center of town, far from the sea's ever-present call. A cozy lunch spot a few doors down offered seafood. Again. She ordered battered fish and crab cakes to go, still thinking about how she had eaten like an animal that morning. She found a bench and ate alone. It was delicious, but she wished the fish had been raw. The salmon at breakfast had been so, so good.

After lunch, she browsed shops to prepare for her journey. Not entirely sure what she'd need for a two-week ocean trip, she wandered and chose carefully. A waterproof satchel. A lined raincoat. Some personal essentials.

Every store impressed her—no plastic bags, no wrapping, no waste. She bought two cloth totes to hold her purchases and was grateful for them; the bags were heavy, and she still had most of her cash. She needed to be careful with her spending, especially if Catalina's "agreement" involved money.

Bay was ready to head back to her room when she spotted an adorable pair of waterproof boots in a shop window. She paused.

Waterproof! Light-Voice squealed.

Bay smiled. She couldn't help herself. She walked in, causing the bell above the lavender door to jingle. The shopkeeper greeted her with a warm hello but did not look up as she was busy helping another customer.

Bay knew what she wanted. She went straight to the shoe section and sat on a white bench between two rows. Out of sight from the rest of the shop, she set her shopping bags down and started sifting through boxes for her size.

The bell above the door jingled again. "Welcome in," the shopkeeper said, followed by a hesitant, "Can I help you?"

"Yes. We're looking for someone."

Bay froze. That voice. Husky, familiar. It was one of the women from the bridge.

"A young girl with blonde hair and dark eyes," another voice added. "About fifteen. Thin. Traveling alone."

They are looking for you!

Bay dropped to her knees and crawled to the end of the aisle. She peeked around the corner and saw two pairs of legs— combat boots, dark trousers. She backed away quickly, heart pounding. She scanned the shop and saw a dressing room. Leaving her bags, she crawled toward it and squeezed under the door, then locked it from the inside.

She stood up and stared into the mirror. Right into her own terrified, black eyes. What if this was the danger her dad had warned her about? *What if Dad called the police?*

Do mermaids have police?

Bay didn't want to find out.

What are you going to do?

I don't know! Bay thought, trembling. Her long, golden-blonde hair shone like a beacon. Her palms were sweaty, her breath shallow. The shopkeeper would see her the moment she left the stall.

I wish my hair was black, she thought in a panic, clenching her eyes shut. A bitter cold pooled at her toes. Pain shot through her fingertips. Her internal Darkness came to greet her fear. Copper and salt flooded her mouth, metallic and raw, like blood in seawater. Her breath turned cold as Light-Voice cried out in pain, the sound sharp and disoriented.

When Bay opened her eyes, she let out a loud gasp and quickly covered her mouth to stifle the sound. She was staring at her reflection, but she was no longer the girl she had been moments before.

CHAPTER EIGHTEEN

The Empty Room

Trent ran his fingers through his sweat-dampened curls, breath heavy in his chest. The morning had been agony since he discovered the empty bed. Atlantis was gone. Or Bay, as she preferred now.

Even after all of these years, it was still hard not to call her Atlantis. The name echoed through his chest like a lullaby from a time before the world fractured. Atlantis had clung to his neck when she was scared of thunder. Bay had run straight into a storm.

He had risen early that day with plans for them to grab breakfast before putting as much distance between them and the ocean as possible. He had been so relieved the night before when he had rescued her just in time. Before the Plowmans could deliver her to the sea. And yet suddenly she was gone! How had he been so careless? He knew what was at risk, and still, he let her go.

The room was stripped of her presence, the bedsheets unruffled, the silence far too loud. His heart had plummeted in his chest. At first, he had bolted from the room, calling her name and sprinting through the quiet neighborhood like a madman, hoping and praying she hadn't gotten far. A flicker of hope sparked when he remembered her phone. She'd left it on. Maybe he wasn't too late. But tracking her location only confused him more. Her signal pinged erratically, looping around a town about an hour away, lingering only minutes in each place before darting somewhere new. He chased her digital ghost through stoplights and backstreets, every turn gnawing deeper into his panic.

Finally, the signal stopped moving. He pulled into a grocery store parking lot, pulse pounding in his ears, scanning every corner for a sign of her. The map led him to a dark green car with tinted windows.

Empty.

As he leaned down to check again, a young woman approached the car. Her brow furrowed, and she was clearly unsettled by the stranger peering through her window.

"I'm sorry," Trent said quickly, raising both hands. "I—I think my daughter left her phone in your car." He pulled up a photo of Bay, his voice tight with desperation.

The woman studied the photo, then bit her lip. She ran a hand through her short strawberry-blonde hair. "I'm a delivery driver," she said. "I give rides sometimes too. I think… yeah, she was with me last night."

Relief and dread tangled in Trent's stomach. They checked the backseat and found her phone jammed between two cushions, switched to silent. He didn't know whether she had done it by accident or on purpose. Either possibility chilled him.

"She asked to go to a gas station near the edge of town," the driver said, voice laced with guilt. "I didn't realize how far I was taking her. I'm so sorry—"

But Trent was already moving. He climbed back into his car and peeled out of the lot; the card still clutched in his fist. There was no time for apologies. He didn't blame the driver. He blamed himself.

He realized that he should have told Bay the full truth. But he hadn't wanted to hurt her. He foolishly thought he could shield her from the worst of it. That a slower reveal would make it easier.

Now, his protective silence might have cost him everything. It pained him even to think of her name, but if Allura found her first...

He didn't finish the thought. He just pressed harder on the gas. The coast was drawing closer. Too close.

CHAPTER NINETEEN

The Wish

Bay stared at herself. Her long blonde hair was gone. In its place, midnight black strands tumbled down past her shoulders. A sharp, metallic tang still clung to the back of her tongue.

How is this possible? Light-Voice asked, startled.

I don't know, Bay thought, grabbing a few strands and holding them up in front of her, just to be sure the mirror wasn't playing tricks.

What are you going to do? Light-Voice asked again.

Bay had no good answer. She knew only that she needed to get out of this store and back to her hotel room as fast as possible. She could hear the shopkeeper wrapping up the conversation with the two people who were looking for her. She kicked herself for not paying closer attention. She should have made an effort to figure out who they were.

"Well, I'll keep my eyes open. I sure hope she's okay. You'll have to excuse me; I'm going to check on a customer. I think I heard something over in the dressing area."

Bay held her breath. Then she heard it: the bell above the door. A departure. She exhaled in relief. Then a sharp knock sounded on the door of the changing room, making her cry out.

"Oh! I'm so sorry! I didn't mean to frighten you," the shopkeeper said gently. "Can I help you with anything?"

"No...I'm fine, thanks," Bay replied, trying to steady her voice.

"All right, then, I'm here if you need anything!"

Bay waited until she was sure the shopkeeper had returned to the counter. Then she turned back to the mirror, running her fingers through the black strands again.

"Please, please stay black," she whispered under her breath and stepped out of the stall. She walked back down the shoe aisle, snatched up her bags, and with her eyes glued to the floor, marched toward the door.

"Thanks for stopping by! Come again!" the shopkeeper called out behind her.

Bay didn't respond. She was already halfway through the door when suddenly she collided directly into someone. Her bags slipped to the ground.

"Oh! Here, let me help you with those," a familiar voice said as a young man crouched down beside her.

"Thanks. I'm so sorry for running into you like that—" Bay began, flustered and scrambling to collect her things.

"It's fine—Ba-Brittany, is that you?"

Bay looked up and saw him: the handsome teen from the fountain, with the same teasing smile stretched across his face. Cyrus. He lifted one of her bags and tucked it behind his back.

"You!" Bay exclaimed, reaching for the bag.

"Wow, you sure found your way around town fast," he said with a grin. "High maintenance are we?" he added, gesturing to her overflowing shopping haul.

"Give me my bag, Cyrus," she said, stretching to grab it.

"I would love to, but my arm hurts where you ran into me," he said pitifully, cradling his biceps with a dramatic wince.

"I'm sure you'll manage," Bay replied, unimpressed, holding out her hand.

He handed the bag back with a smirk. "The black hair looks good," he said, suddenly more sincere. "When did you have time to do all this? I'm actually impressed."

"None of your business," Bay muttered, snatching the bag and stepping around him.

"In a hurry, I see. More shopping to do?" He called after her.

"None of—" she began, turning to glare.

"Yeah, yeah, I know. None of my business. You really should expand your vocabulary."

Bay rolled her eyes. "Thanks. I'll work on that."

"Later, newb!" he called with a wave.

She didn't stop walking until she was back in front of the Red Sea Inn. She was flushed, flustered, and exhausted. Once again, Cyrus had completely knocked her off her rhythm.

Bay eased open the hotel doors. The innkeeper was busy speaking with another guest. Perfect. She darted up the wooden stairs, careful not to draw attention to herself. She didn't want anyone to notice her new hair or all her shopping bags. It hadn't been very long since she'd left the hotel, and there was no way to explain how she'd gone shopping and dyed her hair in such a short time.

Once she reached her room, she locked the door and went straight to the mirror above the dresser. Jet black. Still there.

Black. It looks so depressing. Can you change it back?

I kind of like it. Plus, there are people looking for me, remember? Doesn't hurt to look different.

I wonder who they are, Light-Voice mused.

I'm sure my dad alerted someone, Bay thought. Probably mer-police or something.

But they were already looking for you last night—while he was still sleeping. How did they even know what you looked like?

Bay blinked. *I… I don't know. Maybe he woke up during the night and…* But it didn't make sense. She paused to consider the possibilities. She hadn't seen their faces. Could one of them have been Allura? No. The image didn't fit. She couldn't picture her mother in combat boots. Best not to assume anything. Better to keep hidden.

How did you change your hair? Light-Voice asked, her tone laced with awe.

Could it be a mermaid thing? Part of the transformation? Bay sighed. *There's so much I don't know.*

Maybe mermaids have powers. Your dad did talk about mer-magic, Light-Voice offered.

Bay paced the room, considering. One thing was certain: she couldn't stay here another night. Even though she'd paid in advance, it was too risky. If the searchers came and told the innkeeper her age, she'd be exposed. The woman might've guessed, but it was easier to feign ignorance than to ignore the truth when it was confirmed out loud. Adults never trusted teenagers.

Bay unpacked her bags and started organizing them. Most of her purchases fit into her backpack. The waterproof satchel held her flip-flops, deodorant, shampoo bar, and purse. She would carry everything to the Sweet Cream Bakery and hope Catalina would take her aboard, even beg if she had to. She had to get out of Avalon Cove. She had to reach her mother.

Okay. But do you want to maybe try a different hair color?

Bay ignored the comment. Since when did Light-Voice have so many opinions? It was getting crowded in her thoughts lately. Probably the stress. Or maybe it was the loneliness. She missed Izzy. She missed her dad.

Still, she liked the black. It matched her eyes—dark and endless, like deep water. Something about that depth soothed her. It felt... honest. And no one who saw her now would connect her to the missing little blonde girl.

But how had she done it? The moment had passed too quickly to understand. She'd figure it out later.

Bay straightened the room out of habit. She wanted to leave it just as she had found it. Maybe that would make up for her unannounced exit. She waited until the lobby was empty and the innkeeper was gone. Only a couple sat chatting at the bar. Perfect.

She placed her room key on the large oak desk and then slipped out the door with her backpack and satchel. She unfolded the visitor's map and traced the route with her finger to The Sweet Cream Bakery, her next stop.

At least the map showed her where to go, even if nothing else in her life did.

CHAPTER TWENTY

Sweet Cream Bakery

Bay hustled along the cobblestone streets, avoiding eye contact as she weaved through the late afternoon crowd. Her head stayed low, her backpack heavy on her shoulders, sweat beginning to collect at her lower back. Just when she thought she couldn't take another step, she spotted the shop's sign.

A few minutes later, she stood in front of a periwinkle-blue one-story building. She stepped inside and immediately took in the warm, sugary scent that wrapped around her like a hug.

Powder-blue tables and white chairs dotted the room, matching the striped walls with pink trim. A long glass counter displayed small decorated cakes and treats, pastries too beautiful to eat. Some were frosted with glittering designs, while others were topped with buttercream or shaped like sea creatures, their icing rippling like waves.

Scanning the tables, Bay saw no one sitting alone. Tempted by the aroma, she ordered a seashell-shaped cookie and found a table tucked into the far-right corner. She dropped her bags at her feet and nibbled her treat slowly, watching the door and glancing at the large, sunshine-yellow clock above the register.

At exactly four p.m., a tall girl strode in. She had brown skin, lavender-blue eyes, and a cascade of wild brown curls that tumbled like waves in a storm. Her high cheekbones, sun-warmed complexion, and full red lips gave her an effortless elegance, but there was something roguish in her posture, something daring in the way she moved. She wore fitted black trousers, a flowing white shirt that caught the breeze like a sail, and weathered brown boots laced to the knee. A leather cord was wrapped twice around her wrist like a tether. Something about her seemed familiar.

"You must be Jo?" the girl asked, her voice crisp as she approached.

"Huh? Oh, yes, I'm Jo. And you are...Catarina?"

"Catalina," she corrected, smiling.

"Oh, sorry—Catalina. It's a pretty name."

"Thanks. So, you're looking to go to the Pacific Palace?" Catalina asked, narrowing her eyes slightly as she sat down.

"Well, yes. Didn't you say you offer that trip?"

"Yes, but it's unusual for human women to be in our shore villages—let alone ask for passage to the palace port."

"Human?" Bay repeated, brows lifting.

"Look, it's in the middle of the ocean. The port village services the kingdom below, mostly for merchant trade and transport. Our clients are usually mermaids who cannot transform for very long or those carrying goods."

"Why do you think I'm—oh, no..." Bay groaned.

Oh, yes! Light-Voice chimed as Cyrus sauntered through the door and approached their table wearing a half-smile that immediately made Bay roll her eyes.

Catalina followed her gaze. "You two know each other?"

"Yes," Bay muttered, slapping Cyrus's hand away from her cookie. "But I don't know what he's doing here."

"Ladies," Cyrus said smoothly, bowing with mock elegance before straddling a backward chair between them.

"Oh, me and Ba-Brittany go way back," he added, stealing a piece of Bay's cookie. "My arm still hurts, by the way."

"Cyrus is my brother and business partner," Catalina began, then turned sharply. "Wait—who's Brittany?"

Bay groaned and dropped her head onto the table.

"That's Brittany," Cyrus said, pointing at her. "Isn't it?"

"She told me her name was Jo."

"Interesting..." Cyrus said, casually taking another bite of the cookie.

"Excuse me, everyone."

Bay immediately recognized the husky voice. All heads turned as two women entered. One had short, bright red hair;

the other wore hers pulled into a ponytail. Both wore seafoam-green collared shirts and black pants with shiny metal badges clipped at the hip. Not police, but official. Her heart sank slightly as she saw that neither was Allura.

"We're looking for a human girl, fifteen years old," the redhead announced. "She has long blonde hair and dark eyes. About five feet tall and thin. Traveling alone."

Cyrus raised his eyebrows at Bay. She turned to him, eyes wide, silently shaking her head. A low murmur spread through the bakery as customers glanced around.

Oh no, Light-Voice whispered.

Bay's stomach dropped. Had any of these people seen her earlier today—blonde, alone, browsing the shops? She didn't know who these women were. Had her father sent them? Or were they something worse?

The brunette stepped forward. "If you've seen her or know anything, it's imperative—"

"Oy!" Cyrus called, leaping from his chair.

"No, please," Bay whispered after him.

Catalina turned toward her, brows pinched in concern, as Bay scanned for other exits. There was only one behind the counter. Too far. No way she'd reach it in time. She gripped the table, shutting her eyes. Her toes went cold as Darkness slithered through her veins.

No, no, no..., Light-Voice cried out, beginning its battle against the spread.

"I saw that girl last night," Cyrus announced brightly.

"What's that?" the redhead asked, scrutinizing him.

104

"Yeah. Scrawny thing. Met her by the fountain. Tried saying hi—real feisty. She wasn't very polite."

What an ass! Light-Voice hissed, halting the internal battle to make her thoughts known.

Bay remained frozen, trembling as her heart pounded. If they took her now, she would never know the truth about her mother. And she would never see her father ever again.

"Where is she?" the brunette demanded.

"Hmm...let me think," Cyrus said, tapping his chin. "Is there a reward?"

Bay dared a glance. Catalina's lavender-blue eyes narrowed, locked on her, expression unreadable, the pleasantness gone. Her panic spiked. They were going to turn her in. The coldness crept to her ankles.

"This is not a game," the brunette snapped. "Tell us where she is, or we'll take you in for questioning. And you'll be banned from all mer-villages. Human." The word "human" sounded like venom.

Bay blinked. Cyrus was in fact the only man she had seen in town. Was he the only one?

"Oh, right!" Cyrus said, snapping his fingers. "She said she needed to get to Dremwell. Asked for directions. Seemed in a hurry. I told her about the ferry between here and there, and she was gone without so much as a thank yo-"

"When exactly was this?"

"Last night. Ten, maybe ten-thirty."

"Anything else?"

"Nope. Just happy to help!" he beamed.

The two women exchanged a look and turned sharply, leaving the shop. The doors shut behind them. Conversations resumed, and Bay let out a shaky breath. Her toes warmed again as Light-Voice pushed back Darkness.

Cyrus returned and sat beside her—his smile gone.

Catalina leaned forward, eyes sharp. "Who are you really? And why are the *Magistrata* looking for you?"

Bay looked down. "I can't tell you. And I don't know who the...magi-strata are."

"Oh, you owe that and a thank you," Cyrus said.

"A thank you? For scaring me half to death?"

What?! Light-Voice echoed.

"For throwing them off your scent," Catalina said. "Dremwell is a three-day trip. If we're lucky, they'll be gone a while."

"Oh..." Bay murmured, cheeks flushing.

Catalina leaned closer. Her voice dropped. "Now, who are you?"

CHAPTER TWENTY-ONE

The Truth

Bay hesitated, then decided to tell them the truth, including her real name, and how she had ended up here. Something about the quiet understanding in Catalina's face and the way Cyrus had so smoothly handled the *Magistrata* made her feel like she could trust them. So she began, carefully laying out the events of the past few days. She told them how she had learned that her mother was not only alive but a mermaid. How her father had hidden it from her all her life.

She recounted the glowing stones that had called her to the bridge, the feeling of being chased, the haunting glass shop, and the paralyzing fear. She shared her father's vague warning that danger was coming and finally confessed that, with no idea who was looking for her or why, they should assume the worst.

"So that's why you dyed your hair," Cyrus said.

"Y-yeah," Bay replied. She didn't want to explain the part about how her hair had changed color on its own.

Cyrus raised an eyebrow. "Look, I hate to be the one to say it, but your father lied to you. Again."

Bay shot him a puzzled glance.

"You're not a mermaid," he added, shrugging like it was obvious.

"Cyrus!" Catalina snapped sharply.

"What? I'm just telling her the truth," he said, holding up his hands.

Catalina turned her attention back to Bay, softening her tone. "What he means is that your father may have been mistaken."

"No. He was certain," Bay said, already reaching into her satchel. "He even had a picture that proved it."

Catalina's brow furrowed. "What picture?"

"It matched the poster and the fountain in town," Bay answered, now digging with more urgency.

"Fountain?" Cyrus echoed, confused.

"Yes, the green serpentine one," she said, pulling open her backpack.

"What about it?" Catalina asked.

"The figure in that fountain," Bay said, as her fingers closed around the folded paper. "That's my mother."

Cyrus and Catalina stared at her.

"She's the mermaid in the fountain and on the poster in the glass shop. Her name is Allura."

"We know who she is," Catalina said, her voice suddenly guarded.

"You think your mother is Allura? Un-real," Cyrus said, letting out a laugh.

Bay's frustration flared. She yanked the photo free and shoved it toward him. "If my father was lying, then explain this."

Cyrus snatched the photo from her hands; the smirk faded from his face as he looked at it. His posture changed, stiffening. Catalina leaned in and gasped.

Without warning, Cyrus ripped the photo into shreds.

"What are you doing?" Bay shouted, shoving her chair back so hard it scraped the floor. She lunged for the pieces as they fluttered to the powder-blue tabletop, but Cyrus swept them into his fist before she could reach them. "You destroyed it!"

"You can't wave something like that around," he hissed under his breath. "Do you have any idea what might've happened if someone had seen it?"

"You could have asked before destroying it!" Bay snapped. Her voice rose, and several people in the small café turned their heads.

"Both of you—enough," Catalina said, stepping in between them as the tension thickened. "Bay, sit down."

Bay clenched her fists, but after a moment's pause, she sat back down. Her cheeks burned, and her chest heaved with adrenaline.

Catalina turned to her brother. "She didn't know, Cy."

Cyrus exhaled and nodded. "Fine."

Catalina turned her gaze back to Bay, her expression more serious than before. "Something like that photo could unravel everything," she said as she lowered herself into her chair again. "If it got into the wrong hands, especially the Believers."

Bay's brow furrowed. "The Believers?"

"They're humans who hunt for proof of merfolk," Catalina explained. "Some are obsessed with proving our existence. Others... want revenge. There are entire families who have been abandoned by mermaids as well as lovers who were left behind when the truth came out. Some of them want back in. Some just want to punish us for leaving them behind. And others, the worst of them, want to exploit our kind—to sell us, to experiment on us, to crack open our magic like it's something they can own."

Cyrus leaned forward, arms folded on the table. "There are strict laws about this kind of contraband. If anyone else in here had seen that photo, you could've been in serious trouble. And it wouldn't have just been you. Catalina and I would've been arrested for helping you. Even the café owner could've been dragged in for questioning."

Bay's anger crumbled into guilt. Her shoulders slumped. "I didn't know. That photo meant everything to me. I am sorry."

"It had to be destroyed," Catalina said gently. "But Cyrus could've handled it better."

Bay looked down at her lap, nodding slowly. "I get it."

There was a pause before Cyrus spoke again, his tone quieter this time. "I'm sorry about the photo."

Bay gave a small shrug, trying not to let emotion rise again. "Thanks. And... sorry I almost punched you."

Cyrus grinned. "I would've liked to see you try."

Bay cracked a reluctant smile. The tension broke just enough to breathe again.

The moment of levity softened something in her chest. Then she turned to Catalina. "So, if you know my mom... then you must know my father, Trent Sideris?"

Catalina and Cyrus exchanged a look.

"But... he's dead," Cyrus said, looking uncertain. "He died years ago."

"He's not," Bay said quickly. "He raised me."

Another look passed between the twins, more loaded than the last. Entire thoughts seemed to move between them in silence. Bay didn't need to hear their conversation to know something had changed.

Catalina leaned forward slightly, folding her hands on the table. "Allura is the Queen."

Bay blinked. "Queen?"

"Of the Pacific Ocean," Catalina clarified gently.

Bay's thoughts tumbled over each other. "Then... my father is the King?"

Catalina gave a small shake of her head. "There are no kings. Mermaids don't have them. Allura is one of the Seven Sea Queens."

Bay stared at her, stunned. "Then what was my father?"

"He was her *Socius Animae*."

"*Socius Animae*?" Bay repeated, the term unfamiliar on her tongue.

"A soulmate," Catalina murmured. "A love so deep it extends a human's life. It allows them to breathe underwater for a time."

Bay frowned. "So... my dad could transform into a mermaid?"

"No," Catalina replied. "He could swim and survive beneath the surface, but he could never fully transform."

Bay's brows drew together. "Do all mermaids have soulmates?"

"No. It's rare. The Queen's *Socius Animae* was the only one we've ever heard of."

Bay sat back, trying to absorb it all. "Then why don't you think I'm a mermaid?"

"It's your eyes," Catalina said softly.

"My eyes?"

"All merfolk have blue eyes. Always."

Bay reached up, almost reflexively, and touched the skin beneath her own. "But I look just like her. And the stones, they lit up for me!"

Catalina hesitated, then admitted, "Hmm...It is true that only mermaids, or those bonded to them, can see their glow..."

"Can you transform?" Cyrus asked.

"I—I tried once," Bay said. Her voice dropped. "But nothing happened." She felt the memory of the water again, the way it had wrapped around her like maybe she belonged to it. That strange pull hadn't faded. Her fingers reached for the chain around her neck, and she absently toyed with the pendant that hung there.

Catalina leaned closer, her eyes narrowing. "That necklace..."

"My dad gave me this when I was little. Said it was an heirloom."

Catalina's expression shifted, and for a moment, she seemed to forget Bay was even there. "That necklace..." she said softly, then gathered herself. "It looks like the Star of Isis."

She didn't elaborate right away. Her gaze dropped to the gem, then flicked to Cyrus, who watched her with a rare stillness.

"It was lost during the Great Storm," she said, her voice quieter now. "The same night Queen Allura lost her baby... and her *Socius Animae*."

Even the air around the table seemed to hold its breath.

"No one speaks of that night," Catalina continued. "Not really. Us merfolk... we keep our secrets close. We protect our own. But everyone felt the loss. The Queen's grief rippled across the ocean. Her power nearly tore apart the currents. The sky wept with her." She paused and then added with quiet finality, "The necklace was never recovered."

She glanced at Cyrus, and the two of them locked eyes. A silent exchange passed between them, heavier than anything that had come before.

Bay stared at the necklace in her palm, the gem still warm against her skin. The words pressed into her like a weight: *The same night Queen Allura lost her baby... and her soulmate.*

Her throat tightened. Ever since her father had told her that her mother was alive, she had wondered what could be keeping her distant and so unreachable. But what if Allura hadn't known they were alive? What if she had believed her child was gone, taken by the sea?

The ache that bloomed and pounded in Bay's chest felt almost unbearable. It wasn't rejection that had shaped her life, it was grief. Her grief. Her mother's grief. Her father's, too.

"She thought I was dead," Bay whispered, more to herself than to them. Her voice trembled. "She didn't leave me... She lost me."

A sharp breath caught in her lungs. "And she never knew," she said again, this time with more force, as if saying it aloud might anchor her.

She mourned you, Light-Voice said gently. *But she never stopped loving you.*

Bay blinked rapidly, trying to hold back the flood of emotion. She didn't know what scared her more: the thought that her mother had never known she survived, or the fear that, after all this time, the truth wouldn't be enough.

Catalina turned back to Bay. "That necklace is passed down from Queen to Queen. It was given to the first Queen of the merfolk by the Sea Goddess Isis herself."

A gentle warmth pulsed against her skin, like a heartbeat where her necklace sat. Soothing. Steady. Almost alive.

It remembers us, Light-Voice whispered.

She tucked the necklace back beneath her shirt, her hand trembling slightly. She didn't want to lose it too. Not like the photo.

"This is indeed strange..." Cyrus muttered, running his hands through his hair.

"My dad... he never told me any of this," Bay said quietly. Her voice cracked despite her effort to stay steady.

"I believe you," Catalina replied. Her voice was calm, and her eyes were kind.

Cyrus leaned forward again, his tone shifting back to something more practical. "So, what's your plan? Just walk into the palace and say, "Hi, I'm the Queen's long-lost daughter'?"

"She has evidence," Catalina interjected before Bay could answer. "And the *Magistrata* are after her. That's not a coincidence."

Bay nodded, the words forming before she could stop them. "I need to find her. If I could just see her face to face... maybe she'd know. Maybe I'd know."

Cyrus and Catalina looked at each other again. They didn't speak, but Bay could almost hear the decision forming in their silence. Twins, she realized. Their symmetry wasn't just physical, it was in how they moved and how they weighed a choice together without needing to speak.

Finally, Catalina nodded. "Alright. We'll take you."

Bay's heart skipped. "Really?"

"You can stay with us," Catalina added. "At least until we figure out what's going on. You shouldn't be out there alone."

Cyrus gave a half-shrug, trying to sound casual. "*The Contessa's* not fancy, but it floats."

Bay smiled, small but real.

"Let's finish this conversation on the *Contessa*, though," Catalina said, already rising.

"Anywhere but the glass shop," Bay muttered, standing to gather her things.

As she reached for her backpack, Cyrus grabbed it and slung it over his shoulder. "Don't worry," he said. "I won't destroy anything."

Bay smirked. "Thanks."

She followed them out of the Sweet Cream Bakery, heart pounding, hope flickering back to life in her chest.

CHAPTER TWENTY-TWO

The Weight of Shadows

Until recently, Bay's mind had always been calm. Even when the world around her spun wildly, there was a stillness beneath it. I was always there, nestled in the quiet spaces between her thoughts, like a whisper, a guide. It was effortless. Natural. She moved through the world with a sharpness I admired, a quiet strength. I was the part of her that kept her grounded.

But now...something is different. I can't name it. I can barely feel it. But I can sense things, and I know this: I am growing weaker and more distant, while something else, something darker, is growing more powerful. Her hair, the way it changed without dye, without reason, wasn't natural. Not even mer-natural. It happened after the fear. After the wish. After Darkness.

I've tried not to name it. The thing curling at the edges of her soul. I can't see it, not really, but I feel it. It presses against me like a rising tide. Not her thoughts, or her dreams but something other. And when she makes those wishes—I burn. With a kind of pain that doesn't belong in thought. A crack in the space where I live.

Still, I try to hold on. I remind her of right and wrong. I steady her when she doubts. I love her, though I have no name for that kind of love. I am her, and she is me—or she was. Lately, it feels like I'm being pushed aside. Not silenced, not yet. But I wonder: if she grows too powerful, if she forgets the sound of my voice...

Will I vanish?

At first, I felt awe. She's so strong. So brave. She dares to want more. But now I feel something else: fear.

Because this new power inside her doesn't love her. It doesn't guide. It uses. It slithers through her veins when she's scared or aching. It rises when her desire is strong enough. Each wish brings it to life, and I crumble with pain.

Thoughts aren't supposed to feel pain. I never used to. I ache in ways I don't understand. I used to think I could protect her from anything. I used to push back the dark. Now, I can barely hold my shape when it arrives.

And it's not just Darkness anymore. It's him. Cyrus. I want to talk to him, and not just through her. Not just in the echoes of her thoughts. I want him to hear me. I want him to see me. When he laughs, something in me flickers.

She doesn't know. I don't even know what it is, this new ache I carry when he's nearby. Not quite longing. Just...the sharpness of being unseen.

But I stay. Even when I feel myself dimming. Even when her power pulls toward something ancient and wild and terrifying. Even when she forgets how to listen for me.

I stay. Because she is mine. And I am hers. And whatever comes next...

I won't let it take her.

CHAPTER TWENTY-THREE

The Dock

As the three of them headed to the northern side of the island, the late afternoon sun dipped lower in the sky, casting a golden glow over the water, while the cool ocean breeze chased away the heat of the day. Their footsteps echoed in rhythm on the cobblestone road, a soft, comforting sound in Bay's ears.

"If you take a look to your left," Cyrus said in a mock tourist-guide voice, "you'll notice the ever-so-subtle Fans of Fins shop, where you can find everything needed to treat and pamper your scales." He pointed to a bright neon yellow sign shaped like a giant tail fin, the words Fans of Fins written in navy blue across its center.

"Why, thank you, Tour Master," Bay laughed.

"Hey, I'm just making sure you get the full experience," Cyrus replied, continuing to point out various landmarks around Avalon Cove. Bay, entertained, was enjoying this new, whimsical side of the island village.

Bay let out a small sigh of relief as they drew closer to the eastern docks. Her eyes drifted toward the horizon where the sun dipped low and streaked the waves in gold. The Glass Shop, marked in red ink on the innkeeper's map, was tucked safely on the opposite side of the island, near the northwest cliffs. Even now, with Cyrus walking just ahead and Catalina bringing up the rear, she couldn't summon the courage to pass it. Some part of her still trembled at the memory of its sharp angles and shimmering danger. It was easier to keep her focus forward, to let the wind pull her toward the promise of sea and salt.

With each step, the magnetic tug of the ocean grew stronger, coiling itself around her chest and whispering things she didn't quite understand. The waves pounded rhythmically against the dock pylons, loud enough that Cyrus's voice became little more than a muffled hum. When the shoreline finally came into view, her breath caught in her throat. For a terrifying second, she nearly dropped her satchel to heed her reckless urge to run full tilt toward the edge and dive in. Her hands tightened. Her jaw clenched. She shook her head and blinked hard, forcing herself to stay grounded, to remain in her body. The sea had been calling to her, but this felt different. This felt urgent. Hungry.

I'm here whispered Light-Voice gently, a thread of calm through the rising tide of emotion.

Swallowing hard, Bay forced her feet to follow Cyrus onto the long stretch of cement dock where several boats bobbed and creaked on the water. The dock had been painted an unapologetic bright pink, and though the paint was chipped in places, it still offered a bold contrast to the dark sea beyond. Its surface was rough beneath her shoes, scraping lightly on the soles with each step. Shallow puddles dotted the walkway, but her footing remained firm as she moved farther out onto the pier.

Though the salty breeze calmed her body, Bay trembled slightly as she walked behind Cyrus, and she was relieved to have Catalina following her in case she slipped into the deep water. She gulped as the water lapped below them, a dizzying blue-green blur that made her stomach clench. She swallowed again, painfully aware that she still didn't know how to swim.

Then, she saw it.

The Contessa.

It was the last boat on the dock, rising like a ship from a dream. Sleek and elegant, its polished wooden hull caught the sun's final light like a mirror. The cabin was painted a vivid teal, bright even in the growing dusk, and the sails stood tall and pristine, white as bone against the shadowing sky. Time had clearly left its mark in subtle ways, with weathered edges and faded trim, but everything about the boat radiated care. It didn't look like a relic or a novelty. It looked loved. Bay guessed that it could hold at least twenty people comfortably, though she suspected it hadn't seen a crowd in years. As she stepped closer, a strange mix of anticipation fluttered in her chest.

Cyrus leapt onto the boat in a single, easy motion. Bay paused at the edge of the dock, heart pounding as she stared down into the churning sea. The water lapped hungrily against the wooden posts, and in that moment, something sharp and cold echoed through her mind. *Jump.* The word came unbidden, like a forgotten command rising to the surface, and her legs trembled beneath her. She took a step back, her breath catching, afraid her body might obey without permission.

"Don't worry, I've got you," Catalina said, her voice a steady presence as she appeared at Bay's side. She placed a hand gently on Bay's arm, guiding her forward with quiet assurance. Bay leaned into the touch, letting it ground her as she edged closer to the boat. With Catalina's help, she climbed onto the Contessa's deck, one hand gripping the rail while the other searched for balance.

After the moment when her feet touched the wooden boards, she felt the gentle sway of the ocean beneath her. It rocked the boat just slightly, like a cradle in motion, and a shiver ran through her—not from the breeze, but from the lingering echo of that voice. It hadn't been Light-Voice, and that terrified her. The voice was colder, foreign. For one awful second, she feared it might have belonged to Darkness.

We're safe now, Light-Voice whispered faintly, as if it had been holding its breath too.

Bay said nothing aloud, but her fingers tightened around the rope railing as she followed Cyrus toward the cabin door. Each step was a study in concentration. Her balance wavered with every subtle shift of the deck, and though the polished wood gleamed beneath her feet like something sacred, her eyes kept drifting to the edge, to the sea that sparkled just beyond. It looked too beautiful. Too easy to fall into. Her legs shook. She forced herself to keep moving, eyes fixed on the teal-painted door ahead.

They reached it together, the three of them, and Bay's gaze lingered on the carvings etched into the wood. Strange creatures danced across the surface—half-goat, half-finned animals with curling horns and scaled tails, all wrapped in circlets of flowers and waves. The images were unlike anything she'd seen before, and she hadn't finished taking them in when Cyrus reached for the handle and swung the door open.

Inside, a narrow ladder led steeply down into the belly of the boat. The space looked tight, but not impassable, and one by one they descended, squeezing through the narrow passage until they reached the lower level. Bay blinked in surprise. She had expected cramped quarters, maybe something musty or mechanical, but instead found herself standing in a room that was, somehow, warm and inviting.

"This is the galley, or, as landlubbers say, the kitchen," Cyrus announced, sweeping an arm with dramatic flair around the room. "There are three bedrooms and an engine room below."

"It's bigger than I thought it would be," Bay said, still adjusting to the swaying floor beneath her feet. She could stand comfortably, and to her surprise, the pull of the ocean had dulled. The ache in her limbs had faded. The cold was gone.

The kitchen burst with color. Drawers painted in faded hues of teal, orange, and purple, their edges smoothed by years of use. A half-shell sink glowed softly, its surface shimmering with a natural, pearl-like sheen. Overhead, four round lights hung from metal rods, each one wrapped with vines or sea plants that pulsed gently with golden flickers, as if lit by heartbeats.

Bay turned in a slow circle, her eyes wide with wonder.

She was enchanted.

"It's not much," Cyrus said with pride, placing Bay's backpack on the kitchen booth. "But it's home."

It's magical, Light-Voice murmured with awe.

"It's spectacular," Bay agreed.

"Thanks," Catalina said with a soft smile. "Cyrus's room is through the orange door. Mine's the red one behind the stairs. You're in the guest room. It is through the lilac door."

She guided Bay to the room and opened it. Inside was a full bed against the far wall, its lavender bedspread matching the door's pastel hue. A small dresser nestled beside a silvery sink, and through a narrow archway, Bay glimpsed a modest bathroom tucked neatly into the corner. Sheer, silvery curtains shimmered at the small circular window, casting reflections that danced across the room. For the first time in days, Bay felt a hint of calm settle over her. It wasn't home, but it felt like she could finally exhale.

After setting her things down and running her fingers along the edge of the dresser as if to test its reality, she returned to the galley. The scent of sizzling fish greeted her. Cyrus stood at the small stove, humming as he fried fillets in a battered skillet, while Catalina chopped vegetables with the effortless rhythm of someone who had done it a thousand times. When Bay offered to help, Catalina handed her a cutting board and a few ripe tomatoes. The three of them moved around each other with surprising ease, the quiet sounds of cooking layered with the occasional clink of cutlery and the rustle of sea air through the open portholes.

They ate dinner on the deck, plates balanced on their laps as the sky faded into a tapestry of peach and violet. The sea glittered beneath them, calm and vast, stretching far beyond the dock into the darkening horizon.

Over the meal, Bay learned, just as she had suspected, that Cyrus and Catalina were twins. Their mother, a mermaid, had fallen in love with a human, an American tour boat captain with sunburned arms and an easy grin. He was charming at first. But when he discovered her true nature, his love twisted into something possessive and controlling. They lived in Avalon Cove while the twins were young, but he became increasingly paranoid that she would abandon him for the sea. Eventually, his suspicion gave way to cruelty. He took the family far inland, away from the ocean, and the abuse grew worse.

When the twins were twelve, their mother finally fled with them, returning to Avalon Cove in search of safety and salty air. But the weight of their father's memory was too much. After a few years, she returned to her homeland deep in the Indian Ocean, hoping Catalina would follow. Instead, Catalina stayed behind with Cyrus. They inherited their mother's boat and began to build a life of their own. It hadn't been easy.

Bay could feel the weight of their journey. They didn't have much, but they had each other, and the strength of their bond showed in every motion.

Later, as they cleaned up, Bay watched the way Catalina and Cyrus moved in sync. There was no hesitation between them, no pause in the rhythm. Catalina handed dishes just before Cyrus needed them, and he dried and stowed them with practiced ease. Bay wondered what it would be like to have a sibling. Maybe she wouldn't have felt so alone all those years.

Maybe that's why I have always been with you, Light-Voice whispered.

That night, tucked into her lilac room, Bay fell asleep quickly, exhausted but grateful. She had found friends, a safe harbor, and a boat that felt like it belonged to the sea.

CHAPTER TWENTY-FOUR

Harbor Dues

The next morning, Bay woke up surprised by how comfortably she had slept, despite the gentle rocking of the boat. She heard movement above deck and went to investigate, finding Cyrus struggling to hoist a small dinghy with a pulley system. She rushed over to help, grabbing the other end of the rope a few feet away. Together, they hauled the boat onto the *Contessa's* deck.

Cyrus winked as he strapped it down. "Went out hunting this morning," he said with a grin. "Got a nice catch."

Bay walked over to the bucket he pointed to and burst out laughing. It was full of seaweed.

For breakfast, the three of them ate scrambled eggs and seaweed in the kitchen cabin, Bay's new favorite dish.

Afterward, they headed ashore to gather supplies for their upcoming journey. They planned to leave the next morning. On the way back, just as they were nearing the dock, Cyrus suddenly grabbed Bay and Catalina and pulled them behind an old brick building.

"What's going on?" Catalina asked, frowning.

"Sumner," Cyrus said, nodding toward a short man standing near the *Contessa*.

"Who's that?" Bay asked.

"We rent our dock space from him," Cyrus explained.

"Why are we hiding from him?" Bay pressed.

"We owe him money," Cyrus admitted, his voice tense.

"Money we don't have," Catalina added quietly.

Bay raised an eyebrow. "Can't you just talk to him?"

"He isn't really the 'talking' type," Cyrus replied. "We could lose our spot. He owns every transportation dock in Avalon Cove. If we get kicked out, we'd have to sail to another town and start over."

Bay glanced toward the man, then back at them. "How much do you owe?"

"Two months' rent," Cyrus said, avoiding her eyes.

Bay could see their embarrassment. They didn't have much. It made her think of the comfortable life she had known with her father, and the contrast stung.

"He keeps raising the rent when we're late," Cyrus added. "And since he owns all the docks, there's nothing we can do."

Bay looked from Cyrus to Catalina, then turned and walked straight toward Sumner.

"Bay, wait!" they hissed in unison behind her.

But she didn't stop.

As she approached Sumner, he grabbed her arm roughly. "Hey, you! Do you know where that Cyrus kid is—or his sister?" he barked.

Bay jerked her arm free and faced him. "Yes," she said, surprising herself with the calmness of her voice.

"Well, where are they?" he demanded, his face close enough that she could smell his sour breath.

"Why would I tell you?" Bay asked, meeting his gaze.

"Because they owe me money! Now tell me where they are, you little—"

Bay raised an eyebrow. "Hmm... not sure I want to do that. What's in it for me?"

He scowled. "Or I'll knock some sense into you! They don't care about humans on this island, kid."

Bay rolled her eyes as passersby began to stare.

Bay, don't provoke him. We don't want to draw attention, Light-Voice warned.

"Fine," Bay said, more to herself than to Sumner. "They told me to give you the rent they owe. Actually, I came here looking for you."

"You better not be messing with me, girl," he growled.

Bay reached into her wallet and pulled out the cash. "Here's what they owe you."

He scowled, counting it. "You're twenty dollars short!"

Bay smiled sweetly. "Right, can't forget the twenty dollars." She handed it over. "And here's more for next month."

Sumner stood there, mouth agape, as Bay walked back to the corner, where Catalina and Cyrus were watching, stunned.

"Bay, you didn't... you shouldn't have!" Catalina cried, pulling Bay into a hug and whispering, "Thank you," in her ear.

"It's for me, too," Bay said with a grin. "You guys are taking me to the Palace!"

Cyrus looked uneasy. "This is too much, Bay. You have to get your money back."

"Right, I'm sure that guy would hand it over," Bay laughed. Then, seeing their worried faces, she softened. "I've never been

131

on an ocean voyage, and I don't have any supplies. You can count it toward food, lodging—whatever. I'm happy to help."

"It's still too much," Cyrus said.

"Well, you haven't heard my list of luxuries and the menu I expect," Bay teased, flashing a grin. "I'm 'high maintenance,' remember?"

Cyrus smiled shyly. "You're probably right."

Bay gave him a playful smack on the arm, and the three of them laughed their way back down to the boat. As she followed them, the laughter still warm in her chest, she glanced once more at the sea. She had no idea what lay ahead—but for the first time in her life, she wasn't facing it alone.

They had barely set foot on the *Contessa* when Catalina leaned in close to Bay.

"Thanks again," she said softly. "Really."

Bay smiled. "Anytime."

Catalina gave her arm a quick squeeze and started to turn away when Cyrus raised an eyebrow.

"Where are you off to, Cat?" he asked, a teasing note in his voice.

Catalina shot him a knowing look over her shoulder. "Just helping someone dock."

Cyrus smirked. "Uh-huh. Real helpful."

Bay followed his gaze as Catalina made her way toward a small skiff pulling in. A beautiful young woman stood at the helm, her sun-bleached hair tied in a careless knot, guiding the boat with practiced ease. Catalina called out something, and the girl grinned. Together, they secured the lines, laughing as they tied off the skiff.

Cyrus crossed his arms, watching them with a small smile.

"She's one of Catalina's exes. I think there are still feelings there."

Bay glanced over thoughtfully. "Still? So...why'd they break up?"

He shrugged. "Catalina doesn't talk about it much. But they're still close."

Bay nodded, watching the two stroll off down the dock in easy conversation. She tucked the moment away, one more thread in the tapestry of people she was starting to care about.

CHAPTER TWENTY-FIVE

Jump

Bay woke up early the next morning, her entire body tingling with excitement. In two weeks, she would be at the Pacific Palace—her mother's palace. The thought made her breath catch and her chest tightened with possibility and nerves. She couldn't stay in bed a moment longer. Hearing no sounds from the other rooms, she quietly climbed the little ladder and unhooked the latch to peek her head above deck. A hush lay over the world. The morning was crisp, cool, and kissed with the golden hue of the newly risen sun.

Bay stepped fully onto the deck and wandered to the boat's edge. Grabbing the rope siding, she leaned over, staring into the water below. It shimmered like pink and gold glass.

Jump, the word struck her thoughts like a bell. Not loud, but impossible to ignore.

"Jump?" She repeated timidly.

But you can't swim, Light-Voice reminded her.

Jump.

The call wormed itself into the marrow of her bones. Bay had always assumed that her fascination with the water derived from her father's mysterious prohibitions. But this current overwhelming compulsion to jump in was downright scary. The pull she had felt for days now paled in comparison to this. The ocean thrummed in her veins. The land and air were suddenly suffocating. She ached to be submerged.

Go back downstairs! You can't swim!

But the call grew louder. A command. A hunger.

She stood transfixed, staring at the waves lapping the side of the boat. Bay tried to take a step forward, but her foot refused to move.

Snap out of it! Light-Voice cried. The strain echoed through her. Bay's muscles tensed, trembling beneath the surface. She couldn't move forward. Light-Voice was holding her still.

"Let go," she cried, as she gripped the rope siding, using it to drag herself closer to the edge. She was speaking to the voice inside her. The ocean's call sliced through her, demanding an answer.

Please, I'm trying to protect you! Let me help!

Bay closed her eyes and focused. With everything in her, she tore herself free of the invisible grip. She took a step forward. Her whole body lifted onto the balls of her feet, straining toward the sea.

Don't do this! Light-Voice shouted, the sound ragged and full of panic. *Bay, please!*

Too late. Her upper body tilted. She fell forward and plunged into the water.

The plunge took her breath away. For one impossible moment, she felt relief. The water wrapped around her, cool and quiet. It was a return, a homecoming. It held her.

Then, her lungs spasmed. Her eyes stung. Panic surged. She kicked hard, limbs flailing as she surfaced. A wave smacked her in the face. She inhaled salt water, choking. Her arms clawed upward. She broke the surface again and cried out into the air. She felt herself sinking and kicked harder, but the weight of her limbs dragged her down.

Bay, kick! Light-Voice cried.

She kicked and flayed, but she was still sinking.

Then, arms wrapped securely around her. She was pulled, chest to chest, with someone steady and strong. They broke the surface, and she inhaled sharply. Her arms wrapped tightly around sturdy shoulders.

Cyrus.

She clung to him as he cut through the water, dragging them both toward the *Contessa*. Catalina appeared above, calling their names. The rope ladder dropped, and together they climbed. Bay collapsed onto the deck, coughing, sputtering, shivering.

"What were you thinking?!" Cyrus shouted as he kicked off his soaked socks and stormed toward her. His clothes were soaked. Water streamed from his hair.

Bay stared at her hands, unable to speak.

Catalina dropped beside her with a towel, wrapping her gently. "Bay, what happened? I thought you couldn't swim."

"I can't," Bay rasped.

"Then why jump?" Cyrus's voice cracked with intensity.

"I didn't mean to," she said, her voice breaking. Her chest heaved, and the tears started. "I didn't mean to."

"Was it an accident?" Catalina asked, eyes full of concern.

"That wasn't an accident," Cyrus snapped. "And no, I'm not going away!"

Bay blinked, confused. "What?"

"Fine," Cyrus muttered, turning. He stomped below deck, the hatch slamming shut behind him.

"I'm sorry," Bay called weakly after him.

"He's just worried about you," Catalina said, pulling her into an embrace. "That scared him."

Bay allowed herself to be held. Her body still trembled, not just from cold but from the memory. The pull.

After a few minutes, Catalina asked again, her voice calm and quiet. "What really happened?"

Bay hesitated. "I had to jump," she said finally. "The ocean... it called me. Every day, the urge gets stronger. It's not just a want. It's like if I don't go in, something inside me will break."

Catalina's eyes narrowed. Thoughtful. Concerned.

"Is that normal?" Bay asked. "For mermaids?"

Catalina shook her head. "No. Mermaids feel connection. But not compulsion. Not like this." She paused. "That wasn't a calling. That was dangerous."

"But mermaids can't drown."

Catalina looked at her carefully. "I don't think you're a mermaid."

Bay's breath caught. "But you said you'd take me to Allura. I thought you believed me."

"I believe your father believed it. I believe you deserve to know the truth. But this... this isn't normal."

Bay swallowed hard. The tears slipped quietly down her cheeks.

"Look," Catalina said gently, "you can't do that again. Until we figure out what's going on, you need to stay below deck. Promise me."

Bay nodded. "I promise."

I believe you, Light-Voice whispered.

Bay leaned into Catalina's side. Just for a moment.

Later, Cyrus returned. His face was unreadable. He set a plate of scrambled eggs in front of her, and next to it, a bright orange life vest.

"You wear this," he said. "Always. Until you can swim."

Bay nodded, meeting his eyes. There was no teasing in his voice, only certainty.

"I will," she said.

Drowning, she decided, was not something she ever wanted to repeat.

Even if Cyrus was the one to save her.

CHAPTER TWENTY-SIX

Loose Threads

The chamber rose high above the crashing surf, a throne room suspended at the heart of the Pacific Palace, its white marble walls veined with opal and saltstone. Shifting blue fire danced in suspended sconces along the walls, casting flickering waves of light across the vaulted ceiling and polished floor, as if the sea itself moved within the stone. Coral spires climbed up each corner, luminous and ancient, reaching toward carved arches that framed the endless ocean beyond. At the chamber's center stood a massive marble table, its surface inlaid with silver currents and an enormous map of the Pacific territory, studded with colored glass markers that glinted like scattered treasure.

Queen Allura stood motionless at its center, a figure carved from the very bones of the sea.

Maris and Delmar knelt before her. Maris, with her lower-pitched, throaty voice, was the first to speak. "Your Majesty. We tracked the girl into the lowlands near Avalon Cove. We had a clear trail—footprints and recent disturbances along the cliff paths."

"Then where is she?" Allura asked without looking up from the map.

Delmar shifted, restless. "She was ahead of us on the bridge. We had her cornered. She couldn't have crossed into town without us seeing her."

"And yet, she did." Allura's voice was calm, razor-sharp.

Maris inclined her head, her short red hair swaying slightly. "We...lost the trail, Your Majesty. She vanished."

"Vanished," Allura repeated quietly. The word echoed like a memory.

"There was no splash," Delmar added quickly. "No fall into the sea. No scent trail. Nothing. One moment she was there. The next...gone."

For a moment, only the crackling of the firelight filled the silence.

"And the boy?" Allura asked.

Delmar hesitated. Though she stood taller than the Queen, Allura still seemed to tower over her. "A human with brown hair, tall. Met us outside town. Claimed he saw her running toward Dremwell."

Maris scoffed. "It was a lie. Dremwell's roads were untouched. A fool's errand. He sent us away on purpose."

Delmar added, "We believe he is aiding her."

Allura tapped one long finger against the map. "A human ally," she mused. "Curious."

"We should seize him," Maris growled.

"No," Allura said sharply. "Not yet. His usefulness is not exhausted."

Delmar exchanged a glance with Maris but said nothing.

Allura's gaze traced the coastal towns etched into the map—Dremwell, Avalon Cove, Seastar Bluffs, and farther south, Crystal Cove. "If she slipped through Avalon," she said thoughtfully, "she'll need shelter. Familiar ground." She tapped Crystal Cove once, lightly, a pearl ring glinting on her finger. "Quietly," she ordered. "Put feelers there. No grand sweeps. No scare tactics. I want her flushed, not warned."

Delmar bowed. "Yes, Your Majesty."

Maris bowed as well, though slower, more reluctantly.

"Dismissed," Allura said.

They rose and left without another word, their shadows merging with the undulating light. When the door sealed shut behind them, the weight of the chamber seemed to shift.

Allura exhaled slowly, removing her crown and setting it down with a soft, deliberate clink against the marble. Her reflection shimmered in the polished surface, sharp, regal, and weary. They had to find her.

Before he did.

Her hand drifted over the map, pausing above Crystal Cove. The coastline there was broken and wild, caves hidden by tide-shift, cliffs veiled by mists. A perfect place for fugitives and for her to lose them once more. For old mistakes to rise again. She could almost hear Trent's voice, low and unyielding, echoing from a memory she had buried beneath duty and salt and time.

Allura pressed her hand flat against the table, steadying herself. *I will not fail them again.* Her fingers curled into a fist. She would be found. She would be secured before Trent reached her.

Before the past could reclaim the future she had fought to protect.

CHAPTER TWENTY-SEVEN

Tangled Knots

Bay sat on a deck chair, life vest securely fastened, fiddling with her necklace as she stared off into the sea. The pull to dive into the water was strong as ever, but something else tugged at her mind too, more restless, more confusing. Then she heard footsteps on the cabin stairs.

Cyrus.

He moved with easy, careless energy, and Bay couldn't help but smile as he passed her. He pulled a long, thin rope knotted in several places from under a bucket and sat cross-legged on the deck, his bare foot tapping an idle rhythm against the wood.

"What are you thinking about?" Cyrus asked, his voice casual but curious.

"My dad," Bay said quietly, still twisting her necklace between her fingers.

"Oh."

"I miss him."

"Yeah, well, he's probably more than missing you," Cyrus said. "He's probably terrified for you right now."

Bay tensed. "Don't you think I know that?" she asked sharply, glancing down at him.

Cyrus shrugged, not looking up from the rope. "Still worth mentioning."

"What choice did I have?"

"Stay with the parent who loved you, who raised you. Enjoy it."

"And forget about my mom? About all of this?"

"At least you had one parent who loved you," Cyrus muttered, fingers working through a stubborn knot. "You're taking a gamble that could cost you both."

"Cost me both?" she echoed.

"What if you never find your mom? What if you made your dad so angry that he never wants to see you again? I mean..." He finally looked up; his eyes were sharper and sadder than she had ever seen them. "You stole a lot of money from him. You ran away."

Bay's breath caught. His words hit harder than any scolding could have. But then, she remembered Catalina's stories of their father's cruelty, their mother's betrayal—how she had wanted Catalina to abandon Cyrus just because he was a boy. Cyrus wasn't trying to hurt her. He was expressing something broken inside himself.

Bay's dad would be upset and worried, but he would always love her. Nothing could change that. But she couldn't tell Cyrus her dad could never abandon her, that dads don't do that. Because his parents had done that to him.

"I'm sorry," the words poured from her mouth, unbidden. She hadn't meant to say them. "About your parents." Light-Voice finished, using Bay's voice like a portal.

Cyrus glanced at her, something shifting in his expression. It softened. For a moment, it looked like he might say something, but instead he gave a small nod and made room for Bay to sit.

She hesitated, still reeling from what Light-Voice had just done, then slid down beside him. Their shoulders brushed. A warm jolt ran up her arm. She looked away, pretending to focus on the knots.

They worked in silence. The rope moved steadily through her fingers. So did the quiet weight of Cyrus beside her. Both felt strangely grounding.

Then, without warning, a thought filtered into her mind. It was sharp and unfamiliar. *I wanted to go back to Dad. I bet Cyrus would like that.*

A chill skipped across her skin, like a ripple of wrongness. Bay furrowed her brows. The words didn't sound like hers. They didn't even sound like Light-Voice.

What do you mean? she asked silently, a flicker of unease curling in her stomach.

Light-Voice hesitated longer than usual, then brushed the thought away almost too quickly. *Nothing. Forget it.*

Bay shifted uncomfortably, heart thudding. The strange tension lingered in her chest, a knot she couldn't quite untangle.

CHAPTER TWENTY-EIGHT

The Journey

Bay felt better after breakfast. Catalina and Cyrus did not bring up her jumping overboard, although Bay caught Cyrus glancing at her from time to time, no doubt making sure she wouldn't dive into the water again.

Bay furrowed her brows, considering the strange thought from earlier. *I wanted to go back to Dad—I bet Cyrus would like that.* The thought had come from Light-Voice, but it felt like it came from somewhere else too, somewhere deep within. That unsettled her.

After the meal, the twins busied themselves preparing the *Contessa* for departure. Bay tried to help but quickly realized they had a rhythm perfected over years of working together. Cyrus hauled up the sail while Catalina untied the ropes with a kind of effortless grace. It was like watching a practiced dance. Bay sat back and observed, marveling at how nice it must be to have someone who understood you that deeply.

You have me, Light-Voice said.

Bay smiled faintly. It wasn't quite the same as a sibling, but it was something.

Pulling out one of the twins' maps, Bay traced her finger over the wide expanse of ocean, studying the cluster of scattered islands and underwater villages. She found Avalon Cove tucked in the lower left quadrant.

"We're here," Cyrus said, leaning over her shoulder and tapping the map.

"And we're going straight to the Palace?" Bay asked, tracing a hopeful line across the water.

"Not exactly. We'll follow the currents and stop at some of the lesser-known towns. Gotta stay under the radar."

Bay's heart pinched with guilt. "Are you worried about getting in trouble?" She hadn't thought about what she was asking of them until now.

Cyrus laughed. "Nah. We're just helping a kid find her family. Anyone would do the same."

"Kid? I'm almost sixteen! That's only a year younger than you!"

"Are you sure, Ba—Brittany, you got your age right? You act more like twelve," he teased.

"Says the ten-year-old," Bay shot back, but she smiled. "Thanks, Cyrus."

"Don't thank me yet. I plan on escorting you right back to your dad after all of this... unless they put out a reward."

Bay gave him a playful shove, and they both laughed. Together, they mapped out the first leg of the journey to Seaside Island, only a few hours' sail away.

After docking before sunset, Cyrus went ashore to hunt for dinner, everyone agreed it would be best for Bay to stay close to the ship to avoid detection. While Bay was happy that Catalina stayed behind to teach her how to swim, she was disappointed too. She had wanted to see all of the villages along the way and learn more about mer-life.

"You can leave your life vest on the shore!" Catalina called, standing waist-deep in the water.

As she waded in, Bay's feet sank pleasantly into the warm sand. She felt a ripple of pleasure when she stepped further into the water. Smiling despite herself, she joined Catalina, who showed her how to kick and move her arms. Catalina held her gently by the waist, offering encouragement even when Bay's flailing was more chaotic than coordinated.

By the time Cyrus returned, arms full of food, Bay's stomach was growling. They ate their meal on the beach as the sun began to melt into the ocean. Afterward, the twins dove into the deeper water, their movements sleek and powerful. Bay practiced in the shallows, feeling awkward but determined.

Catalina disappeared behind the boat, leaving Bay with Cyrus. When he swam close, Bay noticed something she hadn't before: the webbing between his fingers. Curious, she reached out and traced the delicate webbing.

"I thought boys didn't transform," she said.

"We don't fully," Cyrus said, his voice low. "But we have... gifts."

"Gifts?"

"For instance, my friend Gil has the enchantment gift—the ability to attract someone of interest to you. I thought it was pretty cool too. Until I realized we had the same taste in girls," he said, smiling. He took a step closer.

"Can you do anything else?" Bay asked, heart skipping.

"Maybe," Cyrus said, a glint in his gray-blue eyes.

"Where's Catalina?" Bay blurted, suddenly very aware of how close he was.

Who cares? Light-Voice said.

The words surprised her. Not because they were rude, but because they sounded almost... wistful.

"When a mermaid transforms, it's private. Sacred," Cyrus said, his gaze steady. "You won't see many transform in front of humans. It's to protect all merfolk."

Bay dropped her gaze. "So you think I'm just human too."

"What's wrong with being human?" Cyrus asked, gently lifting her chin. His hand lingered, and Bay's heart thudded loudly in her chest. She could feel the warmth in his fingers, as if he'd branded the moment into the air between them.

"Hey, are you guys still there?" Catalina's voice rang out.

Cyrus dropped his hand and stepped back, both of them pretending nothing had happened.

Back on shore, Catalina and Bay stayed behind on the beach to finish their dinner, while Cyrus headed back to the *Contessa*.

"He has to finish getting ready for tomorrow. We're leaving early," Catalina said, catching Bay watching Cyrus disappear toward the boat.

"Should we go help him?" Bay asked, pulling her attention back to Catalina.

"No, it's not much. Plus, Cyrus likes alone time."

"Really? You two look like you do everything together."

"We do a lot," Catalina said softly, her gaze drifting toward the waves. "We're the only family each of us has."

Bay understood. It had always been just her and her dad.

"It's great you guys get along so well."

Catalina turned her focus back to Bay. "Do you know how mermaids communicate? How they talk to each other?"

Bay shrugged. "I just figured they talked like we're talking right now."

"What about underwater?"

Bay blinked. "I hadn't thought of that."

"In the water, we communicate telepathically. We can speak into each other's minds when we're connected by the ocean."

"Wow..." Bay replied thoughtfully, wondering how that would even feel.

"It only works underwater," Catalina continued. "You can direct your words at one person or a group, depending on who you want to hear."

"How do you do it?" Bay asked eagerly.

"It takes practice. You focus on what you want to say and imagine it reaching that person."

"So... Cyrus can do that too?" Bay asked, curious.

"Yes. But Cyrus and I... we can send to each other even on land. Only between us."

"You can read each other's minds?"

"Not exactly. We still have to project on purpose, but we can hear what the other wants us to hear."

"That's so cool!" Bay said.

"We were close even as kids, but once we realized we could speak without words, it made us... inseparable."

Bay asked about the other gifts mermaid children could have, remembering Cyrus hinting at it.

"Some can speak with aquatic life—like dolphins," Catalina said. "Some older ones can manipulate the water around them."

"What about changing how you look?" Bay pressed.

"Changing how you look?" Catalina tilted her head.

"Not fully, just a part of you. Like hair?"

Catalina smiled faintly. "Mermaid hair behaves differently underwater. It slicks back like a fish's fin and runs along the spine. Sometimes our hair tips change color when we transform."

Bay nodded slowly, filing the information away. "But not on land?"

"Rarely. Maybe a shimmer, but not a full change."

Catalina offered more food, but Bay shook her head. Together they packed up the blanket and headed back to the ship.

Bay was quiet on the walk back. Catalina's explanations had been helpful, but they didn't explain what was happening to her.

She knew she was Allura's daughter. She knew it. No matter what Catalina or Cyrus suspected. Her father wouldn't have lied. He couldn't have. Still, questions tangled in her mind. Why had her hair turned black? How had she disappeared on the bridge? Why did the sea's pull feel so alive?

It's probably just a strange reaction because you didn't grow up near the water, Light-Voice offered gently.

Maybe, Bay thought back. But every step farther from the shore almost seemed to hurt, as if her bones ached for the sea. She slipped on her life jacket, pulling the straps tight—just in case. The call of the ocean wasn't fading. It was growing stronger. And deeper.

Soon, Bay feared, it would be something she couldn't resist.

CHAPTER TWENTY-NINE

A Change

Fortunately, Bay spent the next few days almost entirely in the water. The *Contessa* traveled by day, cutting through deep blue waves, and docked at quiet seaside villages at night. Since Bay needed to keep a low profile, she spent most of her time with the twins, splitting her days between swimming lessons with Catalina and navigation sessions with Cyrus.

Swimming with Catalina was calm, steady, and deeply focused. There was something grounding about it. Catalina moved like someone born to the sea, quiet and sure, her words low and deliberate as she corrected Bay's form or showed her how to glide more efficiently through a current.

Sailing with Cyrus was the complete opposite. It was chaotic, loud, and full of laughter. He barked orders like a pirate captain one minute, then explained knots and compass readings the next, somehow turning every moment into a game. Bay found herself grinning more than she expected, even when she got things wrong.

Both lessons challenged her in different ways, but she loved every minute of them. There was freedom in the salt air and spray on her skin, in the way the sun danced off the waves, and in how the boat rose and fell as if it had its own breath.

She had never imagined her life would be like this. Sailing across open water, chasing the truth about her long-lost mother. But somehow, despite everything, this journey felt like one of the best parts of her story. It was like a chapter in a fairy tale she hadn't known she was part of.

"There it is," Cyrus said, pointing toward a cluster of buildings on a nearby island.

"What town is that?"

"Crystal Cove."

Pretty name, Light-Voice murmured.

"Where does the name come from?" Bay asked.

"Look at the water," Cyrus said with a grin.

Bay leaned over the railing. The sea below gleamed like glass so clear that she could see all the way to the seafloor. Coral glittered like gems beneath drifting fish. It felt like they were flying.

"Wow," she breathed, standing on tiptoes. Suddenly, the ship rocked, and she lost her balance.

"Okay, that's far enough," Cyrus said, catching her by the waist and pulling her safely back onto the deck.

"I didn't do that on purpose," Bay insisted, still peering over.

"Sure," Cyrus said, dry as sand.

Bay turned toward him. She caught the hint of a smile on his lips and realized his hands were still at her waist.

"Well, just in case," he teased, tugging on the straps of her life vest.

Bay laughed and swatted him away. "How much longer 'til we dock?"

"Fifteen minutes. Gonna go help Cat!" Cyrus jogged off, leaving Bay smiling after him.

Nice view.

Rolling her eyes, Bay turned back to the island ahead, heart thudding in a way she didn't want to think about.

While the twins docked the boat, Bay slipped below deck to make lemonade. She rifled through the drawers for sugar and found a jar labeled "sugar" in permanent marker. Just as she opened it, Cyrus's voice called out, "Whoa! Don't do that!"

"I'm just making lemonade," Bay said, confused.

"That's not sugar," Cyrus said, hurrying down. "That's... well, it's sleeping powder. For unwanted guests."

Bay stared at him.

"Not poison," Cyrus clarified quickly. "Just—a heavy nudge to get them off our boat."

Bay blinked, then laughed. "Do you have 'make-you-sick soup' or 'give-you-the-runs milk' too?"

"Maybe," Cyrus said with a wink.

Bay shook her head in amazement. The twins had survived so much more than she ever had and had obviously learned to adapt.

Catalina came below deck and asked if Bay wanted to swim again. Bay quickly agreed and after changing, the three stepped onto the dock. Cyrus went to gather supplies while Bay and Catalina wandered to find a secluded beach.

Swimming was getting easier. Bay wasn't graceful, but she no longer needed Catalina to hold her up.

"You're getting better!" Catalina said warmly.

Bay beamed. "At least I'm not a soggy sack of seaweed anymore."

Catalina laughed. They swam to a shallow spot where Bay could stand if she needed to.

"Is it hard to transform?" Bay asked.

"At first," Catalina said, "you have to sit still, clear your mind, and focus. Now it just kind of happens. But staying human gets harder with age."

Bay floated on her back, staring up at the sky. "Really?"

Catalina nodded. "Some mermaids lose the ability to stay human altogether."

Bay's heart squeezed. Could her mother have struggled too?

"I think my mom did," Catalina said quietly. "She fought so hard to stay for us. Maybe, near the end, she just didn't want to anymore." Her voice trailed off, her gaze fixed on the horizon.

"Has she ever tried to contact you?" Bay asked.

"No. It's been years. Maybe she thinks we wouldn't forgive her."

"Would you?" Bay asked softly.

Catalina shrugged, offering a crooked smile. "Doubt it. But I think Cyrus would."

Bay tilted her head. "Why?"

"He always thought he should've protected her—from our dad."

"But he was just a kid," Bay offered.

"Still. He thinks he should've done something. And I..." Catalina hesitated, "I think I'm angrier at her than he is. She made me choose. It was her or my brother. And I chose him. I'll always choose him."

Bay waded closer and wrapped her arms around her. "I think you made the right choice," she whispered.

Catalina smiled sadly. "Thanks." She brightened. "Wanna see me transform?"

Bay's eyes widened. "Seriously?"

Catalina slipped behind a large rock and tossed up her swimsuit. When she reemerged, fully transformed, Bay gasped. Her tail shimmered red and orange, fanning like a phoenix plume. Her scales glittered in the clear water, and her spine was crowned with a delicate translucent fin. Her hair, slick and fine, rippled like flame beneath the surface, the tips gleaming crimson.

Bay twirled around her, laughing in awe as Catalina darted and spun like a giant koi fish. Each time her head broke the surface, her hair flopped down as normal, then snapped back into a fin underwater.

Bay was amazed. *I wish I had a tail*, she thought. The wish burned through her like fire. A sharp metallic taste surged up her throat, bitter and briny, like copper soaked in saltwater.

Without warning, pain tore through her, and she doubled over and toppled into the water.

Catalina rushed to her. "Bay! Look!"

Bay blinked down and froze. Her swimsuit bottoms floated nearby, and from her waist down stretched a shimmering salmon-pink tail. Tears welled in her eyes. Light-Voice, though faint, cheered from somewhere deep inside.

Bay kicked experimentally, her new tail propelling her forward. Catalina steadied her, laughing joyfully as she taught her how to move. They stayed near the surface since Bay couldn't breathe underwater yet, but she had never felt so alive.

After a while, Catalina slipped back into her human form and retrieved her swimsuit. Bay, however, stayed stubbornly transformed.

"How do I change back?" Bay asked, panicked.

"Stay calm. Focus on your legs," Catalina said.

Bay tried. And tried. Nothing.

Catalina reassured her, but after more time passed, she said, "I'll go get Cyrus. Stay hidden behind the rock, okay?"

"What if a shark comes?" Bay asked, trying to sound brave.

Catalina laughed. "Sharks? Oh, Bay, it's really rare for them to attack a mermaid."

"Rare, but possible?" Bay pressed.

"You'll be fine! I'll hurry." Catalina splashed off through the shallows, disappearing into the brush.

Bay bobbed in the darkening water, fear tightening her chest. *Worst mermaid ever*, she thought miserably.

No you're not, Light-Voice whispered. *At least now you know your dad wasn't wrong. And*

Allura—she's definitely your mother. Look at your tail!

It was true. A real tail. Allura was her mother. A mermaid queen. Bay hugged that small truth to her heart, clinging to it even as the sky darkened to indigo.

Minutes later, Catalina and Cyrus splashed into the water toward her. "Still no change?" Catalina called.

"Not even a scale," Bay muttered.

Cyrus grinned. "Show off."

Bay managed a small laugh. Frustrated, she blurted, "I wish I could just change back!" The wish sparked through her. A sharp, metallic tang flooded her mouth, copper and salt. Then, searing pain shot through her legs. She gasped as her tail shimmered and shifted back into legs.

Ahh, Bay! Light-Voice whimpered, like a cry echoing from deep underwater. *It hurts…*

Bay winced. She could feel it, that shared pain, raw and unexpected.

"Towel, please!" she cried.

Catalina tossed her a towel. Bay scrambled to wrap it around herself, heart hammering, as they made their way ashore. Just as she tied it, Catalina stiffened and pointed down the beach. Two flashlights bobbed in the distance, coming closer. They weren't alone.

And whoever was coming was searching.

CHAPTER THIRTY

An Evening Sail

Two figures approached from the far end of the beach, flashlights slicing through the darkness.

"Bay, get behind me," Catalina commanded in a low whisper.

Bay complied instantly. It was strange hearing her bark orders like that, her usual warmth completely gone. Her shoulders were square, her stance immovable.

Bay crouched low behind her, heart hammering. Every instinct screamed to run, but she didn't. She trusted Catalina. Still, a thousand thoughts raced through her mind. Was this her fault? What if Cyrus and Catalina got hurt because of her?

"Hey, you over there!" a gruff voice called. "What are you doing out here this time of night?"

Two men emerged into view, the beams of their flashlights sweeping the sand. One was tall and broad-shouldered, with a scruffy beard flecked with gray and sea-worn clothes. The other was lean and rigid, his cold blue eyes sharp and calculating.

"We were just finishing an evening swim," Cyrus answered smoothly.

The younger one stepped forward. "Bit late for a swim, don't you think?"

"Is one of you a young girl?" the older one asked, narrowing his eyes.

"This one is!" the cold-eyed man cut in, shining his flashlight directly onto Catalina's face.

"And?" Catalina replied, not flinching, still shielding Bay.

"There's a bounty out for a girl about your age," said the scruffy one, his voice gravelly, like stones dragged across the shore.

"Your point?" Catalina asked flatly.

"I think you might be her," the younger man said with a thin smile.

"Didn't that bounty say the girl had long blonde hair and was traveling alone?" Catalina asked, her voice cool and steady.

"Maybe it did, maybe it didn't," the younger one said. Then he turned to his partner. "Mitch, do you remember the details?"

"Nah, Dan," the older one replied, scratching his beard. "I don't remember nothin'."

Bay stiffened as the names landed. Dan. Mitch. She locked them in her mind like a warning.

"You obviously have the wrong person, and we were just leaving," Cyrus said, stepping in.

"You can leave anytime you like, boy," Mitch replied, stepping forward, "but she's stayin'."

He lifted his flashlight and pointed it at Catalina again. Though she stood tall, nearly eye to eye with Mitch, she wasn't wide enough to fully block Bay from view.

"Well, looky here. Another girl," Dan murmured, voice almost amused.

Bay flinched. Her stomach twisted. She felt exposed, even in the shadows.

"You better leave them alone," Cyrus warned.

Dan chuckled coldly. "Two teenage girls, no guardians, hiding out at night. Definitely not locals. I like our chances that one of you is the girl we're after."

He pulled out his phone. "Mitch, call it in."

The three of them froze. Bay could barely breathe.

"No reception," Mitch muttered, thumbing at his old screen.

Dan scowled. "Fine. You're both coming with us."

"Now!" Catalina called just as Mitch laid a hand on her shoulder and Dan reached toward Bay.

Cyrus grabbed Bay's arm and yanked her out of reach, causing Dan to dive forward and land face-first in the sand. From the corner of her eye, Bay caught a glimpse of Catalina—spinning, driving her knee into Mitch's stomach. He crumpled with a groan.

"Follow me," Cyrus whispered, pulling Bay up the sandy slope and into the brush.

Bay raced after him. Sand slipped beneath her feet, bushes scratched at her arms, and every breath came with a sting of salt. Her legs burned. Her lungs ached. Cyrus darted like a shadow between the trees, never more than a few feet ahead.

A root snagged her foot. She tripped, hit the ground hard, then scrambled up again.

At last, Cyrus pulled her behind a thick tree, finger to his lips. They crouched low, side by side, backs pressed to the bark. Bay's heart thundered. She could hear her pulse in her ears. The only sound was the distant rush of waves.

Where is Catalina? Light-Voice asked quietly.

Bay was still trying to catch her breath, and the fear of having lost her friend made it even harder. "What about Catalina? We have to go back!" she said to Cyrus in full panic.

"She's fine."

"How do you know? They could've caught her!"

"She made it to the water. Trust me."

"But how—?"

"She told me," Cyrus said, glancing at her.

Bay blinked. Then it clicked. "You were talking. In your heads."

Cyrus nodded. "She said she'd draw their focus and meet us back at the boat."

She shielded you.

"But what if they'd both gone after her?"

"And survived?" Cyrus smiled weakly, "She would've gone with them."

Bay's brow furrowed. "But they would've taken her in."

"And?"

"And... oh. Right. They're not after her."

"Exactly."

Bay sat back on her heels, the realization settling like a weight on her chest. "She stood in front of me on purpose."

Cyrus nodded, his expression unreadable.

"Wow," Bay breathed. "And I thought you were the tougher one."

"Me? Ha. Catalina's better at almost everything—except good looks and a dashing personality."

Bay let out a shaky laugh, the adrenaline finally thinning.

"She's stronger, faster. She's a mermaid," Cyrus added, glancing out toward the dark sea.

"Still, she could have been hurt."

"Not by those two. We've dealt with worse."

Bay looked down, shame rising like a tide. "I'm sorry. This was my fault."

Cyrus's posture softened. He placed a hand on her shoulder, firm but kind. "Don't worry about it, Bay. You're with us now."

When they got back to the *Contessa*, Catalina was already there, dripping wet, wringing out her hair.

"You okay?" Bay asked, breathless.

Catalina looked up and grinned. "What took you so long?"

Bay ran forward and hugged her tightly. "Thank you," she whispered.

Catalina hugged her back. "We're leaving tonight."

"Isn't it too dark to sail?"

Catalina shook her head. "The water's calm. The sky's clear. It's a perfect night."

Later, they sat on the open deck, the ship gliding silently through moonlight. The sea mirrored the sky so perfectly it felt like they were sailing among the stars.

Bay exhaled slowly and turned to Catalina. "Why did you protect me like that?"

Catalina shrugged. "Because you're one of us."

Bay's throat tightened. "You risked yourselves for me."

"And we'd do it again," Catalina said.

Cyrus raised an eyebrow. "Even after that landing punch to the jaw?"

"Especially after that," Catalina replied with a smirk.

They laughed, and Bay leaned back against the railing. For the first time since she had left her father and Izzy behind, she understood what it felt like to belong. Not because of blood, but because someone had stayed. Someone had chosen her.

Above them, the stars burned brighter than ever. She still longed to meet her mother, but tonight, she did not want the journey to end. Cyrus and Catalina were no longer just guides. And now she knew, without hesitation, she would fight for them too.

CHAPTER THIRTY-ONE

Salt and Sweets

The *Contessa* glided across the water, its sail catching the breeze like a secret. Bay leaned on the railing, watching the reflections. The air was cooler now, the salt brushing her cheeks in soft kisses. Behind her, Catalina and Cyrus adjusted the rigging, working in tandem with practiced ease. There was comfort in their quiet rhythm, as though the sea itself recognized their bond.

Only one more night, Catalina had said, before they reached the Pacific Palace. Bay let that sink in. She was almost there. She should've been nervous, but all she felt was a gentle, aching pull — like something was still unfinished.

Light-Voice stirred gently, a warm flicker under her ribs. *They're good*, it whispered. *They make us feel real.*

Bay didn't answer. She just listened.

"Everyone says the stars look closer out here," Cyrus said, voice soft beside her now. He was close enough for her to feel his warmth.

Bay didn't turn. "Yeah. Like they're twinkling right on top of the water. I just need a bottle so I can catch one."

He leaned on the railing, eyes on the sky. "Maybe they're closer because they're watching."

"Watching for what?"

"I don't know. For someone to finally get it right or something." He said it like a joke, but it didn't quite land that way.

Bay looked over at him. His hair was damp, his face glowing in the moonlight.

"That sounded almost poetic."

"Yeah, I'm pretty impressive," he said with a shrug.

Bay smiled. "Yeah. Okay."

Catalina came up from below deck, wiping her hands on a rag.

"Talking about me again?"

"Only nice things," Bay promised.

Catalina gave her a small smirk. "Better be."

She moved past them to the helm, but not before resting a hand on Bay's shoulder. Just for a second, just long enough. The stars above seemed to twinkle brighter.

Later, they sat together on the deck, the three of them wrapped in their bedroom blankets, sharing a tin of sweet biscuits Catalina had stashed away. The night sky pressed down, so vast and close it felt like the sea might open up and carry them into the stars.

Cyrus tossed a shell between his hands, frowning slightly. "You know what happened back in Avalon and Crystal Cove wasn't normal, right?"

Bay looked up. "What do you mean?"

"The *Magistrata*. The way they were hunting you. That's not standard, even for fugitives," Catalina said, her voice low.

"We've seen bounty hunts before," Cyrus added. "This was different. Too quiet."

Bay did not reply right away. The wind lifted a strand of her hair and tugged at the edge of her blanket.

"We were thinking..." Catalina said carefully, "what if you didn't go all the way to the palace? Not right away."

"You could stay with us," Cyrus added. "Just for a little while. We can poke around the capital and see who's asking questions. Make sure it's safe."

Bay smiled, but the expression was softer than her usual ones. "Thank you. That means more than you know."

For a moment, she let herself imagine it. Staying. Sailing with them. Waking up to sunlight on the water, laughing over breakfast, never needing to explain who she was or where she came from. It would be easy to disappear here. Easy to feel safe.

And she wanted it. Just a little too much.

Then, Light-Voice stirred again. Not warm this time, but weighted—like a hand pressing gently against her heart. *She still thinks we're gone. And he's missing you too.*

Bay looked down at her hands and flexed her fingers once. "I trust my dad," she said. "He wouldn't lie about Allura. He said she was my mother, and... look at me. I transformed. I became a mermaid." She glanced up at them, her voice steadier now. "He was telling the truth. I can feel it."

Light-Voice pulsed in quiet agreement. *We're close. So close now.*

Bay let out a breath. "I have to see her. I know once I do, it'll all make sense."

They didn't press her.

"We should sleep soon," Catalina said eventually, stifling a yawn. "We'll want to be rested."

"One more night," Cyrus murmured. "And then everything changes."

Light-Voice hummed again, like a small sigh of contentment.

Still, Bay felt it, woven through the peace like a subtle weight, the sense of something ending. No one said it aloud, but they all felt it. The journey was almost over. Tomorrow, they would be in the palace. Under scrutiny. And nothing would ever be this simple again.

Beneath the stars, their small trio felt sacred. Quietly unbreakable. They were no longer just traveling together.

They were becoming a family.

CHAPTER THIRTY-TWO

The Stars Are Watching

The deck of the *Contessa* was quiet at night, save for the soft slosh of waves and the occasional creak of wood adjusting to the sea's rhythm. Above, the stars shimmered in a scatter of silver, and the moon, half-full and hanging low, cast a glow that painted the sails in soft outlines.

Cyrus stood near the railing, arms resting along the worn wood, watching the water roll past like a never-ending dream. The breeze carried the scent of brine and rope oil, and something else—orange, maybe. A trace of Bay's hair from when she passed him earlier, half-asleep, smiling in a way that made his chest feel too tight.

He didn't move when he heard footsteps behind him. Catalina joined him without a word, mirroring his stance, her fingers drumming idly on the rail. They stood in silence for a while, comfortable in the quiet. The kind of siblings who didn't need to fill space with words to know something was wrong.

Catalina broke the silence. "She's out already?"

Cyrus nodded. "Yeah. Barely made it to her room."

Catalina gave a short laugh, but it faded fast. "Good. She needed it."

The waves filled the pause. Cyrus leaned forward, his voice low. "We gotta watch out for her, Cat."

Catalina was quiet for a second. Then, "Yeah. We will."

"She's not just some runaway," Cyrus said. "There's more to it, stuff she doesn't even get."

Catalina nodded. "I felt that too. That story she told... it's got holes. Big ones."

"Like why her dad bailed from the palace," Cyrus said, frowning. "Why no one's seen him since. Why everyone thinks they're both dead."

"She acts like she doesn't even know people think that," Catalina said quietly.

"She doesn't. You saw her face. Either someone's been feeding her lies her whole life—"

"Or she's lying to herself," Catalina finished, voice low.

Cyrus ran a hand through his hair. "I don't think she is. Lying, I mean. I think she's scared. And whatever went down... I don't think she even knows the full story."

Catalina glanced over at him. "And what if the truth's bad? Like... really bad?"

Cyrus met her eyes. "Then we deal with it. Like always."

Catalina gave him a crooked smile. "You're turning into a softie."

He rolled his eyes. "Shut up."

"No, really. All this protective big-brother energy? Should I be jealous?"

Cyrus let out a short laugh. "It's not like that."

She raised an eyebrow. "Hmm. No. It's not. I know that look."

"What look?"

"The one you had when we first saw her. Like you'd finally found something that mattered."

Cyrus stared down at the waves. "There's just... something about her."

Catalina leaned in a little, her voice light. "You mean besides the whole tragic past, those big dark eyes, and how she somehow always keeps you guessing?"

Cyrus smirked. "You done?"

"Almost."

He shook his head, then went quiet. "It's not that. It's... the way she is. She doesn't try too hard. Doesn't want anything. She's just there. But when she's around, the boat feels different. Lighter, I guess."

Catalina's teasing faded. "Home."

Cyrus looked over at her.

"She makes it feel like home," Catalina said again, softer this time, like she wasn't even talking to him.

He nodded. "Yeah."

They stood together, silent for a while, the ship groaning under their feet, the sky slowly turning above them.

"I used to think the sea was it, you know?" Catalina said. "Like... drifting forever. Never really belonging anywhere. I didn't hate it. You didn't either. But now..."

Cyrus waited.

"I think I care now," she said quietly.

He reached for her hand, something he hadn't done in years. "We're allowed to want more," he said.

Catalina gave a small nod. "We just have to keep her safe long enough to get there."

Cyrus gave her hand a quick squeeze before letting go. "I keep thinking about the *Magistrata* chasing her," he said. "What are they so scared of?"

"Yeah, I don't get it either," Catalina murmured. "They must think she is dangerous or something."

"I don't buy that," he said. "Not after what we've seen. Not after how she looks at people, like she's waiting for someone to flinch. She doesn't even get our world."

Catalina's brows pulled together. "But that's the thing. There's gotta be more to it. Something even she doesn't know."

Cyrus glanced over. "You think she is dangerous?"

Catalina hesitated. "The way she transformed... it freaked me out a little. I can't piece it all together, but it almost looked painful. I just think we don't have the whole picture yet. But I trust her."

Cyrus stared out at the water. "Yeah, me too. Still feels like we're flying blind."

They fell quiet again. This time it felt heavier, not awkward, just... full. The stars shimmered on the waves like pieces of something they couldn't quite reach.

"You think she'd stay?" Cyrus asked, barely above a whisper.

Catalina looked at him. "If we asked her?"

"If it doesn't go how she's hoping. You think she'd still stay—with us?"

She didn't answer right away. Then, "Yeah. I think she would."

She gave a small, almost secret smile. "We just have to make sure she gets that choice."

CHAPTER THIRTY-THREE

Left Behind

Catalina didn't watch as Cyrus made his way below deck. She didn't need to. She could feel his movements now, the subtle shifts in the ship that told her where he was without seeing him.

Had it really been three years since they had been on their own? She let out a slow breath, her gaze drifting toward the horizon, lost in a memory she couldn't forget.

It was nearing dusk when their mother told them.

The sun spilled gold across the cracked kitchen floor, slanting through the crooked blinds like a goodbye. The little rental house perched on the cliffside had always smelled faintly of salt and tea leaves. Today, it smelled like endings.

Cyrus sat at the table, elbow-deep in repair parts for the Contessa's broken gear shaft, his fingers smudged with grease. Catalina leaned against the counter, arms crossed, chewing the inside of her cheek.

Their mother stood by the sink, staring out the window at the restless gray ocean.

"I'll be going soon," she said, her voice barely louder than the waves below.

Neither of them moved. Cyrus kept threading wire with too much force. The strand snapped in his hands.

"To the sea," their mother added. "Back to where I belong."

Catalina's jaw tightened. Cyrus dropped the broken wire on the table.

"What do you mean?" he asked.

"I mean, this world is closing in," she said, still not turning to face them. "Too many neighbors. Too many questions. I can't stay any longer."

"You've said that before," Catalina said coolly.

"This time I mean it." There was silence except for the ticking of the stovetop clock and the kettle beginning to hum. "I've stayed longer than I should have. For you. For both of you. But it's different now. You're not children anymore. You'll survive."

Cyrus's voice cracked. "You're just...leaving?"

She turned slowly, her long black hair loose around her shoulders, eyes the color of sea-stone. "You don't understand the danger I've been in all these years. Your father— your father changed after you were born. He grew jealous. Possessive. Violent."

"We know that," Catalina said. "We remember."

"No. You remember pieces." Her mother's voice hardened. "But you don't remember what it was like to live every day wondering if he would drag me inland. Lock me away. Use me to bargain with others. Humans do that. They cage what they fear or what they want."

She turned her gaze to Cyrus, and something cold slipped into her expression. "And now I see him in you."

Cyrus blinked. "What?"

"You're almost grown now. And I see the same stubbornness. The same heat in your temper. You don't belong in the sea, Cyrus. You'll never fit there. You belong with the humans. You are one."

Cyrus stood up fast, the chair scraping behind him.

"I tried," he said, voice shaking, "to protect you. When I was a kid. I tried."

"I know," she said, but it didn't sound like comfort.

"You're saying I'm like him?"

She looked away. "I'm saying, I can't protect you anymore. And I won't be caged again." Silence pressed against the walls like a rising tide.

Cyrus walked out. The front door slammed behind him, the echo cutting the room in two. Their mother stayed by the sink, fingers gripping the edge so tightly her knuckles paled.

Catalina watched her. "You know," she said quietly, "I used to be proud that I took after you." Her mother turned sharply as Catalina continued. "I thought you were brave, strong. A mermaid. Someone who survived and stayed. But now I see you're just scared."

"That's not fair."

"No. What's not fair is watching your son try his whole life to protect you, only to be told he reminds you of the man who hurt you." Her mother's face hardened, but Catalina wasn't finished. "What you survived was real. I'll never say it wasn't. But Cyrus? He's never hurt anyone. He's good. He's loyal. And if you can't see that, maybe you have been living on land too long."

"I'm doing what I must to stay alive," her mother said, low and cold.

Catalina stepped closer. "We're mermaids. We don't run when it gets hard. We don't hide. And we don't abandon our families just because we're scared of loving the wrong person again."

The kettle shrieked. Their mother turned back toward the window, her voice barely a breath. "You'll understand when you're older."

Catalina shook her head. "No. I won't." Then she walked out the same door her brother had.

CHAPTER THIRTY-FOUR

Ash and Smoke

The waters near Avalon shimmered like glass, warm, still, and far too calm for what stirred beneath. Trent hovered just below the surface, a dark silhouette cloaked in drifting seaweed, watching the fractured shimmer of light above him.

He hadn't come this close to the capital in years. Not since he had wrapped a newborn in seagrass and fled from a throne touched by prophecy and stained with blood. Her throne. The thought pierced him behind the ribs like a blade.

He adjusted the shell-wrapped scroll tied at his waist, checking again that it hadn't come loose. Every mark etched onto the parchment was a record of his failures and his relentless pursuit. What kept him going were his cherished memories. Bay's laugh. The way she flinched when people spoke too loudly. The strange habit she had of glancing sideways when she thought no one was looking. As though listening to something he could not hear. As though someone else were there.

Today's lead had been thin: a whisper about two Sea Crown guards returning to Avalon, their errand a failure. Normally, that would have meant nothing. But the name that carried with the tide chilled him.

Allura.

Even now, he felt her presence bleeding through the water. Not a memory, but a bond. The old tether of *Socius Animae*, frayed but unbroken, pressed into him like a bruise, just beneath the skin, just deep enough to drown. Sometimes he imagined he could still hear her voice threading through the currents, a phantom stitched into the tides.

Trent finally swam to shore and rested a few hours, hiding among the grassy sand dunes. Hunger forced him to turn back towards Avalon. He had only been walking for a short time when he heard voices. Quickly, he flattened himself behind a large outcropping of rocks. *Magistrata*. The Queens' silent blades. Part sentry, part executioner, they answered not to kingdoms but to the ocean itself. He had lived at Allura's side long enough to know their power. Where soldiers brandished weapons, the *Magistrata* wielded silence like a knife.

The taller one wore her dark hair pulled back. The other, broader in the shoulders, had short red hair and moved like someone who trusted her fists more than spells. Both women wore dark jackets, damp at the edges from recent surf, their boots crusted with dried salt. They had been on land long enough to dry.

"I wonder why Allura wants this girl," the tall one hissed, "and why she won't let us bring in the human. He lied to us. For that alone he should be punished. He cost us three days."

"I told you the boy was lying," the other grunted. "I should've broken his nose when I had the chance."

"You would've scared the whole island into hiding," came the reply. "Doesn't matter now. We planted the bounty at

Crystal Cove. I'm sure they'll show up soon. And if we get to the boy first..."

Trent's pulse quickened. Bay was still ahead of them. And more importantly, someone had thrown them off the scent. Someone clever. Someone with her.

He pressed tighter to the rock wall, heart pounding.

The tall *Magistrata* turned slowly to survey the surroundings, her voice tight with urgency. "The Queen's patience is running out. If the child reaches the Sea Witch—"

"She could tip the balance," the other finished. "And she's not alone. That's what worries me."

The two started running at a fast clip, churning the dark sand and kicking up the dust into smoky spirals. Trent remained motionless until they were out of sight. Only then did he let out a slow, exhaustive breath. Bay was alive. Still ahead of the hunt, and not alone.

But alliances were dangerous. Allies came with agendas. And Bay was already too powerful, too haunted, too close to slipping beyond his reach.

After hastily swallowing some fried fish that he had brought back from Avalon to his hiding place in the dunes, Trent continued his search into a narrow canyon of sea glass, swimming deeper.

The knot in his chest wasn't fear. It was grief. Allura's name still burned. Not from love lost, but from the kind of loss that takes root. The kind that lingers, stubborn and sharp, long after hope has crumbled. He remembered her voice. The first time they touched. The raw brilliance of the bond that had once been their lifeline, their *Socius Animae*.

It clung to him still, a tether woven from ash and memory.

He wanted to hate her. Some days, he almost managed it. Other days, like this one, he ached only for the woman she had once been. Before prophecy. Before power. Before the words *Sea Witch* shattered everything they were meant to be.

Trent swam harder, ignoring the burn in his lungs. If Bay was headed for the Pacific Palace, she was moving straight toward danger. Toward the sleeping forces and fractured allegiances that coiled beneath its jeweled thrones. Forces even queens feared to stir.

He broke past the edge of the reef and stopped, chest heaving. Ahead, Avalon's spires clawed at the horizon, haloed by the faint glow of dawn.

He unrolled the scroll. Names. Coves. Every lead he had followed. Every false hope. He dipped his finger in ink and circled a new place: Crystal Cove.

He tucked the scroll away. This time, he did not pray to the sea. He did not plead with fate. He simply whispered, "I'm coming, Bay. I'll find you. No matter who stands in my way."

Then he vanished into the deepening blue, smoke trailing behind him like a broken oath.

CHAPTER THIRTY-FIVE

Pacific Palace

ust as Catalina predicted, by morning, they arrived at the massive docking station for the underwater kingdom. It rose from the sea like a cathedral of light. The structure reminded Bay of a giant carved iceberg, but smoother, more deliberate, as though shaped by magic as much as by engineering.

It looked as though it had once been a small island, expanded and transformed with a kind of marble-like material that shimmered faintly in the morning sun. Polished white stone jutted from the ocean, gleaming so brightly it was almost blinding. Towering pillars supported high platforms and terraces, their bases carved with spiraling patterns that resembled waves and kelp gardens, each detail sharp and immaculate.

The entire station felt like an island made of marble, rising untouched and eternal in the middle of the ocean. It was both elegant and imposing, a place that looked built for gods or queens.

The dock itself was vast and efficient. Several large cargo ships waited their turn to unload, while sailors moved about— some clearly merfolk, others likely kin to them. Nearer the shallows, smaller boats carrying visitors and tourists clustered at the docks, where a series of shops and structures stood. These buildings, too, were made from the same luminous material, giving the entire area a pristine, almost surreal quality. Everything here looked impossibly clean, as though the salt and wear of the sea had never touched it.

Now this is what I'm talking about. Look how perfect and polished it all looks.

Bay shrugged, less impressed. While it was huge and gleaming, she preferred Avalon Cove—vibrant, colorful, and alive.

"So, here we are," Bay said, her chest tightening with a mix of anxiety and excitement. She tried to sound calm, but her voice wavered as she looked toward Catalina. "I want to try again. I want to perfect the transformation before I meet her."

Catalina tilted her head slightly but said nothing, waiting.

"I want her to recognize me," Bay continued. "Not just my face, but everything. The tail. The scales. I want her to see the part of me that's hers. The part that proves my dad was telling the truth."

Catalina nodded, her expression softening with understanding.

Bay found a quiet spot near the edge of the docking station, away from the noise of cargo ships and curious tourists. The water shimmered below, clear and cool, stretching out like a mirror. She stood for a moment, staring down at it, her heart pounding. She thought of the first time she had transformed. The weightlessness. The shimmer. The sense of something ancient rising up inside her. She wanted that again. Only this time, she wanted it on purpose.

With a deep breath, Bay bent her knees and launched herself forward, cannonballing into the sea.

Not very royal of you, no? Light-Voice teased with a hint of snobbery.

Bay rolled her eyes. *Just wait 'til they get a load of my swim style*, she shot back, grinning despite herself.

She dog-paddled away from the boat toward a calmer area. Relax, she told herself. Focus.

She closed her eyes briefly, feeling the cool water against her skin, and willed her mermaid form to emerge.

Nothing.

She tried again, staying calm, concentrating. The sea was calm. The sun above was brilliant and clear. Seagulls called overhead, swooping over the ships. The water carried a cool energy, invigorating yet oddly heavy.

Then she saw them—light-blue shapes, smooth and deliberate, circling below her, rising fast.

Fear seized her chest.

Catalina had said sharks rarely attacked merfolk, but fear overrode reason. Bay screamed.

On the dock, she saw Catalina and Cyrus talking to a tall mermaid with broad shoulders wearing a seafoam green shirt and short red hair. The *Magistrata*. No, not now. Please, not now. At her scream, Cyrus and Catalina whipped around. The *Magistrata* immediately pointed at Bay, gesturing sharply.

Bay swam frantically toward the boat, wishing, willing her tail to emerge. Darkness prickled along her toes. She tried to ignore it, focusing harder.

Her legs fused together. A shimmer of pink bloomed beneath her waist.

But her hands stayed human. Her upper body remained bare of scales.

Half-transformed, Bay paddled desperately.

A sharp metallic taste flooded her mouth, copper and salt thick on her tongue. Light-Voice trembled inside her, its presence flickering like a sputtering candle in the wind. Please, it whispered, the sound strained and raw. It hurts.

Bay clenched her jaw. She knew the pain wasn't just her own.

Still, she kept swimming. Kept trying.

Half-human, Bay paddled desperately as the figures below gained speed. She wouldn't make it.

She cried out again.

Cyrus tried to leap into the water, but the *Magistrata* yanked him back. They began to argue loudly. Catalina, without hesitation, dove in, slicing through the water toward Bay.

Just as she neared, Bay felt a powerful yank on her tail.

She was pulled under.

Everything went quiet. Strong hands restrained her. She flailed, gasping, but more hands grabbed her, dragging her deeper. Darkness crowded in. Bubbles blurred her vision. The pressure in her chest tightened.

Bay, you have to do it. You have to transform! Light-Voice cried, fear and pain threading through every word. *Please, you have to save us!*

Bay felt the light inside her, begging to be released, but she couldn't. She could barely breathe. Her body convulsed as the pressure became unbearable. Her mind screamed for oxygen. Her thoughts spun. She thought of her father. Of Izzy. Of everything she hadn't said.

Please, Bay!

She couldn't hold it anymore.

Water rushed into her lungs. The sea poured through her.

But as she drowned, something stirred. An energy deep and primal, answering her desperation. It wasn't just light. It wasn't just hope.

It was something heavier. Darker. It throbbed beneath her skin, pulsing with the force of a thousand desperate wishes.

Bay opened her mouth to scream.

And the ocean swallowed her whole.

CHAPTER THIRTY-SIX

The Queen

Water rushed into Bay's lungs, stretching them beyond what should have been possible. She panicked, instinctively reaching for something, anything, and the wish formed before she even realized it. *I wish to breathe.*

The now-familiar taste hit her tongue, like blood in seawater. Metallic and cold. Light-Voice gasped inside her mind, not from surprise but from pain. *Bay, stop this. Not like this.*

But it was already happening. A sharp, searing ache tore through the sides of her neck as gills forced themselves open. Water pushed through them, burning at first, then flowing clean and smooth. Somehow, miraculously, she could breathe.

It wasn't like using her lungs, not exactly, but at least it didn't hurt anymore. Her vision sharpened next. It stung for a moment, then cleared with startling intensity. She could see farther and clearer than ever before, every flicker of motion, every shadow, every ripple. Above her, Catalina's crimson tail still flailed near the surface.

Why does it always hurt?

On the deck of the Contessa, mermaids with banded arms, clearly guards, were holding down Cyrus. They looked identical to the two gripping Bay's arms tightly on either side. Bay lunged upward toward her friend, surprised that she could cast one of them off, but another guard seized her tail, yanking her back and giving the first just enough time to reclaim her arm. Surrounded by three very powerful mermaids and not wanting to cause more trouble, Bay stopped fighting and let the guards guide her. She was certain she could get this sorted out once brought to the Palace.

Attempting mental communication, she stared up at Catalina and concentrated: *Catalina, I am okay! I can breathe. Don't worry!*

No response. Catalina didn't react. Bay squinted, but her friend was barely visible now, as Bay's guards dragged her farther into the darkening blue.

Below, the vague outlines of a town began to emerge, or maybe a large city. It was in fact the capital of the Pacific Palace. It shimmered with impossible grace. Towering statues lined the avenues, carved from coral and obsidian, their eyes fixed on the sea around them. Elaborate buildings rose from the seabed like underwater cathedrals, their spires twisting upward as if chasing the currents.

Heavy containers hung on chains from the ships above, lowered methodically into enormous receiving bays. Everything below pulsed with structure and order, gleaming under soft light. The buildings were made of the same sleek, luminescent material as the station above, but down here they glowed like chandeliers catching the light.

Bay took it all in with wide eyes. This was her mother's kingdom. Her birthright. And she had never seen anything like it. Everything was clean, bright, and eerily quiet. Mermaids glided in and out like vibrant fish in a giant aquarium, their scales flashing like gemstones. Vendors whispered silent messages to passing merfolk. It was a different world.

She didn't have long to admire it before being pulled toward a guarded entrance, a massive cave that descended into darkness. The mouth of the cave had been carved directly into the side of a towering undersea mountain, its stone surface worn smooth by centuries of current and time. Lights glowed in even intervals along the walls, circular blue orbs connected by clear tubing, but their soft, sterile glow only seemed to make the shadows feel deeper.

Two guards restrained her arms while two others flanked her, one ahead and one behind.

She tried again to communicate. *Hello, I think there's been a mistake. I am the Queen's daughter. I must speak with her.*

No response. Either they were ignoring her, or they truly couldn't hear her.

Must be incredibly useful for keeping secrets.

Or incredibly lonely, Bay replied, clinging to the voice's presence more than she wanted to admit.

This will all be over soon. Allura will fix this.

The thought steadied her for a moment. Surely, when the Queen saw her, everything would be set right. But the silence pressed tighter, and the cave only seemed to grow darker.

Finally, the cave branched left, and they leveled out. A massive door blocked their path. It was made of the same strange material as the buildings above, but unlike those glowing structures, this surface absorbed light, staying dark and cold, like stone pulled from the bottom of the sea.

I do not like the look of this, Light-Voice whispered.

But Bay found the door strangely mesmerizing, like staring into the night sky. Something about it felt ancient and alive.

She reached out, almost without thinking. A guard caught her wrist and gently, but firmly, pushed her hand back to her side.

The lead guard approached the door. Without a visible signal or gesture, it began to rise into the ceiling of rock above. They swam beneath it. Bay glanced up as they passed underneath; the door looked to be a foot thick, and completely seamless. When it closed behind them, it did so with a low, final sound that echoed in her chest.

One of the inside guards handed a key to the one holding Bay's arm.

They're going to be sorry when Allura realizes what's happening to her daughter, Light-Voice huffed.

Bay was led into a wide central chamber lined with barred cells. The water here felt colder, heavier. They turned a jagged corner into a narrower passage, where a single, isolated cell waited at the end of a long hallway. She was pushed inside without a word. Two guards took position outside. One of them pocketed the key.

Now what? Bay wondered. She could see nothing beyond the long, dim hallway and the two guards stationed in front of her cell.

Demand to be seen immediately! The Princess cannot be treated like this! Light-Voice insisted.

But Bay wasn't ready to announce her claim. Not yet. She wanted to meet Allura first, face to face.

Left alone, the weight of it settled on her chest. Just hours ago, she nearly drowned. Now she was locked in an underwater dungeon. But somehow, impossibly, she could breathe and see beneath the sea.

Her transformation, though, was still wrong. Her hair floated wild and black, her hands lacked webbing, and the gills on her neck pulsed uncomfortably. They weren't where they were supposed to be.

She looked down. Her soaked T-shirt clung to her chest, and below it, her gleaming pink tail shimmered faintly in the cell's blue light. This wasn't how she had imagined meeting her mother. She had pictured herself arriving with confidence, fully transformed and radiant, not trembling and incomplete.

Why couldn't she get it right? Even young mer-children could manage a proper shift.

The silence closed in around her. A quiet so deep it seemed to press against her thoughts. Why had they locked her up? Had she broken some rule?

Would Cyrus and Catalina be thrown into cells too?

Trying to pass the time, Bay turned inward. She stared at a strand of her floating black hair and concentrated, willing it to shift, to turn blonde. Nothing. She focused harder. Still nothing. Her head began to throb.

Then she remembered. *I wish my hair was blonde again*, she thought, not just thinking it, but pouring herself into the want, into the need.

Heat flared at her scalp. Copper tang stung her mouth. Her hair lightened in an instant, shimmering gold through the water. The guard outside her cell noticed, doing a double take, but said nothing.

Bay, stop, Light-Voice whimpered. *What are you doing?*

Bay faltered. Her fingers clenched. Light-Voice's panic echoed inside her, but she pushed it down. She had to finish the shift. She had to look right.

It hurts.

She ignored the plea, chill creeping up her tail. She ignored the sting building behind her eyes. If she could change one thing, maybe she could change more. She focused again, harder this time. I want scales, she thought. *I want to look right.*

Bit by bit, they began to form. Small patches of shimmering armor along her hips and thighs. Each one felt like it was tearing through her skin. Her muscles trembled. Her thoughts frayed. Her gills fluttered erratically, and the remnants of her lungs burned with the effort.

It was working. But it was costing her.

Her body burned, her mind throbbed, and still the transformation remained incomplete.

Finally, drained and hollow, Bay slumped against the rock wall, her hand curling around the small starfish charm on her necklace.

Light-Voice had gone quiet.

The silence inside her was worse than the dungeon walls.

Time blurred.

Then came movement. The guards outside her cell shifted. They stepped aside.

Bay looked up.

She felt a shock and then a shiver.

Coming down the corridor, graceful and terrible as a rising tide, was the Queen herself.

CHAPTER THIRTY-SEVEN

Mistaken

he Queen was even more magnificent than Bay had imagined. Pictures did not do her justice. She radiated presence, the kind that pulled the water around her into still reverence. Stunned, Bay realized with a painful jolt that she did not truly resemble the Queen after all. She was only a shadow, a faint and flickering echo of this powerful being, like a dim reflection in turbulent water.

Allura stood as tall and commanding as any of her armored guards. Her long, graceful neck led into a full, curvy figure that exuded effortless authority. Her pink tail shimmered with flawless precision, each salmon-colored scale gleaming and perfectly aligned, curling upward over golden-tanned skin in elegant, intricate swirls that looked almost ceremonial. Her hair, blonde and silken, hung in a straight curtain down her back, and her large, almond-shaped eyes, so blue they seemed almost unnatural, glowed faintly as if lit from within. They did not blink. They did not soften.

She is here! Light-Voice shrieked, giddy with excitement, nearly breathless in its urgency. *You found her, Bay, she's real!*

But Bay could not move. She stood frozen at the center of her cell, her heart overflowing with awe, admiration, and a wild, aching happiness she had never known she could feel. She trembled with anticipation, scarcely daring to breathe. The Queen lingered just beyond the bars, her brow creased as she murmured something to the guards. Her voice, even when speaking low, resonated with authority.

See? I told you they would get in trouble! Light-Voice added, brimming with triumphant satisfaction, but Bay barely heard it. Her focus had narrowed entirely to the figure outside her cell.

Snapping out of her trance, Bay swam slowly toward the bars and placed her hands against them. Her fingers curled around the cold iron. She reached out with her thoughts, sending her words through the water, hoping her mother would hear them even if she could not speak them aloud. *I don't know what to say. I am so happy to see you.*

Allura looked up sharply, her eyes locking onto Bay's. For a brief, blinding instant, Bay's heart soared. She had heard. But then the Queen's expression hardened, and her voice cut through the water like a blade.

"Do not speak to me," she said coldly. The words did not pass through her lips in any audible way, but Bay heard them clearly inside her head, as if the Queen's thoughts had pierced straight through the water. It was not like the telepathy Bay used with Light-Voice, but something more forceful and commanding, a direct mental intrusion that left no room for misunderstanding.

Bay recoiled, stunned. A tightness surged through her chest, and the joy that had been swelling inside her moments before dissolved like mist in the current. Allura had heard her, that much was undeniable, but she had not recognized her. She had not truly seen her.

"No... I am Trent's daughter... your daughter," Bay said, forcing the words into the water around her. Her voice slipped through the current, shaped by her lips and carried by her breath, but she also pushed the thought outward with her mind, hoping it would reach the Queen more clearly that way. Speaking underwater was never simple. Sound bent and faded in strange ways, and meanings could easily be lost. Desperate to be understood, Bay used everything she had. The truth pressed against her chest, too urgent to keep inside. She needed to be known, even if it meant risking everything.

"Do not speak to me again, creature," the Queen said, her voice cold and cutting as she turned away.

"But you're my mother!" Bay cried out, her voice rising, trembling with disbelief. Her body surged forward, one hand reaching through the bars as if she could catch her, as if proximity alone could convince her.

Allura turned back then, slowly and deliberately, her movements steeped in the authority of a queen. Her face twisted into something sharp and terrible, a clear expression of disgust. She looked at Bay as though she had just crawled out of the muck at the bottom of the sea. Her lips parted, but for a moment, no sound emerged. Then she lifted her chin, eyes narrowing, and gave a single, deliberate shake of her head. A silent refusal. A queen denying what stood plainly before her.

"But I look so much like you! Our hair, our nose—my tail! My dad said—"

"Trent lied," Allura said, her voice carrying the weight of finality, like a sentence passed. "I thought it was a trick to stop me from killing you, pretending to be her. No doubt something you learned from the Sea Witch. But it isn't working."

Bay blinked. Her thoughts skidded and collided. The Sea Witch? What was she talking about?

"I'm telling the truth!" she begged. "I ran away from my father to find you, to be with you. Please, speak with him! He'll tell you!"

"You will not get away again. I will kill you this time." The Queen's voice was measured, but behind it was the force of a vow carved in stone.

Bay staggered back, as if the words themselves had struck her. Her mind spun, her thoughts unraveling faster than she could catch them. *Kill?* That word echoed, louder and louder, louder than her heartbeat. Darkness stirred, subtle at first, like smoke curling at the edge of her vision. Then it rose, cold and biting, crawling up her tail like frost. She tried to hold onto something, whether an image or a thought, but everything slipped through her fingers.

Her chest tightened. Her breath came in short, shallow bursts. The water felt colder, suddenly thick around her limbs, pressing in from all sides. She reached out with her mind, trying to call someone: her father, Catalina, Cyrus, anyone. But the connection frayed and broke. Panic surged.

Light-Voice whimpered. *Why? Why does she hate you? What is wrong?*

Bay could not answer. Her legs trembled beneath her. She pressed her palms harder against the bars, trying to steady herself, to hold on to something solid, something real. But the bars were slick. Her vision blurred. Spots bloomed and danced before her eyes like ink in water. Darkness crept higher, seizing her ribs, sinking cold claws into her chest.

The betrayal burned. It wasn't the angry kind of fire. It was colder than that, colder than the deep trenches, colder than anything she had ever known. It hollowed her out.

The last thing she saw before everything went dark was the Queen's blue eyes—no longer glowing with awe or power, but with hatred. Unmistakable and burning.

CHAPTER THIRTY-EIGHT

Eavesdropping

Bay had exhausted every memory she could think of and obsessed over every truth or lie she had been told. But she couldn't crack this puzzle. She didn't understand why her mother refused to claim her. Why she hated her. None of it made sense, no matter how many times Bay turned it over in her mind.

Darkness gnawed at her from the inside, and the silence didn't help. It pressed in on her like the crushing deep. The cold was constant, curling around her bones.

Light-Voice tried to cheer her up, to keep her afloat. But Bay couldn't help in the fight. Not now. She was drained and confused. Her anger had nowhere to go; it just sank deeper, like black ink spilling on white silk. If nothing else, at least the ocean's pull was finally quieted by being here, she thought bitterly.

To pass the time, she numbly took stock of her surroundings. First, she examined every inch of her cell, her eyes trailing across the rough stone walls and floor. Tiny carvings marked the surface, likely the daily count of those who had come before her. Some were worn down to nearly nothing, others were fresh and jagged. It was a quiet kind of desperation, etched into stone.

She also began noticing details she had missed before. The guards, for example, weren't as identical as she had first thought. Though they all wore the same silvery armor and had similar builds and blue eyes, their skin tones, tails, and personalities varied. She tried to keep track of time by their shifts—two during what she assumed was the day and one during the quieter hours, likely night. But the underwater cave offered no sunlight, no natural rhythm. She couldn't be sure if her guesses were right, but by her count, she had been here for about a week.

Today, one of the guards had vibrant green scales that shimmered from neon to hunter green. The other, older in demeanor, had a beige-and-blue tail and always looked exhausted.

I hope Catalina and Cyrus are okay.

Me too, Bay thought back, worry tightening her chest.

Your dad warned there were dangers. Maybe this is part of it.

He didn't say the danger was Allura! Bay snapped, frustration flashing through her. *All he ever talked about was how kind and brilliant she was. That is not the woman I met. He should've prepared me. He should've told me the truth.*

He tried, Light-Voice answered gently. *We should have stayed away.*

This is his fault, Bay thought bitterly. *He basically sent me into the arms of a lunatic.* She knew she was being dramatic, but she didn't care. The bitterness had nowhere else to go.

Maybe Allura is confused or sick, Light-Voice offered. *Maybe she'll come around.*

I won't hold my breath, Bay replied, rolling her eyes.

She was tired. Tired of this place. Tired of talking only to herself. Tired of the madness that had swallowed what was supposed to be a dream. What scared her most was how much Light-Voice had grown. In isolation, it was louder, stronger. Less like a voice in her head and more like someone else. She wasn't sure that was a good thing.

Bay wished the silence would end. She didn't want to lose her mind in an underwater prison.

Suddenly, pain surged through her like a jolt of electricity. The taste of copper filled her mouth, coating her teeth. She collapsed onto the cold stone floor, a silent cry escaping her lips. At that moment, a young voice echoed in her head as clearly as if someone had spoken aloud: "Shimra is covering the shift tonight." Bay froze, blinking in shock. She glanced at the guards. Neither of them moved or turned.

"Well, she's late. Nearly thirty minutes," came a second, gruffer voice. Bay peered down the corridor but saw no one. Still, the conversation continued. Her heart pounded. Somehow, impossibly, she could hear the guards speaking.

"How long 'til this one gets tried?" It seemed that the younger one with green scales was speaking. "It's been over a week. Especially for a kid. Her parents must be losing it."

"No trial," the other replied. "She's charged with *lèse-majesté.*"

"What? How can a child go against the crown? She seems harmless. She can't even fully transform. Look at her hair, it's a mess."

"They say the Queen herself came to confront her."

"So, what's to be done with her?"

Bay saw the beige-and-blue-scaled guard pause and shudder ominously. Then she heard it—clear and horrifying: "She is sentenced to death. By beheading."

"What?" Bay cried out.

"What?" the green-scaled guard echoed in alarm.

Both guards turned abruptly to face her. The older one squinted. "Do you think she heard?" the tired one whispered.

"I don't know," said the green-scaled one.

Bay played dumb, directing her thoughts at them: *What am I doing here? Hello? Will someone answer me, please?*

"I think it was just a coincidence," the beige guard said, turning back around.

"I guess so," the other murmured, though her eyes remained fixed on Bay. "Don't you think it's strange how much she looks like the Queen?"

"I wouldn't say that out loud."

"But it is odd. We're going to execute a kid who looks just like our Queen. Without a trial. She's the same age as—"

"Leave it, Riana. Argh, where is Shimra? I'm going to be late!"

"Go ahead and go, Deptha," Riana said. "I'll cover until Shimra gets here."

"Thanks." Deptha swam away without another glance.

Riana's shoulders slumped.

She feels bad.

And she should, Bay answered. They're going to kill me. Even the guards don't know why.

I'm sure there's some kind of mistake.

A mistake is the wrong dinner order. This is a death sentence.

Try talking to her, Light-Voice urged. *Maybe she can help.*

Bay took a breath and willed a thought toward Riana "Are they really going to kill me?"

Riana did not move at first. "So… you did hear." Then she turned. "Yes. I'm afraid so."

"But why? What did I do?"

"Didn't the Queen tell you?"

"No. She didn't say anything."

"She came here, didn't she?"

"Yes, but…we didn't really talk."

"Then you must know. Don't play dumb, kid. This is serious."

"I don't know!" Bay cried, her voice vibrating through the water. "I don't know why she wants me dead!"

"Why did you come here?"

"To find my mother."

"Who is she?"

"Allura."

Riana's mouth dropped open. "You lie, child."

"I'm not lying! You said it yourself—I look just like her. My father told me who she was. That's why I came."

"Then why weren't you raised with the Queen?"

"I don't know! I didn't even know I was a mermaid until a few weeks ago!"

Bay launched into the whole story: her vacation with the Plowmans, her father's confession, and her journey with Catalina and Cyrus. Riana listened without interrupting, her expression assessing but kind. Bay had just reached the part where she finally met Allura when Riana suddenly stiffened.

The guard turned toward the corridor. A new guard was approaching whose tail flashed with bright streaks of orange and yellow.

"I have to go," Riana said quickly.

"Wait, don't leave me!"

"You must be silent. Don't speak to anyone else. I'll return when I can."

Without another word, she swam away, exchanging a brief nod with Shimra. The newcomer didn't apologize for being late and showed no interest in Bay at all.

Riana disappeared down the corridor, and Bay was left to do the only thing she could: wait.

CHAPTER THIRTY-NINE

Ally

*C*ome on, Riana! When are you going to show up? Bay pleaded in her mind as she witnessed another changing of the guards. Disappointed, she hung her head. No Riana.

It will be soon. She has to come soon! Light-Voice urged.

Bay could still overhear the guards' conversations. At first, she had hoped eavesdropping would help her escape or at least make sense of her imprisonment. But most of what she heard was mundane: complaints about bosses, excitement over promotions, gossip. When Bay was mentioned, it was clear that few knew why she was there. And all of them trusted that if the Queen thought she was guilty, it must be true.

I don't want to listen to this. They don't even know me! Bay thought bitterly.

They must really like Allura.

Bay scoffed. *Yeah, and look where that blind loyalty got me. What kind of people follow orders without question?*

Riana believed you, Light-Voice recalled.

But where was Riana now? The thought that she might never return sent a wave of hopelessness through Bay. Tears welled in her eyes.

She will come. You aren't alone. I am here, Light-Voice said gently.

Bay had accepted it: she was losing her mind. Her little voice was growing louder, more distinct, almost its own person. Yet, ironically, it was the only thing keeping her sane. Though every counselor on land would have warned against "feeding the voice," Bay clung to it. Without it, the loneliness would be unbearable.

Finally, three days later, during a changing of the guard, Bay spotted a flash of green and beige swimming down the hall.

Yes! I told you! Light-Voice squealed.

Riana and Deptha exchanged pleasantries with the current guards. Bay swam up, hands gripping the bars, staring at Riana. But Riana did not look at her.

"Don't look so obvious," Riana's voice whispered in Bay's mind. "No one can know we're talking. Swim away. Act normal."

Bay drifted to the corner of her cell, picking up a rock to scratch idle drawings into the wall.

"I looked into your story," Riana said. Bay remained silent. "I found your friends."

Bay spun instinctively, sending ripples through the water. Deptha glanced at her.

"Kid's acting funny," Deptha remarked.

"I would, too, if I were locked up alone," Riana replied easily. Bay steadied herself.

"Your friends are fine," Riana continued once Deptha turned away. "They're restricted to the docking area but safe. They are worried about you. I let them know you're alive."

Relief flooded Bay. "Thank you," she thought.

"I don't know if there's more I can do. But I'll try."

"Why are you helping me?" Bay asked softly.

"Because you're just a kid. And something isn't right."

"I'm sixteen. Almost."

"The Queen's daughter...she was born sixteen years ago. But everyone knows she died shortly after; so did the Queen's consort, her *Socius Animae*. After that, the ocean raged for days. It's taboo to bring it up."

Bay's questions spilled out: "Why keep me a secret? My father, Trent, is alive. Why deny we exist? Why want me dead?"

"I'll keep digging."

"How long will that take?"

"I don't know."

"But you'll help me?"

"I told you I'd try."

"Don't I get a phone call? A lawyer?"

"No. We do typically have a trial with three Onares, similar to judges, but we do not have lawyers. When two or more Onares agree, then the judgment is decided. Very extreme cases are brought to the Queen for judgment and sentencing."

"Will I get a trial?"

Riana hesitated. "No."

"Not even before the Queen?"

"She has judged."

"That wasn't a trial! It was barely a conversation! She just... she hated me on sight. This is a stupid system."

"There are flaws. But I've never had reason to question it before now. We are a very small community of ancient subjects. We live long lives. Within our culture, there is education, wealth, and care for our subjects. We are not prone to the same circumstances as humans. I have never once doubted the Queen's judgement; she has the best intentions for her people."

"Except now—you're helping a condemned kid!"

"Maybe Allura's judgment is clouded. But I believe she still thinks she's doing what's best."

Bay clenched her fists. "Right. Killing your kid. So noble."

"I'm trying to help you understand the stakes."

"When do I get out of here?" Bay demanded.

"I'm not helping you break out!"

"What? But if I stay, they'll kill me!"

"I hope to uncover something—something that might change the Queen's mind."

Bay sank to the floor, cold fury filling her chest. She lay there, not caring if Deptha guessed that there was something going on. Riana wasn't going to help.

Riana said she would try, Light-Voice whispered.

Yeah, well, she didn't hear what the Queen said to me, Bay thought grimly. *There's no changing that monster's mind.*

How can you call your mother that? There must be something we're missing. Didn't you hear Riana?

How can you defend her? Bay shot back. *A mother should fight for her child. She didn't even try.* Bitterness coiled in her gut. *If Allura ever does reconsider, maybe I'll give her a real reason to lock me up,* she thought darkly.

You don't mean that.

Bay didn't answer. Because, maybe...

Maybe she did.

CHAPTER FORTY

Changing of the Guard

Bay's hair floated around her face, a constant irritation as she swam. She decided to try wishing it back, despite the painful consequences. She focused hard: *I wish my hair would slick back.* Instantly, she felt it pull behind her into a fin-shape. As she touched it, a sharp pain flared at her scalp. The copper flavor mixed with her saliva, Light-Voice flinched, trembling with fear. But it had worked.

Buoyed by her success, Bay tried again: *I wish my transformation would be complete.* Nothing happened. Maybe she needed to be more specific. *I wish my hands would web.* Thick webbing grew between her fingers. *I wish my scales would cover my body.* Nothing.

Bay reached deeper. She touched Darkness inside her, just a little. Molten, metallic water swirled across her tongue. A cold pain unfurled in her tail, stronger than anything she had felt recently.

What is happening? Why is Darkness so strong? Light-Voice cried.

Bay ignored her. She focused harder, willing pink scales to grow across her body. It was like dragging herself through frozen fire. She tore off her T-shirt as the scales climbed up her torso, matching the elegant swirl pattern she had once admired on Allura.

When she finally opened her eyes, she was transformed. A real mermaid. *Finally!* she thought, her happiness barely masking the gnawing pain. But it wasn't enough. *I wish my tail was blue,* she thought, picturing the brilliant sky she missed. The pain slammed into her harder.

Light-Voice screamed, *Stop, Bay! It hurts!*

But Bay clamped down, refusing to slow. The agony was searing, ripping across her body. It mirrored her internal turmoil, and she craved it. She wanted to burn away everything Allura had left behind.

I feel tired.

Ignoring Light-Voice, she focused on her tail. She wouldn't keep her mother's pink color, not after what Allura had done. She collapsed onto the dungeon floor, gasping. When she opened her eyes, her tail shimmered blue, the pain finally easing.

Light-Voice remained silent for the rest of the day.

For days, Bay practiced in secret. The guards barely noticed her anymore. She shifted her tail color from blue back to pink, altered her skin tone, and webbed her hands at will. Each transformation grew easier with time, but the cost never lessened. Pain, exhaustion, and the creeping chill of Darkness followed every wish.

Light-Voice begged her to stop, whispering warnings that became weaker with each passing day. Bay didn't listen. Eventually, the voice grew quiet. Then silent. As her mastery sharpened, the pain and Darkness took its place, filling the space where Light-Voice used to live.

She felt the guilt. She felt the sadness. But they were fleeting, distant. The pain grounded her. It made her feel powerful. And it was addictive.

Bay felt a flicker of hope when she learned Riana would be guarding her alone that night. And when at last she arrived, Riana slipped a small, blue enamel tin through the bars.

"What is this?" Bay asked, sitting up.

"A gift from your friends. I checked. It's safe. I thought you could use some cheering up," Riana said.

"Thank you." Bay cradled the tin, her heart aching. She felt something stir in her chest—Light-Voice—faint but responding to the kindness from the twins.

"I'm sorry," Riana added softly. "I haven't found anything concrete yet."

"Nothing?"

"I think the Sea Witch is involved. She might be the key to this whole thing, but no one will talk. Not about her."

Bay's pulse quickened. "The Sea Witch? Allura mentioned her too. Can't you just—ask her?"

"It's not that simple. She's dangerous. People barely speak her name."

"There has to be someone who knows something."

"I'm trying," Riana said. "I promise."

"How much time do I have?"

"About two months."

Bay let out a hollow laugh. "That'll be a lovely birthday gift."

They spoke a little longer, but Riana had no real updates. Bay was exhausted and clung to the tin like a lifeline. Inside were six cookies, each carefully wrapped in seaweed.

"They're really good," Riana said. "Your friends found the best shop."

Bay was hardly listening. Inside the lid, a message had been scratched with care: *Hope this bit of sugar brings you some relief.* Her breath caught. A signal.

"Want one?" she asked, her voice calm.

"Oh, no, I can get them anytime."

"Go on. I can't eat them all before the guards change," Bay said lightly. She wished Riana to take one.

Riana hesitated, then smiled and accepted a cookie. She devoured it in two bites while Bay slowly nibbled hers, keeping the conversation going. Riana talked about her training and how proud she felt on passing the placement exam and joining the palace guard.

Then she yawned.

Bay's heart pounded. The "bit of sugar" was working.

Another cookie. Another yawn. Within minutes, Riana drifted gently to the ground, fast asleep.

Bay hesitated, guilt gnawing at her.

Don't do this, Bay, Light-Voice whispered. *She was trying to help you. If Allura finds out—*

Bay felt a pang of relief that Light-Voice was speaking again. But she pushed it aside.

"I'm sorry," she murmured, more to herself than to Riana.

Reaching through the bars, Bay slipped the keys from Riana's vest pocket. Her hands trembled as she unlocked the cell. She dragged Riana inside, laid her gently on the floor, and stripped off her uniform.

I wish to look like Riana, she thought, channeling every ounce of her will into the transformation.

The pain ripped through her, searing, paralyzing. The copper-blood taste flooded her mouth, so strong it felt like she might choke. It was worse than any change before. Her body writhed; her vision blackened at the edges. She nearly passed out.

When her eyes cleared, she was staring into the cookie tin lid. Riana's face stared back.

What is happening to you? Light-Voice whimpered.

Bay didn't answer. She gently turned Riana's sleeping form to face the wall. Then she quickly locked the cell, and swam out to take her place in the corridor, posing as the guard. Though this was usually Riana's rest period, Bay was wide awake. Every distant sound made her jump. Every passing second felt like it would never end.

Hours dragged by.

Then, a subtle shift in the water. Two mermaids approached, their movements casual. It was the morning shift.

They swam closer, smiling. "Hey, Riana. Shimra said you had the night shift again. Poor thing. Did Deptha finally switch with you?"

Bay hesitated. Her mind raced.

"Uh... yeah," she said. "Deptha owed me."

The taller of the two narrowed her eyes. "Wait, didn't you have the feast duty tomorrow? Or did someone cover that too?"

Bay's heart pounded. She had no idea what they were talking about.

"I'm sorry," she said quickly. "I'm late meeting someone. Prisoner's fine. Gotta go."

Without waiting for a reply, she pushed off and swam fast, trying to keep her pace just shy of suspicious.

"Okay... see you later?" one called after her.

Bay didn't answer. She shot down the hall, past the heavy door, past the final guard post, and into the shadowy tunnels. Her chest burned with panic and hope. She didn't stop.

Upward she swam, toward the faint shimmer of light above. Freedom called to her, cold and brilliant.

CHAPTER FORTY-ONE

A Salty Goodbye

Bay exited the tunnel and hovered in the open water, staring down at the Pacific Palace. It stretched below her like a glowing dream, quiet in the early morning dark. The lights from the buildings had dimmed to a soft, eerie shimmer, and only a few mermaids moved silently through the stillness. The world was hushed, suspended in shadow and silence.

She drifted there for a moment, stunned by how vast everything felt. After so many days trapped within the narrow stone walls of her cell, the open ocean felt unreal. The current brushed her skin like a forgotten touch. There were no bars, no guards, no constant echoes of her own thoughts bouncing back at her. Just water, open and endless. She could move freely in any direction, and the weight of that freedom made her dizzy.

Now what?

Bay could not afford to hesitate. She swam quickly behind a nearby rock and stripped off the guard's uniform, her hands shaking. *I wish to be myself again,* she thought, keeping the black hair and blue tail. The copper taste rose on her tongue. The transformation surged through her body, painful but familiar. Easier now. Her breath hitched, but she stayed upright, the pain already fading.

Lifting her gaze, she saw the stars scattered above the surface. They twinkled faintly, blurred through layers of water, and she stared at them in wonder. She hadn't realized how much she had missed them. They looked just as they had before— indifferent, infinite, beautiful. A pang of longing pierced her chest. She wanted to stay and watch as the sun rose and chased them away. She wanted to feel the world shift from night to morning, just once, in silence. But there was no time. Not now. Bay swam toward the docks.

The *Contessa* was still there, docked exactly where they had left it. Relief bloomed in her chest. She moved to the rope ladder and raised her head above the water. The air felt sharp and cold. *I wish for legs,* she thought.

Her body responded at once. Scales cracked and peeled. Her tail split down the center, bones shifting and reshaping with a flash of fire that tore through her spine. She bit her lip to keep from crying out.

Inside, Light-Voice screamed.

Bay gasped. Her vision blurred.

Are you okay? she called silently, desperate.

No answer.

She floated for a heartbeat, naked and stunned, her skin prickling in the open air. The sea no longer held her the same way, but it hadn't released her either.

Bay grabbed the ladder and climbed. Each step left her trembling. The wind bit at her wet skin, but the cold didn't scare her.

The silence did.

The ocean was not done with her. Its call surged through her like a current. It clawed at her spine, begging her to return. It didn't want to let her go. It took everything she had to stand. After a few breathless minutes, she staggered below deck and shut the door behind her, the sea's voice still pounding in her blood.

She found the kitchen cabinet where the sleeping powder was kept—half-empty. Smiling sadly, she knew: Cyrus and Catalina had risked everything for her. She filled a teapot with water, stirred in the powder, and set it on the stove.

Still dripping, Bay went to her room, threw on clothes, and headed to Catalina's room. She gently placed a hand over her friend's mouth.

Catalina snapped awake, squirming, until she realized who it was—and then flung her arms around Bay. "Oh my goodness, it worked!" she gasped, hugging her tightly.

Bay sobbed in her friend's arms. After weeks of isolation, the contact unraveled her completely.

"What happened?" Catalina whispered.

"I'll explain. I started some tea," Bay managed.

"I'll wake Cyrus. Meet you in the kitchen," Catalina said, tossing her a towel.

Bay dried herself, lingering in the little room. She touched the smooth wooden walls, committing every detail to memory. This boat, this wonderful boat, had become home. And after everything she had been through, she didn't want to leave it again.

She made her way to the kitchen, where Cyrus paced nervously. When he saw her, he crossed the room in two strides and swept her into a hug. "Bay," he breathed.

She nestled against his shoulder before pulling away, urgency sharpening her resolve. "Hi, Cyrus," she whispered.

They sat. Bay told her confusing tale while Catalina prepared the tea.

Why aren't you telling them about the transformations? Light-Voice asked weakly. Her voice was faint, barely a whisper in Bay's mind.

Because they'll be questioned when I leave, Bay replied, relieved to hear Light-Voice again.

But the calm didn't last.

What do you mean? We can't separate! We can't leave Cyr—

Enough, Bay snapped inwardly, the tension and fear boiling over before she could stop it.

She finished her story. Catalina set three cups on the table. Cyrus added honey to his and drank deeply.

"Oh, Bay, I'm so sorry," Catalina said, face pale.

"We have to stop her—the Queen is crazy!" Cyrus slammed his fist on the table.

"No," Catalina said firmly. Taking a thoughtful sip of her tea. "Forget the Queen. We need to leave. Now."

"I needed to see you one more time," Bay said, voice trembling.

"What do you mean?" Catalina demanded.

"Bay, we're not leaving without you," Cyrus insisted.

"I know," Bay said tearfully. "That's why I have to do this. I will try to meet you in Crystal Cove in a couple weeks' time."

Cyrus opened his mouth—but then slumped over, the sleeping powder taking effect.

"Don't do this, Bay!" Catalina cried, realizing what was happening.

"I love you guys," Bay whispered, catching Catalina as she wobbled and helping her collapse into a chair.

How could you do that? Light-Voice asked, horrified.

Bay ignored her. She retrieved some rope and scarves, quickly binding their wrists and mouths. She packed her waterproof satchel with some money leaving the rest under Catalina's pillow, as well as food, water, maps, and a change of clothes.

Trumpets blared from the docks. Heart hammering, Bay dashed onto the deck. She threw everything into her waterproof bag and dove into the sea just as footsteps thundered toward the *Contessa.*

Relief sang through her veins as she hit the water. *I wish I was an old mermaid with a green tail and white hair,* she thought. Pain ripped through her, but she forced herself to swim, ignoring Light-Voice's desperate cries. Ignoring the metallic taste of blood flooding her mouth. Her legs fused into a powerful tail; her arms grew frail and wrinkled. She was unrecognizable.

The city blazed in alarm—orange lights flashing, sirens wailing, guards swarming door-to-door. Bay stayed low, pressed against the rocky seabed. She followed a canyon path winding far from the Pacific Palace, swimming as fast as her battered body would allow.

How can you leave them like that? They could be in trouble! Light-Voice wept.

I had to. It's safer for them, Bay thought grimly.

We need to go back! Light-Voice cried.

Bay sobbed silently as she swam. *We never would have escaped together, and I couldn't risk their lives. They could have been imprisoned, or worse.* Bay gave up trying to convince Light-Voice she had done the right thing. *First prison, now this*, she thought bitterly. *I'm alone again.*

You are not alone, Bay.

Bay swam until she could barely move. Exhaustion dragged at her, but fear kept her arms stroking weakly forward. Finally, she spotted a narrow crevasse in the rocks where she wedged herself inside, trembling.

Bay squeezed her eyes shut and let the saltwater carry her silent tears away.

It was a long while before sleep found her.

CHAPTER FORTY-TWO

A Shiver

Bay woke to turbulence in the water around her. At first, she thought it was another changing of the guards, but when she opened her eyes, she saw only the dark corners of the cave where she had fallen asleep. She turned toward the crevasse opening. Then let out a horrified scream, forgetting she was underwater.

Stay calm, Light-Voice urged. *Catalina said they don't eat mermaids.*

Bay pressed herself against the sharp rocks, scooting as far back as she could. Just feet away, a massive tiger shark was forcing its way toward her. *Okay, would you mind telling the shark that?* she thought back, heart hammering.

The shark backed away, only to reveal a whole school of tiger sharks. Some of the smaller ones might have been able to reach her if they tried. The large shark resumed its effort, thrashing and slamming against the stone. Bay pressed herself harder against the back wall, feeling the tip of its nose graze her stomach.

Grab a rock and hit it!

Bay froze, paralyzed with fear.

Grab a rock now!

She shut her eyes, inhaled deeply. The water flowed through her gills, forcing her to focus. Above her, a jagged purple rock balanced on a ledge. Keeping herself pinned to the wall, Bay reached up, grabbed it with both hands, and raised it over her head.

The tiger shark lunged again. Bay felt the blast of water against her skin—and the graze of teeth just inches from her ribs. With a desperate cry, she slammed the rock down with all her strength onto the shark's nose. The beast recoiled, thrashing violently and backing away from the crevasse.

You did it! Light-Voice cheered.

But Bay didn't celebrate. She stayed frozen, rock clenched tightly, as the school of sharks glided past her hiding place. She kept the rock raised, muscles trembling, adrenaline crashing.

Put the rock down.

Bay's arms ached. She wanted to, but she was trembling too hard.

They're gone. It's okay now.

Eventually, Bay lowered the rock. Her hands still trembled, her chest ached, and her limbs felt hollow from holding herself so still. She waited a long time before daring to move again. When her stomach growled, she knew she couldn't stay hidden forever. Clutching the purple rock like a lifeline, she slipped out of the crevice and kept close to the canyon floor. Every flicker of shadow made her flinch. Every shift in the current felt like another threat. Her body was sore, her nerves frayed.

Are you heading back to where your dad is? Light-Voice asked gently.

Bay didn't answer at first. She swam in silence, her limbs shaking from fear or fatigue, she couldn't tell which. Her mind still replayed the moment the shark's nose had brushed her ribs, the weight of its body pressing against the rocks. It made her want to crawl back into the crevasse and never come out. But she was done hiding. Done waiting for someone else to fix everything.

No, she thought at last. *I'm going to find the Sea Witch.*

She didn't feel brave. She felt wrecked. But she kept swimming anyway.

If the world wants me dead, she thought, it's going to have to catch me first.

CHAPTER FORTY-THREE

A Twisted Smile

What are you saying? You should find your dad first! He can help, Light-Voice urged.

Help against a whole army of mermaids? Bay was doubtful. She couldn't even leave the ocean, even if part of her ached to be wrapped in one of his bear hugs right now. She longed to forget this whole thing and go back to how life used to be. But she knew that wasn't an option.

Didn't you notice how hard it was for me to be on land? Bay thought back. *He would take me somewhere far away from the ocean.*

Would that be so bad?

I don't think I could survive outside the ocean anymore, Bay admitted.

But why the Sea Witch? Riana said most mermaids won't even talk about her.

I know. But she also said the Sea Witch might be the key to finding out what's happening to me.

You don't even know where she is, Light-Voice pointed out.

Yes, but it's the only lead I have.

Are you going to keep this skin? It feels weird being old. Can't we be young?

Bay smiled slightly. *I'm trying to go unnoticed. Young girls traveling alone get noticed.*

Just then, Bay spotted a glowing green light on the ground, a siren stone. The enchanted rocks she had first followed to the mermaid village.

We must be close to a village! Light-Voice exclaimed.

Bay spotted another glowing stone, then another, and another—following them until the water shallowed. Land loomed ahead.

She swam faster, anxious for signs of life. What she found was a village unlike any she'd ever seen. It looked as though it had been flooded and the townsfolk had simply adapted. Half of it was underwater: shops, restaurants, and homes. But just above the surface, a dock stretched the length of the village, supporting dry businesses that catered to land dwellers. Boats floated up and down flooded streets like cars.

Bay longed to stay and explore, but she had a mission. Remembering Riana's warning that "decent" mermaids avoided all talk of the Sea Witch, Bay veered off toward darker alleys and rundown shops. She wasn't looking for pretty.

Where are you going? It's getting creepy, Light-Voice warned.

Bay ignored her. Eventually, she found a barely lit and water-damaged hotel, its doors rotted through. Loud voices spilled out.

You want to go in there?

Bay answered by swimming through the rickety door and entering into the dark and flooded space. Inside, a small, cramped room buzzed with noise. Music blared, and brass instruments hung from the low ceiling, casting strange reflections. Mermaids half-submerged in water drank and laughed. Tables floated above the flooded floor.

Serving them all was the strangest little man Bay had ever seen. He rode a miniature paddleboat. He resembled a frog with his round gut, bulging eyes, and a mouth so wide it looked like it had been slashed across his face. Yet, he moved with ease, weaving expertly among the patrons.

Bay slipped on a shirt, pulled herself onto a stool in the back, and tried to blend in. She was about to wish herself back to normal when—surprisingly—she realized she could already breathe and speak above water. Her hair fell flat, no longer shaped into its sharp, spine-like fin.

Then, across the room, came a grunt.

A towering mermaid in layered kelp armor had a scrawny boy by the wrist. "You think you can take what's mine, human?"

The boy thrashed, barely twelve. "I didn't take nothing! And I ain't human!"

Bay felt her pulse spike. Before she could move, her body moved without her.

She stood. Her arm shot forward with terrifying force, seizing the armored mermaid's wrist in a grip like iron. Bay watched, stunned, as the woman flinched.

"Let. Him. Go." The words rasped from her throat, low and dangerous.

The room fell quiet. Even the music dimmed.

The mermaid stared at Bay's hunched, cloaked figure—frizzed gray hair, weathered skin—and blinked. "What in the Deep..."

Her arm was released. She hesitated, then turned and slithered off, muttering as she went.

Bay's hand dropped. She staggered back, dizzy.

What was that?! she shouted inside.

He was just a kid, her Light-Voice replied, quiet but firm. *I wasn't going to let her hurt him.*

The boy stared at Bay like she'd grown horns. "Thanks," he said, cautious but sincere as he inched past her. His red hair clung to his forehead, and a faint sliver of a scar cut through one brow. Then he darted through the tables and vanished into the back.

Bay sat down, still rattled, her hands trembling.

We shouldn't be here. This is a bar, and you're only fifteen.

I'm almost sixteen, Bay thought, grinning. *And I look about a hundred.*

"What can I get you, young lady?" croaked a voice.

Bay turned and looked straight into the frog-man's bright green stare. Her mouth went dry. *Young lady? He must be joking,* she decided. "I don't want...anything," she stammered.

"Would you like me to come back?" he asked, raising one eyebrow.

"Yes, please," she mumbled.

The frog-man turned away, but Bay's stomach betrayed her, rumbling loudly.

"Wait."

"Yes?" he spun expertly back around.

"Do you have any food?"

"Seafood soup, kale burgers, fried shrimp," he recited.

"I'll take one of each," Bay said eagerly. She hadn't eaten real food in months.

The frog-man gave her a curious look, bowed, and paddled off.

You should ask him about the Sea Witch.

I will, Bay promised.

When the food arrived, Bay dug in, listening to the conversations around her. No one spoke of the Sea Witch. But from a shadowed corner, a low voice muttered: "It's the mermen you forget. That's the curse."

Bay blinked, but when she turned, no one was there. Just then the frog-man returned and asked if she wanted anything else. She forced herself to act.

"No, or...yes," she blurted out. "I do have a question."

He tilted his head, waiting.

"Do you know anything about the Sea Witch ?"

"As much as anyone does," he said calmly.

"What if I don't know anything?"

"Curious," he said. "A lady of your maturity, and yet so innocent." He smiled, and Bay wished he hadn't. The expression stretched his froggy mouth into something grotesque. A shiver raced down her spine.

He turned to leave. "Wait!" Bay slapped half her remaining cash onto the table. "Just tell me where to find her." The frog-man eyed the money, then Bay. For a moment, Bay thought he might refuse.

Then, without a word, he zipped off, only to reappear moments later. He handed her a thick, aged scroll. Bay unrolled it with shaking fingers. A star marked a spot with a neatly penned label: *Sea Witch's Lair.*

It should have made her feel better. Instead, she felt the knot of fear tighten in her gut. The path was clear. And it was waiting for her.

CHAPTER FORTY-FOUR

Shards of Truth

Bay moved slowly through the coral-stained alleyways of the mer-city, bent beneath the weight of her disguise. Her back curved with practiced stiffness, and kelp-gray hair twisted behind her in a sharp fin over hunched shoulders. She had enchanted her tail into folds of mossy robes, frayed and clinging, aged by illusion. The old woman's spell held, for now. She didn't speak. She hadn't spoken aloud in hours; she didn't dare.

The mer-city was a small trading outpost between Hydrous—where she had acquired the map—and the mostly uninhabited region known as the Outer Drop, where the Sea Witch lived. Shops were half-shuttered. Guards drifted in twos; their movements were slow but alert. The farther she swam, the colder it got. Not water-cold. Soul-cold.

In a narrow corridor, Bay ducked beneath a low stone arch draped in netting. Above her, a window shutter slowly closed, its octopus occupant watching her through cloudy glass eyes. She bowed her head and waited. Every sound felt sharp, amplified. Each whisper echoed like broken glass across her skin.

She no longer had Catalina's quiet strength beside her. No Cyrus watching the shadows. She had left them behind, drugged by her own shaking hand, their trust folded under a blanket of sleep. She hadn't stopped moving since. Her hands, twisted into claws by the spell, ached from the cold. She flexed them once, then tucked them back into the robes.

I'm sorry, she thought. The words didn't echo. They just dissolved under the pressure in her chest. Light-Voice didn't answer. Its silence scraped harder than any guard's gaze.

A slow current nudged her as she turned down a tighter passage. Fewer merfolk lingered here, just a few scavengers and traders. One glanced her way and quickly looked away. That was the advantage of appearing old and bent and harmless: you became invisible.

But Bay didn't feel invisible. She felt fractured. Like something inside her was unraveling one strand at a time. It wasn't just fear. It was also grief for every truth she'd lost in the last few days.

Her father had always been evasive, but she had trusted him. Trusted that if he were protecting her, it was because he loved her. That love had never been in doubt. Until now. Allura, the Queen she had believed to be her mother, had looked her in the eye and said, "You are not my daughter."

Bay's chest tightened at the memory. That single sentence had ripped the ground out from under her. She didn't know if Allura was lying or not. It didn't feel like a lie. It felt too practiced. Too hollow.

And yet, if Allura was not her mother, then why were there so many similarities between them? And why had her father allowed her to believe otherwise? *Why won't anyone just tell me the truth?*

Her fingers tightened around the straps of her waterproof satchel. She had thought that knowing her mother would be the key to understanding herself. But every step closer to the truth had led only to more jagged pieces. Half-answers. Dead ends. Silence.

You shouldn't be here.

Bay paused in the shadows beneath a glowing sign, letting her thoughts settle.

You shouldn't be here, Light-Voice repeated, louder this time. *The air feels wrong. The current is poisoned. The deeper we go, the more I feel it. Darkness is breathing now. It's watching.*

Bay closed her eyes. Weight settled behind her ribs—not from fear, but from something heavier. There's no other way, she whispered inside herself.

Light-Voice trembled. *Please. Turn back. We can find another path. There has to be another way.*

Bay opened her eyes again, staring out across the bioluminescent coral ridges in the distance. There isn't. If she didn't go forward—into the Sea Witch's lair, into the heart of whatever curse her life had become—then she would never understand who she was. Never know what had happened to her. Never be able to fix whatever was broken.

I have to finish this, she thought.

Waves ripped behind her. Too heavy. Bay's pulse stuttered.

She slipped into a recessed archway between two market dens. Two Queen's guards passed slowly. Their shoulders were broad, posture alert, as they scanned the street, asking questions in low voices.

Bay flattened herself against the coral wall, holding her breath. The illusion flickered for half a second. Her heart seized. She clenched her fists, forcing the spell to hold. The guards passed her without a glance.

She waited a long moment, counting her heartbeats before she dared to move again. Her limbs were shaking. The farther she traveled, the harder it became to hold herself together, not just the illusion, but her very self.

She didn't know when Darkness had started whispering. Maybe it always had. Maybe it simply waited, quiet and patient, while she wrestled with her heartbreak. Her betrayal.

But now it was growing again. Feeding. As though strangely pleased with the charted path and wanting her to press forward. It did not speak in words, but rather as a hunger behind her ribs, a shadow pressed along her spine. It urged her forward, deeper. Promised answers. Power. Closure.

Bay stumbled through another tight turn and stopped. She ducked behind a broken pillar and slid to the ground, pulling her fin up to her chest. The ache of loneliness crashed into her. She missed her dad, even though he had lied. She missed Catalina and her quiet, steady strength.

And she missed Cyrus. The thought of him made her eyes burn. His voice, his crooked grin, the way he looked at her like she was just...a person. Not a burden. Just Bay. She missed his stories. His reckless bravery. His stupid jokes. She missed how he made her feel real. A sharp pang twisted inside her, and she tried to swallow it back.

Don't think about him, she told herself. *You can't afford to.*

He was kind. He made me feel—

Bay shut her eyes tighter. No. Not you too. It seemed somehow wrong that Light-Voice should feel the same as she did about Cyrus. The way it echoed her attachment and shared her longing. It made Bay feel hollow and doubled. As though even her own feelings weren't entirely hers. She shook her head. *I don't want to talk about this. Not now.* The quiet between them was louder than any scream.

Bay rose slowly, her limbs stiff from sitting. The city was thinning now, the outskirts giving way to deep water, canyon paths, and broken reefs. In the far distance, past the drop-offs and fog-thick water, she knew what lay ahead.

The Outer Drop. The place where the Sea Witch waited.

She was almost there. Her disguise rippled faintly. She let it drop, just for a moment, just to feel her own skin again. The water pressed cold against her arms. She exhaled, steadying herself.

There would be no turning back after this. Not from the Sea Witch. Not from the truth. Not from herself.

CHAPTER FORTY-FIVE

The Sea Witch

I t had taken eight days to reach the Sea Witch's Lair from Hydrous, the village where Bay had found the map. Light-Voice, of course, had begged her to find her father or reunite with Cyrus and Catalina. But Bay could not. This was her burden to carry, a matter of life and death. She refused to endanger the ones she loved.

The entrance to the Sea Witch's lair was deep underwater, buried in the cold, crushing dark. Catalina might have made the dive with her, but allowing her to do so would have felt wrong. Cyrus would've tried to stop her. Her father would have, too. He would've begged her to leave the ocean behind, to flee to some place dry, far from tides and monsters. But Bay understood now. There was no separating herself from the sea, it had claimed her too completely. As long as she drew breath beneath the waves, Allura would never stop hunting.

By the time she approached the Sea Witch's stronghold, the waters had turned murky and unpleasant. Bay passed the crumbled ruins of a drowned town, consumed by the ocean long ago. Fallen towers, broken arches, the skeleton of a world devoured. According to the map, the entrance lay hidden among the wreckage. Her tail shivered with unease.

We should turn back. Please, Bay. I'm scared.

Bay felt it clearly, the fear in Light-Voice rising stronger than her own. It was a deep, trembling dread that soaked into her bones. But Darkness inside her pulsed with hunger, pulling at her and urging her forward. Even as Light-Voice begged to escape.

"No," Bay said quietly, steadying her breath. "Not this time."

She pushed ahead, deeper into the dark.

Inside, the cave was not the black void she had feared. Instead, it burned with eerie blue torches that shimmered beneath the water, casting a ghostly light across the stone. Along lengthy, ornate tables, treasure sparkled: crowns, coins, and sapphires the size of her hand. A jeweled tiara caught Bay's eye. The massive sapphire at its center reflected her face in a haunting glow. She reached out, fingers trembling, drawn to the silent song it seemed to sing.

Don't touch anything! Light-Voice snapped.

For once, Bay obeyed. She pulled her hand back and drifted onward. The water began to shallow until her tail brushed the rocky bottom. When it became too shallow to swim, she wished herself human again. She surfaced, gasping as air flooded her lungs. Her gills closed. Her tail split painfully into legs.

Wobbling and slipping on slick rocks, she made her way up the passage, ignoring the furious pull of the sea behind her. Her feet felt relief even as they scraped along sharp rocks, simply from remaining in the water. The shallows clung to her like a final comfort. The current narrowed to a thin ribbon around her ankles, and though her body longed to sink into it, she pressed on. Every step sent pain through her chest, as each breath of dry air burned.

At last, the passage opened into a vast circular chamber. A table stood ahead, piled with towels and robes. Bay realized she was naked and hurried to wrap herself in one of the robes, strangely warm and fitted perfectly to her body. She grabbed a towel, and when she unwrapped it from her head, her hair had dried into thick, silky, silver waves.

Another table appeared, laden with clothing: gowns, tunics, and dresses fine enough for queens. Bay chose a simple olive-green sundress and pulled it over her unfamiliar frame.

"You become accustomed to it," said a voice behind her.

Bay spun around. The tables, robes, and towels had vanished. In their place stood a large dining set with delicate, high-backed chairs carved from pale wood. A table glittered with crystal and polished silver.

Before it stood a woman, radiant and strange. Her skin shimmered cobalt blue, her long dark hair cascading in dark waves down her back. She wore a gown of mysterious white fabric that rippled like a living creature, swirling like waves with every movement. Small and slender and with an elven poise that felt both delicate and eternal. She raised one hand and gestured toward a chair.

Bay hesitated, then stumbled to a seat beside the glowing table, her heart pounding. The woman smiled and lowered herself across from her.

"It has been long, has it not, since you last walked above the waves?" she asked. Her voice was old and strange, as if carried from another time. It floated through the air, ethereal and enchanting.

Bay ignored the question. "I need answers. About my mother. I was told you could help."

The Sea Witch's smile deepened, slow and dangerous. "Did they not warn you? Everything has a cost, Grandmother."

Bay flinched at the title. The illusion still clung to her, leaving her frail, hunched, and hollow-eyed.

"What is it you seek so desperately?" the Sea Witch asked, her voice as smooth and cold as the stone walls around them.

"Why won't my mother accept me?" The words escaped before Bay could steel herself.

The Sea Witch tilted her head, a flicker of something unreadable in her dark eyes. "Your mother must be long dead. Why do you still care?" She spoke as if the question itself were foreign to her, as if she could not grasp the shape of that kind of longing.

"No... she's alive." Bay's voice wavered, and she hated the weakness in it. "But my father told me who she was, and now I'm not sure he was right. I need the truth. I have to know."

"He was wrong?" the Sea Witch repeated softly, as if speaking to herself. Her dark eyes narrowed in thought. She studied Bay with growing suspicion, as though she were seeing someone who should not exist.

She thinks you're mad, Light-Voice whispered urgently. *Remember, you still look like a frail old woman. Slow down. Explain.*

"I know that!" Bay hissed, her nerves fraying.

The Sea Witch straightened. "Are you feeling well, Grandmother?" she asked, her tone polite but laced with mockery.

Bay clenched her fists at her sides. "Yes!" The word came out sharper than she meant. She drew a shaky breath, fighting back the panic rising in her chest.

"I was told you could help me," she said, her voice cracking with desperation. "Please. Can you, or can't you?"

The cold crept up her legs, winding around her like a noose. A terrible thought arose in her chest. What if the truth she was chasing didn't save her? What if it broke her instead?

The Sea Witch smiled, a thin, knowing curve that never touched her ancient eyes. "You have come for answers," she said quietly. "But nothing in this place is given freely."

Bay's chest tightened. She hadn't realized there would be a price.

"What... what do you want?" she asked, her voice low.

The Sea Witch tilted her head. "That depends. What have you brought me in offering?"

Bay hesitated. She had nothing of value. She looked through her satchel, no gold, no power. Then she ran her fingers to her throat, the Star of Isis.

She reached up and touched it, fingers brushing the smooth metal. Her last treasure. Her mother's, or so her father had claimed. The only piece of herself she still believed in.

Don't give it to her, Light-Voice whispered, urgent and afraid. *Please. Not that. It's important.*

Bay swallowed hard. Her hand brushed the pendant.

"It's all I have," she said, and lifted the chain from her neck.

The Sea Witch's eyes flicked to the pendant. Her expression sharpened, just for an instant. Then she looked away, almost too quickly.

"I have no use for another trinket," she said, her tone too smooth, too controlled.

Bay didn't lower her hand. "Please. It's worth more than it looks."

The Sea Witch gave a slow, cold smile. "Perhaps. But I prefer a different price." She leaned in slightly, her voice quiet. "I want five years."

Bay choked slightly. "What... what does that mean?"

"You will age. Five years lost to you. Five years added to me."

The smile returned, thinner than before. For a moment, her eyes flicked to the necklace again. Something dark passed through her gaze, but it vanished as quickly as it came.

Bay's pulse thundered in her ears. Five years. Could she afford that? Would it destroy her?

She gripped the necklace tighter, chest tightening.

Please, Light-Voice whispered again. *Don't do it.*

But Bay stepped forward anyway.

She slipped the necklace back over her head.

Her heart pounded. Five years of her life, ripped away. Would she survive it? Then again, if she didn't get answers, she might not survive the next five years anyway.

"Will it hurt?" she asked, her voice barely audible.

"Very much," the Sea Witch said.

Bay took a shaky breath. "Will it kill me?"

"No."

"Okay," Bay said, Light-Voice shrinking back inside her. "But I want my answers first."

"Payment is always first," the Sea Witch replied.

"But what if you don't give me the answers I want?"

248

"Exactly," the Sea Witch said calmly, meeting her gaze without blinking.

Bay didn't look away. "Will you answer my questions? All of them?"

"Yes."

"Truthfully?"

"Yes."

Bay took a deep breath. She closed her eyes tight and stiffened, bracing for the pain. "Okay," she said. "I agree."

Nothing happened. She opened her eyes slowly.

"Don't you want to eat first?" the Sea Witch asked, her smile curling with mischief.

"No, thank you. I'm not hungry," Bay replied, even as her stomach growled.

"I see." The Sea Witch stood, and the dining table vanished, swallowed by the cave floor. Blue light flared around them, casting sharp shadows across the walls. "Give me your hands."

Bay stumbled forward and placed her hands in the Sea Witch's. At first, there was warmth and then a soft pulsing that felt almost comforting. A metallic tang budded on her tongue. Copper. But this time, it wasn't repulsive. It was alluring. Her jaw tensed. Her throat tightened with longing. Some primal part of her wanted to bite down, to taste the power in the Sea Witch's blood, to swallow it. Her hands trembled. Not from fear, but from want.

"What have you done?" she shrieked.

Then the Sea Witch screamed. She tore her hands away, stumbling back. Her palms were blistered and raw, burning bright red.

"I didn't do anything!" Bay stammered.

"The green bottle. Cabinet. Go!" the Sea Witch barked.

Bay rushed to the cabinet and grabbed the emerald bottle.

"Open it and pour it over my hands," the Sea Witch commanded, her voice strained, the pain sharp in her velvet-black eyes.

Bay uncorked the bottle and gently poured its contents over the burns. The Sea Witch gasped as the liquid touched her skin. The blisters began to cool and fade.

Bay reached out to help her stand, but the Sea Witch recoiled. "Do not touch me."

They faced each other now, the air between them charged and brittle.

"Who are you?" the Sea Witch demanded.

"I... I don't know," Bay said helplessly.

"Your name."

"Bay."

"That is not your real name."

"Atlantis Bay," she whispered.

The Sea Witch's face lost all color. "How old are you?"

"Fifteen. Almost sixteen." Bay closed her eyes. She focused, letting go of the illusion. In a breath, the old woman's form melted away. Midnight hair spilled over her shoulders, her limbs were young and strong again, and her eyes were stormy and fierce.

True terror flooded the Sea Witch's gaze.

"So," she whispered, voice trembling, "you have come to kill me at last."

CHAPTER FORTY-SIX

A Love Story

Bay pressed her hands to her face and groaned. "I don't know you. Why would I want to kill you? How could I kill you?" Her irritation at not knowing anything, combined with the ocean's constant pull, was beginning to override her fear. Ever since she had stepped into the sea, nothing had made sense. Everyone else seemed to be following a script she had never been given.

"I just want to know who my mother is."

"You truly don't know?" the Sea Witch asked. Her voice had changed. The sharpness had faded, replaced by something quieter. Curious. Tentative.

"No. I don't." Bay's voice cracked. The cold prickling over her skin was spreading faster now. The sea pulled at her, an ache in her bones that would not ease.

She missed her father. Missed Catalina. Missed Cyrus. She was so tired. Tired of guessing. Tired of being alone in all of this. Tired of fighting.

"Then why come here?"

Bay played with the chain of her necklace, fingers moving slowly over the cool metal. "Because it's the only place left. The only clue I have. The only way to get answers."

The Sea Witch studied her for a long moment, the flickering torches reflecting off her sharp cobalt skin.

"Do you know what can kill a Sea Witch?" she asked at last.

Bay shook her head, her heart pounding in her chest.

The Sea Witch leaned back in a chair that appeared for her, the blue firelight dancing across her face and accentuating her cold features.

"Years ago," she said, her voice soft but entrancing, "this cave sat at the edge of a thriving fishing village. You passed its ruins on your way in, didn't you?"

"Yes..." Bay whispered.

"I found this place when it was still alive. Cloudy skies, cold waters, the ocean brimming with creatures. It reminded me of home, long ago, before all of this." She gestured around the elaborate cave, her hand sweeping through the blue-lit air.

"They hated me," the Sea Witch continued, her voice laced with something almost proud. "And yet they needed me. They came seeking wishes. Power. Beauty. Wealth. They bartered years of their lives, slivers of their souls. And when the town began to rot under the weight of its own greed, they blamed me."

Her mouth curled into a bitter smirk. "So they summoned a champion. Santiago." She spoke his name like a prayer steeped in venom. "He had left them long ago, wandered the world in search of knowledge and forbidden magic. They begged him to save them from me. And so, he came back. A scholar. A traveler. Beautiful and cunning."

A chair appeared beside her, and Bay sat without thinking. She leaned forward, drawn in despite herself.

"He was beautiful," the Sea Witch said softly. "Golden skin. Auburn hair. Eyes like molten bronze. The town paraded him through the streets like a prize."

She paused, the smile slipping from her face. "He came to my door, and he lied. He acted as though meeting me had fulfilled his life's dream. That he had wasted years seeking magic, but now wished only to serve such great power."

"So... he didn't mean it?" Bay asked, her heart tightening.

"He meant every word," the Sea Witch replied, her voice hollow. "He meant to flatter me. Enchant me. Make me love him."

The sorrow in her voice hit Bay like a weight for which she hadn't been braced. "And he succeeded. Slowly, skillfully, he fed my loneliness and my pride. We spent hours together, poring over books, diving for rare ingredients, chasing new spells. I taught him more than he ever taught me. Somewhere along the way, our souls entangled. We both desired power, and that made our bond easy to form."

Bay caught her breath. "You were *Socius Animae*."

"Yes," the Sea Witch whispered. A single word, heavy as stone.

Bay hesitated. "Was it real?"

The Sea Witch's face closed, ancient sadness flickering through her dark eyes.

"It was real. But it was twisted."

She stared into the blue flames, her gaze distant. "He confessed the night he broke the enchantment over me. But it was too late. By then, I was already pregnant with his child. She would be born of our bond. I didn't even know I was with child. He had clouded my mind so deeply; I couldn't see the truth."

Her voice sharpened, splintering into rage. "He had learned how to kill a Sea Witch!"

Bay said nothing. She was beginning to panic about how she fit into the story that was unfolding.

"He thought he was so clever—that all he needed to do was to break his enchantment over me, beg forgiveness, and then all would be well. To prove that he was sorry about what he had done, he even shared his original plan on how he was going to have me killed. First, he would steal the child. Then raise her in secret. And when she came of age, she would kill me. Fulfill the ancient curse I was born beneath."

She paused, then turned her dark eyes back to Bay. "You see, we are not born as humans are. When a Sea Witch is ready to create an heir, the mist of her essence leaves her body and seeks out a host, a pregnant mermaid, often very powerful. The mist merges with the unborn child. For years, they grow in one body together."

Bay gripped the chair so tightly her knuckles turned white.

"At sixteen," the Sea Witch continued, "the host's soul is consumed. The Sea Witch awakens fully. And upon her first return to the ocean, she absorbs her mother's magic from the very marrow of her bones. Only then does she become unstoppable."

Bay pressed a hand to her mouth, stomach turning.

"But until that final moment, before she re-enters the water," the Sea Witch said, her voice soft again, "the child can be killed. If the birth mother, the mermaid, acts in time. If she beheads the child before the ritual is complete, she cannot save her daughter's life, but she can protect her soul."

Bay's heart stopped.

"I wanted to kill my daughter," the Sea Witch said suddenly, her voice cracking under the weight of memory. "I wanted to save myself. But I couldn't. Our magic binds us. A Sea Witch cannot harm her child, no matter how much she may wish it."

Bay shuddered violently.

"Santiago begged me to destroy the child. Promised we could live together. But he did not understand. We are bound by laws older than the ocean itself."

Her hands curled into fists. "And so," she said, her voice turning to ice, "I chose vengeance. I summoned the storm. I tore the village from the mountainside. And I made him watch as I drowned his family and those he loved."

Bay shivered, the memory of the ruined village rising fresh in her mind. "And the child?" she managed to ask.

"The mist drifted away," the Sea Witch said, her voice lowering to a near whisper. "Lost to the waves."

Bay hardly dared to breathe.

"Until," the Sea Witch continued, her voice barely audible, "I received a summons. A queen. A desperate mother."

Bay's heart pounded against her ribs.

"I met her in secret. She held a child. Strong. Cursed. Beautiful. She begged me to save her daughter and offered her life in return."

The flames flickered, casting strange shadows that danced across the stone walls.

"I told her the truth. The child would devour her daughter's soul. Only the birth mother could stop it. She would have to behead the child herself. And she was resolved to do it."

Bay gripped the edge of the table, her fingers aching.

"But she hesitated. Her partner begged for more time. He told her to wait until after their daughter's sixteenth birthday. He pleaded with her. And together, they made an unbreakable vow, sealed by ancient magic that could not be undone. The plan was to raise you, love you, and end it when the time came."

The words sank in slowly. And Bay's heart sank with them.

"But after the vow was sealed, he ran. He took you and disappeared. He didn't understand ocean magic, not then. And when he did, it was too late. Their bond, their *Socius Animae*, was shattered."

A cold numbness spread through her. She could feel herself slipping into it.

"And so," the Sea Witch said, smiling faintly, "you come to me, asking who you are."

Bay's voice cracked into the silence. "So, you're my mother?"

The Sea Witch's smile deepened. Not warm, not cruel. Just inevitable. "Yes."

Bay sat frozen, the truth hammering into her chest. She had dreamed of crowns. Of belonging. Of finally finding her place. Instead, she had found ruin. Not a princess, she was a monster.

A monster who ate the princess.

CHAPTER FORTY-SEVEN

Inside

This can't be right. This monster can't be your mother. No, something is terribly wrong. Light-Voice's panic echoed Bay's own thoughts.

Bay had no answer. She didn't know how to steer the conversation, didn't know how to hold the weight of what she had just heard. She wasn't ready to absorb it, and she couldn't sit in silence. The truth hovered like a storm, waiting to drown her.

Desperate for something, anything, to hold onto, she blurted out the first question that came to mind. "What's your name, anyway?"

"Which one?" the Sea Witch asked, her voice almost bored, as if reciting items from a list. "Do you want the name of the girl whose body I stole, or the one I created for myself?"

Bay faltered. "Um... the one you chose, I guess."

"Ceto."

Bay licked her lips. "Can you really not hurt me?"

"I cannot."

"Did you ever have a name for me?"

"I did not," Ceto said, her tone flat.

Bay shouldn't have felt surprised, but the emptiness of the answer hit harder than she expected. She swallowed the lump rising in her throat and pressed on. "Do I have magic too?"

"I believe you have already proven that you do," Ceto replied coolly. "Did you not come to my cave as an old woman, hair gray with age?"

Your transformation. Wasn't it mer-magic? Light-Voice whispered.

Bay nodded slowly, her mind working back through the moments that had brought her here. "I can hear mermaids' thoughts sometimes. I can turn into a mermaid. I can change my hair color. Can I do anything else?"

"Transformation is a natural ability for every Sea Witch," Ceto said. "We can become anyone, or anything living, with minimal effort. Except for the eyes. The eyes stay the same."

There was almost a note of pride in her voice as she continued. "We can mimic speech easily. Even learn the languages of other species."

"Across species?" Bay echoed.

"Yes. Animals, mostly."

"But I have to wish for it?"

"Yes. Even the simpler magic, like transformation, requires a wish. All magic stems from wishes. And every wish has a cost. It will be as limitless as the price you are willing to pay or the price someone else pays."

"Pay?" Bay echoed.

"The pain you feel. The wild force inside you creeping and hungry?"

Bay shivered. She hated thinking about Darkness. Speaking of it made it feel stronger, closer.

"The bigger the wish, the greater the cost. For you. For anyone who asks for your help."

Bay stood abruptly, her chair scraping against the stone floor. Her head throbbed. Heat coursed through her body, sharp and urgent. The ocean pulled at her, relentless and deep, whispering promises she no longer trusted but couldn't ignore. She stumbled to the water's edge, dipped one foot in, then the other, and finally sank into the shallows, cross-legged. The sea wrapped around her like silk, its coolness easing the fire in her skin.

When she looked back, Ceto was watching her with a detached sort of curiosity, like someone studying a creature they half recognized.

Bay forced the words out. "If I'm not actually a mermaid, then why do I feel like one? Why does it feel like the only time I'm really myself is when I'm in the water?"

Ceto shrugged. "A Sea Witch is a creature of both land and sea. We breathe air and water. We prefer the sea because it strengthens us, but we are not bound to it."

"But I feel called to it. I feel like it owns me."

"I do not know why," Ceto said simply.

"Maybe I can wish it to stop." Bay seized on the thought. "I wish the pain would stop," she whispered, stepping out of the water. Nothing changed. The pain tightened its grip on her spine, clawed at her chest.

"I wish the pain would stop!" she cried louder, clenching her fists and willing it with everything she had. Darkness rose around her feet like tendrils of smoke. She gasped as the familiar, awful pain surged through her, the same one she felt every time she transformed.

She concentrated harder, desperate for relief, but the urge didn't ease. The pain only grew sharper.

At last, she collapsed onto the cold stone and slid herself back into the water. The sea's cool embrace calmed her skin, but the ache inside remained. "Why didn't my wish work?" she asked, her voice shaking.

"It could be that you are new to casting. Or that you have not yet absorbed all of my powers. You may not be strong enough," Ceto said.

"I don't want your powers!" Bay cried.

"We do not have a choice."

Something is wrong. You are kind, and she is cruel. You don't crave power; she lives for it. You can't leave the ocean, and she can. Maybe she's wrong. Maybe she isn't your mother.

Bay bit her lip hard enough to taste salt. "Do you ever...hear voices?" she asked suddenly.

Don't tell her about me!

Ceto tilted her head. "Voices? Oh, you must mean your wish-magic's voice. That was a bit frightening at first, wasn't it?"

"No, not Darkness. I-I mean something else..." Bay hesitated, heart pounding. "A voice. Inside me. Talking."

"It has been a couple hundred years," Ceto said slowly. "I had almost forgotten. The voice you hear is your host."

"My what?"

What?

"Your host. Atlantis. The Queen's daughter." Ceto said, almost lazily. "She will be gone soon. Once you turn sixteen, your body will start to consume her. I am surprised you still hear her now. Mine had gone quiet years before the consumption."

She turned slightly, smiling in memory. "Oh yes. I remember that voice. Mine begged. Clung on for years. But wish-magic wears them down, you know. The more you use it, the faster the voice fades. I stopped hearing mine long before the end. That silence was... peaceful."

No-o-o-o! Light-Voice screamed, not a whisper, not a thought, but a full, desperate cry.

Correction: Atlantis screamed.

The sound didn't just echo in Bay's mind. It came from deeper, from the girl within. From the sister she never meant to harm.

Bay sat frozen.

The word *leech* clawed through her thoughts. Her stomach twisted, a rising nausea that tasted like guilt. She didn't want to believe it. Didn't want to imagine that the tiny light inside her was a person, a soul, someone real. Someone she was destroying with every breath she took.

Maybe she was just insane. Maybe that would be easier.

But even as she tried to reject it, the truth slithered in, cold and slow, wrapping itself deep around her heart.

A parasite.

And she was running out of time.

CHAPTER FORTY-EIGHT

The Cure

But there has to be some way to stop this!" Bay said finally, looking up angrily.

She had taken a long moment to absorb the fact that she was stealing someone's life. Light-Voice's life. The one who had always been there to support her and help fight off Darkness. If she was supposed to consume Light-Voice, then what or who would be left? Would she be a monster like Ceto?

"To stop what?" Ceto said with annoyance.

"Everything. I don't want it! Any of it. I don't want your power—"

"You don't want to be the most powerful creature throughout the entire ocean?" Ceto said, staring at her as though Bay wasn't being honest with herself.

"No!" Bay shouted. Yet, even as the word tore from her throat, a tremor of doubt whispered at the edges of her mind. She remembered the luxurious pleasure she felt when she touched the Sea Witch's hand, the magic thrumming warmly through her body, filling every hollow space.

You could have it all, a voice inside her whispered. Darkness had been waiting. It would answer the silence Atlantis would leave behind and was eager to take her place. It would happily fill the void in Bay's mind with something else. Strength. Freedom. Power beyond imagining.

For a moment, she almost wanted it. Bay clenched her fists. "No," she said again, fiercer this time, steadying herself.

"It is your fate, child."

"But can't I choose my fate? Isn't there anything I can do to stop this? Couldn't I leave her body and just...go somewhere else?"

"It is impossible to fight off the desire. Once you turn sixteen, the final phase begins. You will be called to the power. It will be overwhelming. Every act of magic will pull you deeper until you understand this is your true path."

"What if I can fight it?"

"Like you are fighting your desire to be in the ocean? Ha! That desire is nothing compared to what you will feel."

Bay looked down, still sitting in the water, the waves rippling around her as the Sea Witch's hard, dark eyes—black and unforgiving—stared back. Bay's eyes.

"Isn't there some way to stop it? Any possible chance at all?" Bay pleaded.

Ceto was silent for a long moment, her gaze growing distant and strange, as though she were searching through a private cache of buried memories. "There was something Santiago once spoke of. 'A cure,' he called it, when he confessed his plans to me. What was it...? A legend of the Enchanted Witch who refused to absorb her host. He called it separation."

"So it is possible? There's a cure?"

"It was only an old legend," Ceto said, waving a hand in quiet dismissal.

"You were a legend to me until a short time ago," Bay reminded her.

Ceto almost smiled. A tired, bitter twist of her lips. "Even if you could gather what you needed, it would be nearly impossible. The spell was difficult. After the separation, the host lived, but the Enchanted Witch died."

Bay was silent.

No.

"If you can perform it, which is unlikely, it will almost certainly kill you," Ceto added.

"Is there any way I can survive?"

Ceto looked at her for a long time. For the first time, there was something almost sad in her expression. "Once," she said softly, "I thought I could change my fate too. I was young, like you. Hopeful. It broke me."

Bay swallowed hard. "Can you show me how to do it—the separation spell?" she asked.

"Child, you're not listening. It won't work. And if it does, it means death. Why choose death?"

"Because I don't want to end up a monster." She said it too quickly, before thinking about who she was talking to. Then more quietly, she added, "I've taken enough from... Atlantis. She's saved me from Darkness more times than I can count."

"Saved you from Darkness?" Ceto scoffed. "Nonsense. You are meant to embrace it. To feed it. She has only kept you from your true potential."

"Tell me how to do the spell," Bay said, her voice steady, stubborn.

Ceto let out a long, dramatic sigh. "You will need Allura's blood."

No, you can't kill her! Atlantis cried.

Bay's breath caught. "I... I have to kill the Queen?"

She gulped, the words tasting like ash.

"No. You need only some of her blood. Her blood will strengthen you and her child. Once the clock strikes midnight on your birthday, the desire will awaken. You will be drawn to the wish magic inside like never before. You will begin to consume the soul within you."

Light-Voice—Atlantis—let out a small, heartbreaking whimper.

"You must hold the blood in your hands," Ceto continued, "and something that belonged to your host. Then, you must wish to separate from her."

"And?" Bay asked.

"And that is it."

"I thought you said the spell was difficult."

"It is. It will require powerful focus and complete concentration. Fighting that level of temptation will not be easy, especially for a new witch. You must channel all your thoughts like never before."

But we don't know what will happen to you, Atlantis muttered softly.

"Will you help me practice?" Bay asked, nervously fidgeting with her necklace.

"It is hopeless, child." Ceto turned away and began closing the doors of her potion cabinet.

"But if there's a chance," Bay said, her voice rising, "doesn't that mean you might have a chance to live too? That I might not absorb your power?"

The Sea Witch paused, her hand resting on the cabinet door. Bay stepped out of the ocean water, her body aching as she walked slowly toward her.

"Don't you want a chance to live?" Bay asked, inching closer. "A chance to keep your power?"

"I know my fate. You should come to terms with yours. Let the light die."

A long silence stretched between them.

Bay saw then that the Sea Witch would not change her mind.

"I guess I should get going then," she said, her voice small as she reached for the edge of the green dress.

"No need. The clothes will disappear when you transform." Ceto glanced over her shoulder with a twisted smile. "I wish you good luck."

Bay hesitated. The hairs on her arms rose.

What if this was exactly what Ceto wanted? What if the Sea Witch was sending her straight to Allura, hoping the Queen would kill her?

Her mind raced, but she forced herself to stay calm.

"How can I trust you?" she asked carefully. "How do I know this isn't a trap?"

Ceto turned fully, her eyes glittering. "Because I am bound by the old magic. I cannot lie to the daughter of my line. You are blood. Even if I wanted to deceive you, I am forbidden."

She smiled again, slow and cold. "Of course, the truth is convenient. It's unlikely the spell will succeed. And if it doesn't, Allura will likely kill you anyway."

Her voice dropped, quiet and final. "Goodbye, daughter."

Bay flinched. She stared at her, searching for any crack in the words, any hint of deception.

There was none.

CHAPTER FORTY-NINE

A Secret

eaving her mother's lair, Bay swam above the remains of the decayed town, feeling a shiver run up her spine. The real story of what happened to all those people and buildings was worse than she had even imagined.

Bay was surprised to be leaving the Sea Witch's cave unscathed—physically, anyway. It had devastated her to learn the truth, what her mother really was, and what Bay herself could become. But she had to press forward, so she tucked the pain away where it wouldn't hurt so much. She had years of practice hiding heartache; at least it was good for something.

Are we really going to do this? Atlantis asked weakly.

What other choice do we have?

You have other choices, Atlantis insisted. *Bay, you don't even know if the Sea Witch was telling the truth. She could be hoping you'll get yourself killed by the Queen.*

The Sea Witch was telling the truth, At—. Bay stopped herself. It still felt too strange saying Atlantis's name, even inside her head.

She can't harm me. Remember what happened to her hands?

Atlantis was quiet. Bay swam faster, worried the silence meant her light was growing weaker. She rushed past the tiger shark cave without looking, not daring to linger. The trip passed like a dream. Bay wasn't sure how long it took. She didn't know what she was allowed to feel anymore. And with Atlantis hearing every thought, she didn't dare try. So, she didn't think. She kept herself silent, swimming ever forward.

Near the coast, she found what looked like a mermaid park, with young mermaids playing in massive sea anemones. She rested nearby, eating a small lunch while watching them. It was silent compared to land parks, and for a moment, it felt like watching an ocean documentary with the sound turned off. Mothers scooped up their little ones and carried them to the surface to breathe, and Bay's chest tightened painfully. She turned away before despair swallowed her.

She pressed on toward Crystal Cove, where she had asked Cyrus and Catalina to meet her. As she neared the beach, Bay transformed, pulled on a swimsuit and shorts from her bag, and headed down the dirt path toward the dock. Her clothes dried quickly under the sun, but the heat was almost unbearable. The air was dry, scorching against her skin. Every breath made her lungs ache. Her body itched and burned, desperate for the sea. The pull toward the water grew stronger with each step, and she had to stop and breathe just to keep from turning back and diving in.

Then, ahead, she spotted the *Contessa* and broke into a run, heart pounding.

They were here.

Not just passing through. Not just waiting out the tide.

They were waiting for her.

Cyrus. Catalina. The only two people in the world she still had.

"Cyrus!" Bay called, her voice catching in her throat.

Cyrus! Atlantis cried with sudden joy, the name ringing bright in Bay's mind. The happiness in her voice was unexpected, too light for everything they'd been through, and Bay wasn't sure how to feel about it. But for once, she didn't silence her.

Cyrus turned. The moment he saw her, he ran, arms open, feet kicking up sand. He didn't wait for her to reach the dock. He met her halfway, scooping her into a hug so fierce it knocked the breath from her lungs. Bay clung to him, the warmth of his arms and the steadiness of his breath grounding her in a way nothing else had. The way he held her, as if she might break apart at any moment, undid her.

Then Catalina appeared, bursting from below deck. Her face lit up as soon as she saw Bay. She didn't hesitate. She ran straight to them and wrapped her arms around both of them, pulling Bay into an embrace that was softer but just as full of love. For a long moment, they stood there, tangled together beneath the bright sun, and Bay didn't move. She didn't want to. She was surrounded by the only two people who had never turned their backs on her.

She was with her people. After Ceto. After the prison of Allura's power. After all the coldness and confusion and lies. She was here. Safe.

They found a quiet patch of beach nearby. Bay sat half-submerged in the shallows while Cyrus and Catalina laid out a blanket and brought her food. Her head throbbed with the ocean's call, insistent and heavy, but she forced herself to stay on shore. She didn't want to miss a second with them. For the first time in what felt like forever, she didn't have to be a prisoner or a witch or a girl with a ticking clock.

She could just be Bay.

"How could you do it?" Cyrus asked once he settled on the blanket. The hurt in his voice stung.

He's angry, Atlantis said faintly. *Tell them it was your idea to tie them up. Not mine.*

Bay laughed before she could stop herself, a short, sharp sound that cracked the tension, but only for a moment. Seeing the look on Cyrus's face, the way his jaw tightened, she sobered quickly.

"Sorry," she said, her voice earnest now. "I couldn't risk you getting caught. Not after seeing how much the Queen hated me. What if she wanted to kill you too?"

"You should have let us make that choice," Catalina said, her voice calm but firm.

"There wasn't time. I was scared for you both."

"We have more experience than you," Cyrus snapped. "You can barely swim."

"Yeah, but I have this talent," Bay shot back. "I knew I could get myself to safety. I wasn't sure I could save all of us."

"We don't need you to save us!" Cyrus said, louder now, the frustration in his voice cracking through the calm of the beach.

"What talent?" Catalina asked suddenly, her tone sharper than before.

Bay hesitated, her heart pounding. "You were right. I'm not a mermaid. And I'm not Allura's daughter. Not really."

"Wait, what? You are a mermaid. We saw your tail," Cyrus started, confused.

"Let her finish," Catalina said, cutting him off gently. Her eyes stayed on Bay, watching her closely.

You can trust them.

I know. They deserve the truth.

So Bay told them everything—escaping the underwater cell, the road map from the frog-man, meeting the Sea Witch, the truth about her identity, and the cure that might save Atlantis.

The twins listened silently until she mentioned returning to the Palace.

"But what happens to you?" Cyrus asked.

"What do you mean?" Bay said, stalling.

Tell him the truth, Atlantis urged.

"What happens after this separation?" Cyrus pressed.

"It's only happened once before..." Bay answered reluctantly.

"And?" he asked.

Bay drew in a breath and looked away. "The Enchanted Witch died."

Neither of them spoke. Bay didn't need to look to know their faces were full of shock and worry.

"What's your plan?" Catalina asked at last, her voice steady but quiet.

Bay let out a long sigh. "I have to get some of Allura's blood and perform the separation spell at exactly the right time. After that?" She shook her head. "I don't know."

Cyrus's expression hardened. "What is with you and these reckless plans? You're going back to the castle, where the Queen wants you dead, to cast a spell that could kill you—based on what some evil Sea Witch told you? How do you even know she wasn't lying?"

He stood, voice rising. "You're not a Sea Witch, Bay!"

"I am a Sea Witch," Bay said firmly.

"How do you know?" Cyrus pleaded.

Bay focused on Cyrus. She examined his face, his shoulders, the way he stood. She let the image settle in her mind and wished herself into his shape. Darkness curled at her toes, wrapping around her like smoke. The taste of copper swirled around her mouth.

Atlantis gave a soft sigh, and went quiet. Not gone but dim. Like a candle flickering behind fogged glass.

And then, before their eyes, she changed. Her body shifted, stretched, and reshaped. In a breath, she became a mirror image of Cyrus.

Catalina stepped forward, reaching out to touch her brother's double. Her fingers brushed Bay's shoulder. "It even feels the same," she whispered, laughing softly. "Cute shorts."

"This isn't funny," Cyrus snapped, crossing his arms.

"Cyrus, cool it," Catalina said, resting her hand on his shoulder. *Let's hear her out.*

Bay opened her mouth to respond, but something stopped her. Catalina's voice echoed in her mind, not out loud.

But she's new to this world, Catalina. I can't let her do this. I—

Excuse me! Bay interrupted sharply, but only in their thoughts. Then she added aloud, "I can hear any mental conversations around me. Even if they're not directed at me."

The twins stared at her in stunned silence as she morphed back into herself, hair lengthening, limbs shrinking, and face reshaping. She was Bay again.

She blinked, trying to reach for Light-Voice, but felt only a faint shimmer in the dark. Atlantis was there but barely.

"And before you ask," Bay said quietly, "Princess Atlantis is inside me. I can feel her. I can hear her." She dropped her gaze, too nervous to meet their eyes.

For a long time, neither of them spoke. Then Catalina stepped forward, her voice steady. "What can we do?"

"I just wanted to tell you the truth," Bay said softly. "Thank you for everyth—"

"We're in this together," Catalina interrupted.

Bay turned to Cyrus.

"This is crazy," he muttered. "But we've got your back, Bay." He avoided her eyes. "And just in case, we're guarding our drinks this time."

Bay laughed and threw her arms around them both.

Please tell them thank you. From me, Atlantis whispered.

"Atlantis says thanks too," Bay said.

"Um... you're welcome?" Catalina replied, a little awkwardly.

Cyrus just looked away.

As they ate, they made a plan. When they finished, the twins left to gather supplies while Bay stayed behind to wait on the beach.

They hate me, Atlantis whispered.

They don't hate you. They're scared.

Cyrus hates me.

He's scared for me.

If you die, Bay, then I'm all alone.

Bay blinked hard, her throat tightening. *You'll have your family. Your kingdom,* she thought back. *You'll have a new life.*

But they're my friends too. I care about them.

It's better than being dead, Atlantis, she answered shakily.

You don't have to do this, Bay. Please...

Bay pressed her palms against her forehead. *Just be quiet, will you?* she snapped. A cold silence fell. Bay instantly hated herself for saying it, but she didn't take it back.

She sat in the shallows, staring at the horizon, waiting for the twins to return.

CHAPTER FIFTY

A Voice Grows Silent

There were only eighteen days until September third, Bay's sixteenth birthday. She should have been preparing for her junior year: finishing up summer assignments, shopping for outfits with Izzy, and talking about what classes they might get together. Instead, she was here. Trapped at the water's edge, unable to leave the ocean. Stuck on an island, risking the lives of her friends and her own to save someone she couldn't even hear anymore.

Atlantis hadn't spoken in days.

Please come back, Bay thought, *the silence is unbearable. I'm alone, and I need you. I need you to be strong with me. Please.*

At first, Atlantis had just sounded tired. It was strange to think of a voice in your head sounding tired. But then came the quiet: hours passed with no words. Then a whole day. Then two. Now, Bay was getting scared. She tried coaxing Atlantis back by thinking about Cyrus, Catalina, and even her father. Sometimes she felt something: a flicker of warmth or a sadness that didn't belong to her. And she made herself believe it was Atlantis, still there, still holding on.

Their last conversation played over and over in her mind. It had happened late one night, a few days after they arrived at Crystal Cove. Bay had been sleeping underwater, drifting peacefully with the waves, when something shifted. A heaviness pressed on her, not hers, but familiar.

Atlantis, are you sad? Bay had asked

I...I don't know. I think so, Atlantis answered.

You don't know?

It's hard to explain. I didn't know I wasn't you. I thought I was you. But now that I know I'm not, I think I can feel it. I can feel myself. And it hurts. Or—I hurt. It's confusing.

Bay didn't know how to respond. She was still grappling with her own feelings about Atlantis being real.

I'm sad. And scared.

Me too, Bay thought back.

What if something happens to you and I can't...

Can't what?

Live. Walk. Breathe. Think. I don't know if I'm really doing any of those things now. I just live here, inside. And you are all I have ever known. Bay, you are my world. How can I live without you?

Atlantis, you're supposed to be your own person. You shouldn't need me. I stole this life from you.

Can you steal something if you didn't know you were stealing?

Yes. I stole your body. Your life. Your family.

Bay, I forgive you. I love you. Please save yourself. I'm so tired, Bay. It hurts. I don't think I can make it.

I love you, too, Atlantis. You can do it! It's only a few more days. You'll be free. Your own person. Please, hold on.

And then what? A few more days and I'll be all alone?

You won't be alone. You'll see. This is the right thing. Trust me.

Like I trusted you when you ran away from your father? Or when you tied up your friends? Or went to see the Sea Witch?

I had no choice! I had to find the truth!

You had choices, Bay. I didn't. I never had any choice. Even now, I don't. It might be my body, but it's all in your control.

That's why I have to save you. I can't take any more from you.

And I'm telling you, I can't live without you! I don't know how! I can't do this alone.

You can, Atlantis. You deserve a chance. A real chance.

Even if I don't want one?

Bay felt the words slice through her.

You have to want it, she thought fiercely, blinking back the tears stinging her eyes. *Because I can't lose you.*

CHAPTER FIFTY-ONE

Learning to Stand

The three spent several days discussing their plan, waiting and working through every detail they could think of. They agreed not to make a move on the Queen's Palace until the last possible moment. If they were caught, it would be only days until Bay's sixteenth birthday, and if the plan failed, at least Allura would have little time to act. Bay wasn't eager to find herself in the Queen's clutches again.

The plan was simple in theory: approach the Palace aboard the *Contessa* under the guise of a routine delivery. The twins often transported shipments to the underwater kingdom, so their arrival at the port would likely go unnoticed. Once they were close enough, Bay would transform into someone trusted by the Queen—perhaps one of the guards she had seen or a royal advisor.

From there, she and Catalina would infiltrate the Palace, while Cyrus stayed behind on the ship, ready to leave at a moment's notice. If the ruse succeeded, they would return to Crystal Cove and anchor in a secluded stretch of shoreline. Cyrus would stand watch aboard the *Contessa* while Catalina helped Bay perform the ritual of separation.

The hardest part would be securing Allura's blood. They hadn't figured out exactly how that would work, but Bay was confident. If she could get close enough, she would find a way.

Then they would run. Far from the Palace. Far from Allura.

If everything went according to plan, Atlantis would return to her rightful body, and Bay would leave with the twins for Avalon Cove. She was grateful they wanted her to come with them. She could easily imagine herself helping out as their shipmate. But the thought of being far from Atlantis left a heaviness she couldn't shake. It had already been unbearable, going days without hearing her voice, without feeling her presence.

Still, this was the only plan they had.

And it was their best chance to save them both.

One morning, a few days before they planned to leave for the Pacific Palace, Catalina approached Bay with an idea.

"I want to help you train," she said.

"How?" Bay asked, curious.

"I've been thinking. It's hard for you to leave the ocean, right?"

"Very."

"So what better way to practice your willpower than by fighting that urge?"

Bay hesitated. It would be difficult and painful, but she had to admit it wasn't a bad idea.

They spent the afternoon swimming, the only place Bay ever felt truly quiet inside. In the water, it was as if the sea could hold back everything trying to pull her apart. With Cyrus off in town trying to secure a cargo contract, the day was theirs.

"Let's begin by getting you out of the water," Catalina suggested.

"Now?" Bay asked reluctantly.

"Now. We don't have that much time."

"Okay." Bay sighed and steadied herself, moving through the clear water toward the shore. She glanced back at her prism-colored tail, longing to stay in the depths.

Bay grew more nervous with each step toward the shoreline. She'd been near the water's edge a lot but never truly forced away from it. Now she would have to leave it behind. She took another step and put one foot on dry ground. It was bliss to feel the warm sand beneath her toes and the waves lapping around her ankles. But when she pulled her other foot out and took another step, panic seized her.

"I need to get back in!" she cried.

"Just try and steady yourself," Catalina's calm voice urged.

"I can't! I have to get back in!" Bay gasped, jumping back into the water.

"Bay, I've seen you out longer than that every day," Catalina chided.

"I can't, Catalina."

"Bay, focus. Try not to think about the ocean."

"It's stuck in my mind!"

"Then clear it."

"What do you mean?"

"Clear your mind. Close your eyes."

Obeying, she felt Catalina gently take her hands and guide her onto the beach. Closing her eyes helped. She didn't see the shimmering blue calling her back.

"Just concentrate on your breath. In—good—now out," Catalina coached.

"It's hard!" Bay whined.

"Shh...save your breath. Think about things that calm you. And breathe."

Bay lasted a full ten minutes out of the water that day. Every day after that, she and Catalina practiced for hours. Just when Bay thought she couldn't take any more, Catalina would make her stay a minute longer.

Bay clung to Catalina's voice like a lifeline, grateful beyond words for the sister she had found in her. Catalina helped lessen the silence Atlantis left behind. Not in the way Darkness had, but soft and gentle.

Cyrus spent his days ferrying tourists and securing cargo contracts for their cover. At dinner, he brought food, and they would swim or talk late into the evening. Bay felt guilty about taking up all of Catalina's time. With only one of the twins working, Bay guessed they were probably not making enough money to survive. In the end, she insisted on spending the last of her money for supplies. They were reluctant, but grateful.

"You're really good at this," Bay said, heaving as they finished the day's training. She wiped her face with the back of her hand and let the ocean wash away the sweat off her body. Eight days of intense work had passed. Bay was fatigued but proud. By now, she could fight the ocean's call for over three hours.

"Thanks, but it's you doing all the work," Catalina said.

"Yeah, but I couldn't have done this without you. You know exactly what to say. And the breathing techniques helped a lot. Where did you learn them?"

Catalina traced little circles in the water, watching the ripples fan out before looking back at Bay. "When we were kids, our parents fought a lot. It was overwhelming. I had to find ways to block out the yelling, the scolding, and the violence."

"Oh... I'm sorry, Catalina."

"Yeah, most of the time it was hard," she said, her voice quiet. "But it prepared me for this. So, you see, sometimes good things come from hard places."

"You're amazing, you know that?" Bay said.

Catalina tried to laugh it off, but Bay pulled her into a hug before she could deflect the compliment. They stayed there for a moment, holding on not just for comfort but in quiet recognition of everything they had weathered.

They finished the day with a long, tranquil swim, the cool water calming them both.

CHAPTER FIFTY-TWO

Pulled Apart

ou're mad at Catalina? She can be pretty tough," Cyrus's voice was low as he silently swam next to Bay. Bay's breath hitched, and her heart skipped. She hadn't heard him approach, hadn't felt his presence until he spoke. She spun around to face him, her tail flicking nervously. "What? No. Not at all. She's great." The words came out too fast, but they weren't the problem. The problem was the fire inside her that threatened to consume her.

Cyrus studied her, his voice quieter now. "I can tell something's bothering you, Bay."

Her jaw tightened. And then the words burst out. "I don't think I'm strong enough for all of this. I'm a monster. Everyone hates me! Everyone I thought loved me in this world hates me." Her voice cracked, and the weight of those words sank in, heavier than she could bear.

"Not everyone," Cyrus said gently, his eyes locking with hers. There was a storm behind them.

Bay swallowed and looked away. "I don't blame them for hating me."

"I do," he said. His voice was raw, filled with something heavier than anger.

Bay glanced back at him, the rawness in his words catching her off guard. "Cyrus, if you met Ceto—my real... you'd understand. You'd see the cruel, cold creature she is. What she did to that town. The people she hurt. You'd hate me too." Her voice faltered, guilt creeping in like a shadow she couldn't shake.

Cyrus's gaze softened, but fire still burned in his eyes. He reached for her, gently gripping her arms, the water rippling between them. "You're not evil, Bay. Just because your parents are doesn't mean you are. They might see a monster, but you get to decide if you become one. Not them. You."

Bay shook her head, frustration rising like a tide. "It's different for you, Cyrus. Your dad might've been a bad guy, but there are good men in this world. Have you ever met a Sea Witch? Have you ever killed someone?" Her voice broke as she wrenched free of his grip and turned away.

He reached out again, his touch gentler this time. "You didn't kill anyone, Bay. You are not evil."

Bay turned back to him, her voice quieter now, raw and filled with fear. "I can't hear her anymore. Atlantis. I can't hear her at all. And I—"

Before she could finish, Cyrus pulled her close. She didn't resist. He held her tightly against his chest as she cried, her body trembling in his arms. The comfort was unexpected, but she let herself lean into it. Her tears streamed down her face and disappeared into the waves below.

CHAPTER FIFTY-THREE

High Tide

On the night they left Crystal Cove for the Pacific Palace, the air aboard the *Contessa* was tight with tension. Bay said nothing, Cyrus snapped at everything, and Catalina paced the entire ship, checking every container and reorganizing the supplies even though she had already done it twice before.

They took the trip slow and steady. There was no rush, and they had given themselves plenty of time. Bay swam alongside the *Contessa* for most of the journey. Staying in the water helped her conserve mental energy, allowing her to move with the ocean instead of resisting its pull. The swimming helped clear her mind. She practiced the techniques Catalina had taught her, and the familiar motion calmed her nerves.

A splash echoed nearby.

Bay turned and saw Catalina slip silently into the sea.

They swam together in easy rhythm, side by side like dolphins rising and falling with the swells. For a while, neither of them spoke.

"You're stronger than you think," Catalina said in Bay's mind, her voice steady and warm. "I've seen how hard you've been practicing. I've seen you fight for people. You always have a place with us. With me and Cyrus. No matter what."

Bay's chest tightened.

"I don't know if I deserve it," she answered, her strokes faltering. "I don't even know what I am anymore."

Catalina swam closer, brushing her shoulder lightly.

"I do," she said. "You're someone who fights for the people she loves. That's more than most people ever do."

The words shattered something in Bay. Her strokes grew uneven, her face crumpling underwater. She was grateful for the sea. It caught her tears before they surfaced.

"I understand what it's like," Catalina added after a pause. "Not having parents you can count on. Having to figure it all out yourself. But you're not alone now. You have us."

Bay wept harder, shoulders shaking with the effort to keep swimming. Catalina gave her space, then slowly rose toward the boat.

Bay surfaced briefly and watched her climb the side ladder, water trailing down her arms. She rejoined Cyrus at the helm without a word.

Below, Bay drifted beside the hull, arms wrapped around her middle. She didn't want to leave them. Not ever.

But the sting in her chest wasn't just love. It was something else. A missing piece.

She missed Atlantis.

More than she could have imagined. More than she could bear.

Atlantis had been part of her. Not just a voice, not just a presence. But a thread woven into her being. And now she was fading.

Bay stared up through the water, her face still wet with tears.

I'm hurrying, she thought. *I will save you.*

She climbed aboard when they were a mile or two from the Palace. The plan was simple: once they entered the city, she would hide below deck. Cyrus and Catalina would alert her with a code word after the shipping crates were unloaded and it was safe to come out.

That was the plan.

But they were still half a mile from the Palace port when everything unraveled.

Palace officials surrounded their boat, informing Cyrus over the radio that an escort ship would direct them to a designated area at the loading dock.

"Bay, you have to jump now!" Cyrus said urgently once the call ended.

"No," Catalina cut in sharply. "They'll arrest anyone who jumps ship now. Bay, hide below deck. We'll stall. Let me think..." Her calm voice faltered for the first time. "How could we have been so stupid to take this boat?"

"What do you mean?" Bay asked, her voice unsteady.

"They impounded the *Contessa* for weeks after you escaped. Of course, they flagged it. We must have been under suspicion before we even left for the Pacific Palace. Especially with you still missing. I should have seen this."

"I have an idea," Bay called out and bolted below deck.

The boat stopped. Footsteps thudded above as guards boarded. Bay scrambled past the kitchen, through the red door and rifled through Catalina's clothes until she found a long, royal-blue dress. It was too fine for daily wear, clearly the nicest one Catalina owned. It hung several inches too long, pooling around Bay like the sea itself. Fighting the rising urge to flee into the water, Bay steadied herself and made a wish.

The dress tightened around her shifting form, adjusting to new curves and added height. Her legs stretched longer, her face sharper. She had become someone else.

At the foot of the stairs, she paused, took one slow breath, and climbed to the top deck.

Palace guards stood around Catalina and Cyrus. One questioned them while the others rifled through crates.

I wish to sound like the Queen, Bay thought, swallowing down a wave of nausea as Darkness stirred and taste of metallic blood filled her mouth.

She stepped forward and fixed her gaze on the nearest guard. "Do I answer to you now?" she asked, her voice sharp and cold. It was Allura's voice.

The guard paled. "No, Your Majesty. It's just that you told us to look out for this vessel and—"

"And now you know why," Bay said. "I was traveling aboard it. This is a confidential mission. I trust you will keep it that way."

"Yes, Your Majesty," she stammered, bowing quickly.

Another guard stepped forward. "And what should we do with the ship and its crew?"

Bay hesitated only a second. "Escort them back to Avalon," she said, forcing her voice to remain calm even as panic clawed at her chest.

"No!" Cyrus shouted.

Catalina grabbed his arm and held him back.

"Do you defy your Queen, boy?" one guard barked.

Please, Cyrus, Bay thought fiercely. *I need to know you're both safe. This is the only way.*

"As I said," Bay repeated, "escort them to Avalon. Speak with the dock manager. These two will never pay another coin for dock space again. They performed a service for me tonight and are to be rewarded. That is a royal favor."

"Yes, Your Majesty."

Bay nodded. "Well, what are you waiting for? Go."

The guards obeyed. The *Contessa* began to pull away.

Bay turned sharply but not before catching one last glimpse of Catalina's pale, stunned face, and Cyrus's expression twisted with rage and heartbreak. She wanted to run to them. To take it back. To beg them to stay.

But if she did, she might not live to see the morning.

"Goodbye," she said softly. It was formal. Controlled. The only kindness she had left to give.

She climbed aboard the patrol vessel.

Rigid and silent, she watched the *Contessa* vanish into the horizon, her body aching for the sea, tears slipping down her cheeks. She didn't wipe them away.

A thought surfaced, sharp and unwelcome.

When they were little, Izzy swore that goodbyes were bad luck. That they made things disappear. First the goldfish. Then the hamster.

Bay had always smiled at the memory. But now, the words felt heavier. Like they might stick.

She hugged her arms to her chest.

When the vessel reached the main wharf, a Palace guard rushed up to meet her.

"Your Majesty, you are needed at once. We're to take the elevator down to the Palace."

Bay blinked, unsure where the elevator would lead, but guessed it was a dry, underground passage, something Allura would have designed to avoid the sea.

She couldn't. Not now. Not when every nerve screamed for water.

"I think we should swim down," Bay said coolly, fixing the guard with a gaze that dared him to question her.

The guards hesitated, but orders were orders. They jumped in, awkward and armored.

Bay dove after them.

The instant the ocean swallowed her, the chill of the saltwater rushed over her skin, a balm to every aching thought. She let herself sink deeper into the dark.

She didn't know if she would ever swim back out again.

CHAPTER FIFTY-FOUR

The Cost of the Bond

The tide shifted beneath the *Contessa*'s sleek hull, sending ripples across the surface like a whispered warning. Her sails strained against the wind, taut and gleaming in the fading light. From his small, weather-worn vessel hidden among the craggy folds of the coastline, Trent raised a spyglass, the chilled glass pressing into the deep lines of his palm as he searched the horizon.

They had her.

The Queen's armada was subtle when it wanted to be. There were no banners snapping in the wind, no full regalia. But Trent recognized the glint of their markings. The formation was too organized, too silent. Three warships flanked the merchant vessel like wolves guarding a lamb. And that lamb, the *Contessa*, was being herded back toward Avalon Cove.

He exhaled slowly, lowering the glass. His heart beat a steady rhythm in his chest, not out of fear but from the brutal urgency that had lodged itself in his veins. It had been months of this: chasing shadows, piecing together half-truths and fragments like a mosaic without a guide. But each step, each rumor, had brought him closer.

Bay had been aboard that ship. He had pieced it together slowly, stitching together truth from scraps. There had been rumors of a human girl traveling along the coast and the Queen searching for her. Then, more recent whispers: sightings in some of the mer-towns, a near-capture at Crystal Cove. She was accompanied by two others near her age, a boy and a girl.

He hadn't caught their names, only fragments. They moved together like a family, but Trent had learned long ago that appearances meant nothing in matters of survival.

Bay was with them or else had been. And now, as the Contessa drifted under the control of the Queen's ships, he could feel the sands of time shifting beneath his feet. The moment was slipping past. Every breath, every heartbeat, carried her farther from his reach.

Trent turned the wheel of his helm sharply, adjusting course. The old boat creaked under the pressure, the wood singing in protest. He needed to stay close without drawing attention. He needed to think. He needed to act. He paced the deck slowly, letting the salt spray sting his face and clear the noise in his head.

He couldn't storm the armada. Not alone, not without raising a war he couldn't win. No, he had to be smarter. If Bay was not aboard, then the boy and girl were still his only lead. He had to find them. Question them. Extract whatever truth they held.

Should he come to them as a friend, a tired sailor offering safe harbor, a hand extended in quiet hope? Or as something else, something harder? A grieving father, stripped raw by months of loss, desperate for a glimpse of the daughter taken from him? Perhaps the better path was colder, one that cast him as a force they could not ignore. Sharp-edged. Demanding.

Relentless. A thug who would make them talk. Make them see they had no choice.

Of course, he didn't know them. Not yet. He didn't know where their loyalties might lie. They could be servants of the Queen, or they could be fragments of Bay's fragile rebellion. There was no way to tell whether they would fight him, run from him, or recognize him as an ally.

The truth that troubled him most was simpler still. He didn't even know if they knew enough about his daughter to be worth the risk.

Leaning over the railing, he stared into the roiling waters below. His reflection stared back, fragmented by the waves. Silver threaded through his dark beard now. Fine lines cut deeper into the corners of his eyes. The slow encroachment of time. He was aging again. The bond was broken.

Once, he had been a young man with the world ahead of him—headstrong, bright-eyed, beloved by a family who dreamed he would carry on their legacy. A family of fishermen, shipwrights, and coastal traders. Salt-of-the-earth people, bound by tides and promises.

He had met her on a deserted shore, where the coral reefs bled color into the waves and the air hummed with sea sounds. Allura. The first time he saw her, she had been standing on the rocks, her hair whipping around her like a banner, her eyes like twin stars burning through the mist. She had not belonged to the world he knew. She was too radiant, too terrifying, too utterly beyond reach.

And yet, the moment their eyes met, he had felt it. The pull. Socius Animae: the soul bond. It had ignited inside of him like a flare. Bright, raw, undeniable. His blood had answered hers; his spirit bent toward hers.

He had tried to resist it. Had tried to reason, to anchor himself to the world he knew. But nothing—not duty, not family, not fear—could sever what had been woven into the marrow of his bones.

Loving her had cost him everything.

As the bond deepened, time slowed its relentless advance. His sisters grew older while he remained unchanged. His parents watched with silent, mounting dread as the seasons carved deeper lines into their faces but left his untouched.

At first, he lied. Said he traveled often and said the sea weathered him differently. Anything to explain the impossible. But lies rot from the inside out. When questions became accusations, he vanished for years at a time. And, when he returned, his father, who had once been a man of warmth and bluster, had become cold, brittle, and wary.

When Bay was born, it only deepened the rift. Even as a child, she had an otherness about her, a brightness too sharp, too knowing. His father had kept his distance, offering stiff nods where embraces should have been and silence where lullabies might have lived. He hadn't hated her; he had been afraid. Afraid of what his son had become and of what his granddaughter represented.

Trent had buried the hurt deep, telling himself it didn't matter. To have Allura's hand in his, Allura's love, was worth the hollowing out of the life he had once known. Their love had been both preternatural and supernatural...Gods help him, it had been.

A gull cried overhead, its sharp call cutting through the haze of thought and pulling Trent back to the present. He straightened and adjusted the wheel, narrowing his eyes as the *Contessa* and her escorts shrank into the southern horizon. They were slipping away, but he would catch them. He would find the boy and the girl, and through them, he would find Bay, even if she came to hate him for it.

Her birthday was drawing near, a date that pressed on his chest with quiet urgency. He had to reach her first, before Allura crossed a line that could never be undone, before she did something he could never forgive.

He flexed his hands on the wheel, feeling the old ache in his joints, the ache of time reclaimed, of a life resumed. Graying hair, aging skin, a body that tired more easily than it once had. He welcomed every sign of it. This was the price of a father's love: the cost of his youth, his bond, his connection to the strange and beautiful world he had once known. And he would pay it a thousand times over if it meant saving Bay.

The horizon swallowed the last of the ships, leaving only the restless sea stretching out ahead. Trent smiled grimly into the wind. He had given up everything once for love. Now he stood here again, proving that a man can make the same mistake twice.

But he would not lose her now.

CHAPTER FIFTY-FIVE

The Return

You think this changes my mind because you came back?" Allura asked, one brow arched.

Bay stared at her silently, hoping it would. From the way she had been ushered directly to Allura's private chambers, Bay could tell that the Queen preferred to keep the dealings with her hidden. The guards had been dismissed, and Allura entered alone through a secret door. She had immediately instructed Bay to return to her original form, likely to avoid confusion or gossip among the staff who might be startled to see two Alluras in the same room.

Bay tried to explain why she was there and that she was trying to do what was in everyone's best interest.

"You went to the Sea Witch?" Allura asked. When Bay nodded, she continued. "And did you find out what you are?"

"Yes," Bay said softly.

"The monster you are?" Allura asked.

"Yes...but that's why I'm here! The Sea Witch said there's a spell I could try... But to perform it, I needed to be close to you. Close to my birth mother," Bay said.

"I am not your mother." Allura corrected coldly. The disgust in her eyes cut like a knife.

Given the Queen's disposition, Bay decided to get right to the point. "Look, Atlantis may need your blood to live."

"You are lying to save your life." Allura accused.

"If I was trying to save my life, why would I come here? The Sea Witch made it clear to you years ago; you are the only one who can kill me. And it must be done after tonight, after our sixteenth birthday. Before I reach the sea again."

"This is a trick by the Sea Witch or you to dethrone me and take my kingdom."

Bay tried reasoning with her; it was like talking to a cold stone wall. "The Sea Witch wants me dead, too, remember? She said only you could kill me. That's why you asked her if there was a way to lift the curse and save your daughter."

"Yes, and she told me 'no'," Allura said coldly.

"No, she said she was powerless to stop it. She said only you could kill me. She couldn't kill me herself, even though she wanted to."

"Your own mother wanted you dead," Allura said slowly and deliberately. "Doesn't that tell you what kind of monsters you are? The only solace I have is that I will kill one of you."

Bay closed her eyes, searching for strength, for her little light, for Atlantis. Allura's words didn't just wound her. They crushed her. More than that, she couldn't find a way to make Allura believe her. Darkness was rising inside her, creeping up her legs like a slow tide. Tonight, she would either take the life of an innocent girl or lose her own to the separation. There was no path forward that didn't end in loss.

She didn't even have her past to cling to anymore. The love she thought had belonged to her wasn't truly hers. Her father's love hadn't been for her. She had stolen it. The cold moved into her stomach as the realization settled fully: she was utterly alone.

Her body folded in on itself, arms clutching her middle. She needed the water. The ocean. The pull of it still clawed at her, wild and relentless, driving her to the edge of reason. Too many things were threatening to tear her apart: the rising cold, the numbing grief, and the sharp, unrelenting pain of rejection.

Then something stirred inside her.

You are not alone, Bay.

Atlantis? Was it really her or just wishful thinking? Bay didn't know. She straightened resolutely. "I am trying to do the right thing."

"Do you think I care what you are trying to do?" Allura interrupted.

Bay didn't answer. She knew she had taken Allura's family from her. In truth, she would have felt the same way if their places were reversed. She hated herself for what she was doing to Atlantis too.

"Don't you understand?" Allura closed her eyes. "For you to be this kind, my daughter must have been so special. Every selfless act, every kind thought, is hers. It's her heart pumping love into your black soul. Every sweet thing you say tears at me all the more, because it isn't her. It's you. And you are fooling yourself into thinking you are anything but a hateful parasite that feeds on goodness and dissolves it. You are a cancer."

Bay silently absorbed the pain, knowing she deserved it.

"You took over her mind, her body... and now her soul," Allura whispered, the words heavy with exhaustion. "You took everything. The love of my life. My precious baby. All my joy. I should never have made that oath. If I had known the pain you would bring, I would have killed you that night."

Bay's hands trembled as Allura continued.

"But Trent was adamant. He wanted time with you, even if it was borrowed. He was afraid I might change my mind halfway through, that I would put my people first. And he was right. He knew me too well. He begged me to promise that I would not harm you until after your sixteenth birthday."

Bay almost laughed; a dry, bitter sound caught in her throat. The irony was cruel. Both of her mothers were bound by oaths that kept them from doing what they most wanted. Both were rendered helpless to hurt her. And both were desperate to do exactly that.

"When he fled, I knew he would never bring you back. He is so loving," Allura said, her voice almost gentle. "But I have powers of my own. I bound you to the ocean long ago. I enchanted you to return, no matter how hard he tried to keep you away. It cost me our bond. But the call would last until your sixteenth birthday."

Bay felt herself reel. Her obsession with the sea had never been natural at all. It had been a death sentence, carefully planned.

"I agreed not to steal those years from him," Allura said, her gaze like steel.

She looked into Allura's ocean eyes. They seemed to carry the weight of the world. Bay felt herself slipping into a hollow emptiness, the final cracks forming where hope used to live. She drew in a breath, steadying it. Her face hardened with resolve.

"Well, this is your only chance to get your family back," she said.

"If not, I will kill you," Allura said coldly, turning to leave.

You will kill me either way, Bay thought grimly as the guards bound her wrists and dragged her out.

CHAPTER FIFTY-SIX

The Weighted Oath

Allura had not wept in sixteen years. Not when Trent left. Not when her daughter vanished with him. Not even when the Sea Witch whispered, "There is no cure. Only the blade."

But tonight, as the moon reached its final hour, Allura felt the ache beneath her ribs swell and crash like surf. Still, no tears came. Underwater, it was hard to tell where the sea ended and sorrow began. The water accepted her like an old friend, as it always did. Her pink tail caught the moonlight in waves, trailing streamers of silken light behind her as she descended into the dark.

It was quiet, deeper down. Even the fish knew to keep their distance. The Hall of Tides lay beneath the western wing of the palace, where the reef grew black and the currents swirled with secrets. Allura swam through a long channel lit only by bioluminescent barnacles clinging to the stone, each glow a ghost of queens long past. No one came here by accident.

When she reached the entrance, she slowed, letting her fin settle her in place as the great arch rose before her. The doors had long since fallen to ruin, now replaced by living strands of sea-vine that parted for her with the slightest thought. The ocean knew its Queen.

Inside, everything was still. Columns of white coral stretched to a ceiling lost in murk, and stone statues floated half-buried in the shifting sands. Their faces were unreadable, some worn down by time, others simply unfinished, as though their sorrow had been too great to carve.

At the farthest wall, etched into a column of black reefstone polished smooth by centuries of current, were the words. The surface shimmered like deep glass.

Allura drifted forward, arms folded across her chest as though shielding herself from something colder than the water. Her wide, unblinking eyes found the first line. She had carved this herself. In another life. In another body, though still her own.

She whispered the title, "The Weighted Oath."

The sea caught her voice and carried it upward like smoke. There was no one to hear. Only the water. Only the silence.

Among her people, strength was sacred. They had no room for weakness. No patience for doubt. They were children of the sea, shaped by currents and storms. Bold in battle, unyielding in rule.

But here, in the hush beneath the palace, where no subjects watched and no expectations pressed in on her spine, Allura let herself be something else. A poet. A mourner. A woman who bled through words instead of wounds. Writing was the only place she could speak freely. The only place she was not a Queen.

The crown is not a circlet fair,
But grief wrapped tight in salted air.
It binds the brow, it seals the fate,
It weighs the heart beneath its weight.
I chose the sea. I chose the throne.
I chose the realm above my own.
No love is held without a cost—
For what I keep, I know I've lost.
The tide takes all, both blood and breath.
It favors law. It honors death.
So judge me not, if I must drown
The voice that cries beneath this crown.

She reached out and pressed her palm to the final line, where the words bled deepest into the coral. Her hand trembled.

To cry underwater was useless. No shimmer of grief, no streaks across her face. But mermaids knew how to grieve without weeping.

"Forgive me," she whispered to the words in stone. Not to the Sea Witch's daughter. Not to Trent. Not to her people. But to Atlantis. To her daughter, if any part of her still lived inside the shell. This was the only mercy left she could offer: beheading the demon to save the last piece of her child's soul from being consumed. Allura pressed her palm harder into the coral, anchoring herself to something she could not name.

Tomorrow, she would choose the crown again. Even if it cost her everything.

CHAPTER FIFTY-SEVEN

Blood

ock her in here and don't allow anyone out of this room, no matter what they look like. Do you understand?" Allura commanded the guards. The guards exchanged uneasy glances but nodded solemnly and took their positions outside Bay's cell, the weight of the Queen's warning settling over them like a fog.

Bay had been escorted out of Allura's watery chambers and into a landlocked holding cell above the Pacific Palace. It appeared to be meant for humans who had violated merfolk law. Though the small window was barred, the room was not desolate. It was far more accommodating than the deep cave cell she had been held in beneath the sea. It was almost cozy.

But it was above the ocean, and Bay's skin had already begun to dry out. The call of the water pulled at her with growing intensity. Each passing minute made it harder to resist; the ocean's will pressed against her own like a rising tide.

Bay knew she could not be in the ocean. Not after what might happen at midnight: she might consume Atlantis's soul or destroy Ceto. She had to avoid the water at all costs. But even her ears rang with pain now, the urge to submerge growing more powerful by the second. The enchantment would last until the end of her sixteenth birthday. She wasn't sure she would survive that long.

She cried out and collapsed to the cell floor.

"Please," she gasped. "Remove the enchantment. You have me."

"No," Allura said, looking down at her with unreadable eyes.

"Please! I need all my strength for this to work," Bay said through clenched teeth, her gaze locked on the Queen's face.

"No," Allura said again. She turned to the three guards and began issuing instructions, her voice steady and dismissive.

Bay watched them talk. Just as they were finishing their exchange, she steadied her breath, remembering Catalina's training. She forced herself to her feet.

"I will need your blood for the spell."

"No," Allura said a third time, already turning away, her steps silent as she headed for the exit.

"I can't do the spell without it!" Bay called out, her voice cracking with desperation. "Please, this is your only chance to get your daughter back. I can't hear her anymore!"

Allura paused at the door for a long moment.

"Bring me a vial," she said at last.

One of the guards left her post without question, jogging out of sight. She returned moments later and placed a slender glass cylinder into the Queen's waiting hand.

Allura pulled a golden hairpin out of her hair. When Bay saw that it was actually a small dagger, she gulped. Positioning the dagger against her index finger, the Queen pushed it into the skin without even a flinch. Red liquid poured into the vial. She filled it to the top and handed it to Bay. The guards, who could not hide their horror, stood at attention as Allura pulled a handkerchief out of her pocket and dried the spot before walking away again.

"Wait! I also need something that belongs to Atlantis. Something that's hers," Bay cried desperately.

Allura turned and stared at Bay with hatred burning in her eyes. "Besides her body, you mean?"

Bay met her gaze and nodded.

"You are wearing her necklace," she said, her voice low and sharp. Then she turned and walked away, each step deliberate, her posture unshaken.

Bay's hands slipped to her neck as she ran her fingers along the chain that hung there. Feeling for the soft, warm pulse of the Star of Isis. Clutching the necklace, she held it close, as if it could anchor her to something that still made sense.

Bay was now locked alone in the small room. She glanced around at its gray-blue walls, taking in the sparse furnishings: a wooden bed, a dresser with a small mirror, and a narrow open bathroom with a toilet and sink. A large wooden clock hung on one wall, its steady ticking loud in the stillness. Above the bed, a barred window framed a fading sky. She could just make out the night pushing against the last light of day.

She didn't have much time.

Bay sat on the bed and put the vial of blood on the small side table. She wanted to wish herself out of this cell and out of this Palace. She wanted to run away with every fiber of her being and escape from what she was becoming and what she had to do. But she did not wish for anything. She knew she needed to save all of her strength for the separation spell.

As she sat on the bed, Bay intended to think only about Atlantis and to try imagining her voice. But the call of the ocean kept crashing into her thoughts and disrupting her every effort. The pain of Allura's enchantment had never been this overwhelming. In fact, she could barely breathe. She had to use all of her willpower not to wish herself out of this room.

Her stomach gave a lurch, and she ran to the bathroom, throwing up from the pain. She sat with her face in the porcelain bowl, feeling tired and hopeless. She looked up at the clock and sobbed when she saw that it was only 7:45 p.m. "I can't do this!" she screamed in agony.

She took a deep breath, focused again, and thought of Atlantis. She fought the desire to jump into the water, but it kept coming back like a wave, over and over, crashing down on her. Ten o'clock. Ten-fifteen. Ten-thirty. She started staring at the second hand, following each little tick with her eyes.

Her thoughts ping-ponged back and forth. Even if she did wish herself out of this prison, what about the guards? Could she wish them away too? How powerful would she be after this? Was it worth trying to get to the ocean? *No,* she fought with herself, *think of Atlantis.* But she didn't even know if Atlantis was still alive.

Bay abandoned that line of thought and instead focused again on the clock, ignoring everything else. Finally, at 11:58 p.m., the fear and anxiousness filled her to an almost overwhelming breaking point. Two minutes. She could do this. She had to do this!

Twelve o'clock came, and, like a sudden relief, her desire to jump into the ocean was lifted. She breathed a heavy sigh of gratitude. But as if mocking her brief victory, a new sensation unfurled within her, a creeping, icy touch that slithered up her legs like smoke.

Darkness was coming.

Bay felt it, the weight of it, the seduction. It wasn't pain this time. It was hunger.

It was desire.

Darkness whispered, its voice velvet-smooth, wrapping around her like a silk noose:

You could have everything, Bay. Escape from this prison. Escape from Allura. Be free.

Her body tingled as the power rose into her chest, into her heart. She could feel it now, the staggering strength thrumming under her skin. She could break these walls apart. She could destroy Allura. For one terrible moment, she wanted to. But a thought, thin as a blade, sliced through the fever: *No. I don't want to kill her.*

Pain crashed into her like a tidal wave. Bay hit the floor, her body convulsing in agony.

Think of the pain she caused you, Darkness crooned. *The rejection. The betrayal. Don't you want her to pay?*

"No!" Bay gasped. But the agony only sharpened, driving her deeper into herself.

She abandoned you. She hated you. And still you want to protect her? Foolish, little girl. The fury that Darkness fanned inside her burned hotter, brighter, until her chest felt ready to split open.

Bay clung to one thought: those she loved. Dad. Cyrus. Catalina. Atlantis. If she gave in now, she would lose them all.

You are a queen among worms, Bay, Darkness coaxed, its voice low and rich with promise. *Now take it! No more weakness. No more pain.*

Bay faltered. She wanted it. The promise of power, of control, of never being hurt again.

But then, a voice cut through the roar, steady and pure: *You are not Darkness, Bay.*

"Atlantis," Bay choked out, a sob ripping from her throat. She felt her, still there, a single glowing thread buried deep in the heart of the storm.

I am here. I will always be here.

Tears blurred Bay's vision even as Darkness screamed in rage, clawing at her, trying to tear her apart from the inside out. "I can't do this, Atlantis," she whispered, her voice fractured.

Promise me you'll save yourself, Atlantis breathed, her presence thinning, her voice unraveling like mist. *Your true self. You don't have to become what they fear.*

Darkness surged, desperate now, shoving temptation against her skin, into her bones.

You will destroy everyone you love. You belong to the Sea!

"No," Bay whispered. And this time, her voice did not shake. She thought of Cyrus's reckless grin. Catalina's unwavering gaze. Trent's silent strength. She thought of Atlantis, her Atlantis, who had loved her when she couldn't even love herself.

With trembling hands, Bay snatched the vial of blood and held it before her.

"I wish to be separated!" she shouted into the night.

The blood began to bubble and hiss, spilling from the vial and pouring over her hands, hot and alive.

You don't know what you're doing!

She didn't answer aloud. Instead, she clung to the thought like a lifeline, repeating it silently, fiercely: *I wish to be separated.* Again, and again. She would not belong to Darkness. She would belong to herself, or she would belong to no one at all.

Darkness shrieked and battered against her. But Bay stood, shaking and bloodstained, refusing to kneel.

I am here, Bay. I am with you, Atlantis echoed.

Through the fire and the cold, Bay held on to that single, saving truth until her strength gave out at last. She fell toward the ground, the world spinning into darkness.

Warm hands caught her before she hit the floor. Weak and trembling, she looked up and found Allura's almond-shaped, crystal-blue eyes staring down at her, filled with unshed tears.

"I'm sorry," Bay whispered, her voice breaking. "I tried."

Blurred Lines

Do we cling to the bendable moods of our emotions
or glide along the steely straight paths of our minds,
or should we dance along the borders of both,
until we see blurred lines?
Who is this gatekeeper and how does he keep time,
can he give us the rhythm to unlock what we crave to find?
Are we plagued in a cloud of mist covering the clarity we seek,
or is there a way to be free of the bonds of our own forged realities?

CHAPTER FIFTY-EIGHT

Separation

Atlantis sat up shakily from the hard floor, her face swollen with tears, her chest tight with dread. She couldn't bring herself to look at Bay's lifeless body, the body that had once been hers too. The separation was a blur. She had been inside Bay, almost gone, nearly disappeared, and then suddenly, she was holding her. For a heartbeat, Bay had looked back at her. Atlantis had begged her to stay, willing her to wake. But Bay remained still.

Bay looked different now. Her black hair floated around her, and her lavender skin glowed faintly in the dim light. Her oval-shaped face was framed by bright pink lips that looked too still. She appeared thin, delicate, almost fragile.

And yet, Atlantis still knew her. Every piece. Even now.

She had felt the pull Bay had resisted. She had witnessed the hunger to grasp that unimaginable power with both hands and never let go. Atlantis wasn't sure she could have done the same. Maybe she would have given in, especially if it all ended like this.

Bay and Atlantis. Separated. Alone.

Atlantis, her name echoed in her mind like a half-remembered dream. Her. She. Who was Atlantis, really? She hadn't even known she existed until a few short weeks ago. For so long, she'd assumed she was something else. A whisper in the dark, a conscience, a memory of someone who once lived. A helper. A guide. Not…a person. The revelation felt like being yanked from the deep and flung onto shore. Blinking, gasping, barely formed. She hadn't lived. Not really. Not the way Bay had. Atlantis had missed an entire lifetime: never tasted food, never danced, never felt her hair tangled by the wind. She was an infant.

Even now, moving her limbs felt foreign. She sat awkwardly on the cold stone, terrified she might not even know how to walk. What if her knees buckled? What if she forgot how to breathe without Bay thinking the rhythm for them both?

What if I can't do this alone? The thought poured over her like a crashing wave. Atlantis began to hyperventilate.

"Why did you do this?" she cried suddenly, her voice breaking, cracking through the small room. "I told you this would happen! I told you to let it end me instead!"

Her voice collapsed into sobs. She crumpled into a corner of the cell, hugging her knees to her chest, rocking back and forth. The terror of being alone, *truly* alone for the first time, was a crushing weight. There was no hum of shared thought, no warmth of a twin presence. Just cold silence.

Bay's body remained still.

Atlantis's voice dropped to a whisper. "Come back," she pleaded. "Please. I need you."

CHAPTER FIFTY-NINE

The First Light

tlantis, Bay called out in her mind. There was no answer. She floated in darkness. A deep, endless cold gripped her, pulling her downward, away from light, away from breath. She fought against it, kicking and screaming, but no sound escaped her lips. Her body was numb, her thoughts slippery, dissolving into the void.

Is this dying? she thought distantly.

She wanted to hold on, to fight, but the cold was relentless. It clawed its way inside her, curling around her bones, seeping through her skin, and gnawing at the fragile spark that had once been her life-force.

She had lost. Atlantis was gone. And Bay was nothing.

The silence roared. Shapes flickered in the blackness around her, shadows that whispered. Their voices sounded familiar but warped, like echoes inside a broken shell.

You're dangerous.

You don't belong.

They were right to fear you.

The shadows circled closer, hissing lies that tasted like truths.

You should never have been born.

Bay wanted to scream, but her throat burned with cold. She clenched her fists, or thought she did. Maybe even her hands were gone now. Then came a flicker. A tiny, stubborn warmth sparked against her chest, like a firefly beneath her skin, so faint she almost didn't notice.

But it was there. Through the suffocating dark, a memory ignited, small but fierce. She was six years old, and she was screaming. The cold had found her then too. It had wrapped around her like chains, dragging her under into a place without names, without time. It wasn't just the cold of winter. It was a bone-deep, soul-freezing emptiness—something hollow and vast, something cruel.

She remembered crying out into the night, kicking off the blankets, and gasping for air. Her body had been warm, but her spirit felt frozen. She couldn't explain it. She didn't have the words. Then she heard footsteps. The door flung open, spilling golden light into the room. Arms wrapped around her, lifting her from the tangle of sheets and panic.

Her father, Trent. "It's okay, baby. I've got you," he whispered, rocking her against his chest. His voice shook with helpless fear.

"I can't—I can't breathe," she gasped between sobs, clutching the front of his shirt. He didn't try to explain, didn't tell her to stop crying; he just held her tighter. Bay could still feel the beat of his heart against her cheek. Steady. Strong. Safe.

After a long moment, he reached toward the nightstand and pulled out a small, worn box. The velvet was frayed at the corners. She hadn't noticed it before. He opened it carefully.

Inside, resting on a cushion of black silk, was a necklace. Star-shaped, with an aquamarine stone set into the center, it shimmered like shallow tropical water. The back bore an intricate engraving: a sea dragon coiled around a trident. The Star of Isis.

Trent's hands trembled slightly as he fastened it around her neck. "This," he said quietly, "was your mother's." His voice thickened with grief and mixed with something else. Hope, maybe. Or guilt. "She would want you to have it."

The moment the golden light graced her skin, Bay felt it. A pulse. A warmth. A flicker of light in the vast, crushing cold. Tiny at first. Fragile. Like the first star piercing a storm-drenched sky.

But it grew. Steady, comforting, alive. For the first time, the cold retreated. For the first time, Bay had felt *something else* inside her—a presence she couldn't name, but one that wrapped itself around her heart like a lifeline.

She remembered clutching the Star of Isis tightly, her sobs fading into hiccups. Trent had rocked her gently, whispering lullabies she barely heard.

Somewhere deep within her, in that fragile moment between fear and warmth, Light-Voice was born.

CHAPTER SIXTY

Awakening

Bay stirred. Her hand moved instinctively to her neck, searching for the familiar weight of the Star of Isis. A steady pulse of warmth answered her, vibrating softly against her fingertips, like a heartbeat she remembered from long ago—the first light that had ever saved her.

Comforted, Bay opened her eyes and looked around, then froze. In the corner sat a girl who looked exactly like her. Not a reflection. Not a memory. Her.

Am I dead? she thought.

She no longer felt the painful pull of the ocean nor the agony of Darkness clawing at her soul. It was surreal, seeing the girl who had stared back at her in the mirror for sixteen years. But that wasn't her anymore. That girl, with long blonde hair, a heart-shaped face, rosy cheeks, and a button nose, was Atlantis now.

Everything about her was nearly the same—except for the golden ringlets that framed her face and the almond shape of her sky-blue eyes. Bay's eyes were round and black as night. Atlantis didn't look delicate or frail either; she stood taller, her frame stronger and healthier. Though something in the way she held herself was awkward, as if she weren't fully used to her body yet.

It must have been Atlantis she had seen holding her, not Allura. Bay flexed her fingers, her body tired and sore. She wondered what she looked like now, who she had become.

"Um... I guess I owe you an apology?" she said, her voice uncertain.

Atlantis jumped to her feet, but she moved too quickly. Her legs gave out, and she stumbled backward, nearly hitting the wall. Pressing herself flat against it, she breathed heavily, her hands trembling.

Bay's heart twisted. "Are you okay?" she asked softly, rising to help, but Atlantis nodded her head, wide-eyed.

"I—I'm fine," Atlantis said, though her body shook faintly at the edges, like a mirage straining to stay together. She slid slowly down the wall until she was sitting with her knees pulled up to her chest.

Bay knelt beside her. "I never meant to... I didn't know... I'm so sorry," Bay whispered, dropping her gaze to the floor.

She had saved Atlantis, she had done what she set out to do. But she hadn't expected to survive it herself. Now that she had, she knew Allura would still want her dead. And, judging by the fear in Atlantis's eyes, maybe Atlantis did too. Darkness stirred in the corners of Bay's mind, feeding off her fear.

Atlantis, still trembling, inched forward, then leaned in and placed her forehead against Bay's. Bay closed her eyes, breathing in the quiet peace between them. Darkness faltered, retreating. They drew apart, and Atlantis wrapped her arms around Bay, who melted into her embrace, feeling acceptance for the first time in what felt like forever.

"But, don't you hate me?" Bay whimpered.

"You're alive," Atlantis said gently, still clinging to her. "I lived in you. I felt every tear, every heartbreak, every hope. I could never hate you. That would be like hating myself."

"But I'm not you," Bay said, pulling away. "I stole your body... I almost consumed you!"

"You had no choice," Atlantis said. "And when you could choose, you chose to save me, even when you thought it would kill you."

"Only because of your heart," Bay argued.

Atlantis smiled faintly. "I know you, Bay. I've lived with you. You have goodness too. I love you."

Bay collapsed again, sobbing into Atlantis's arms.

"Feels like I just woke up," Atlantis said. "Like my life was a blur. But I remember bits and pieces. I remember you. I remember fighting Darkness, and you fighting it with me."

Even as she spoke, Bay felt her own light pushing back against Darkness, reducing it once more to a mist.

Atlantis lifted Bay's chin, forcing her to meet her gaze. "I'm scared too," she whispered. "Scared to be apart from you. Scared to live on my own."

Bay gently pushed Atlantis's blonde hair out of her face. "I loved your happy voice in my head. Your stubbornness. Your faith in me. You're far more impressive than your mother could ever imagine."

Atlantis's smile wavered. "My body still doesn't feel like mine," she admitted quietly. "It's like I have to think every step into place. Even breathing takes effort. I didn't realize how much of that you were doing for me."

Bay's concern deepened. "That sounds exhausting. Are you okay?"

"I think I will be. I just... need to figure this whole thing out."

Bay reached out and took her hand. "Here, I'll show you."

Atlantis hesitated, then nodded. Bay steadied her as they rose together, feeling the slight weight of Atlantis leaning into her. When Atlantis stood on her own, she offered Bay a quiet smile. Bay slipped the Star of Isis from her neck and fastened it gently around Atlantis's. The aquamarine gem pulsed between them, a steady heartbeat of shared light.

Atlantis gasped softly as the cool chain brushed her skin, then stilled as the warmth of the aquamarine gem bloomed across her chest, steady and reassuring, familiar. The two clung to each other again, almost wishing themselves back together.

Suddenly, Allura stormed into the room, her eyes wide with disbelief. Her cool demeanor was stripped away.

"Let her go!" she ordered.

Bay dropped her arms immediately, but Atlantis clung tighter. Her grip was unsteady, trembling, but she didn't let go.

"No," Atlantis said, her voice quiet but resolute.

Allura stood in the doorway, chest heaving, eyes wild. But even as the fury burned in her gaze, she seemed to realize it didn't suit her. Her shoulders lifted with a breath, and when she spoke again, it was softer. Controlled.

"Atlantis," she said, extending a hand, "come to me. I must dispose of the demon."

"But you promised," Atlantis replied, her voice breaking. "You said if she kept me safe, you'd let her go."

"I would have said anything to get you back," Allura answered, and for a moment the edge returned to her tone. "Now come here. Please."

"No!" Atlantis shouted, stumbling as she tried to step in front of Bay. Her form flickered again, like a candle in the wind, but she held her ground. "I lived inside her for sixteen years. I know her. She's not evil."

Bay bowed her head. Her voice, when it came, was quiet. "Your mother's right, Atlantis. I didn't save you. You had to be saved from me." She swallowed hard, forcing herself to look at Allura. "But please. Let me live."

"Never," Allura said, her voice barely above a whisper now—but no less fierce. "I will not risk what remains of you."

Atlantis wavered where she stood, and Bay reached out instinctively to steady her. Still, Atlantis didn't move aside.

"If you hurt her," she said, barely able to stay upright, "I'll leave. Forever. I'll go live as a human. Without you."

Allura's face faltered, the fury drained from her expression, and for the first time, tears fell freely down her cheeks.

Atlantis moved slowly, unsteadily, across the room. When she reached her mother, she wrapped her arms around her, resting her head against Allura's shoulder. Bay watched in silence, heart aching.

"Bay is me," Atlantis said softly. "Closer than a sister. Part of me."

"She stole your childhood," Allura whispered.

"I'm sixteen. There's still time left," Atlantis replied with a tired smile. "And don't mermaids live to be, like a hundred?"

Allura sighed, her voice quieter now. "Fine. If she behaves, she can leave the town unharmed."

"No," Atlantis said, stepping closer to Bay. "She stays. With me."

"It's okay," Bay said softly, meeting Atlantis's eyes.

But Atlantis shook her head. "No," she said again, more firmly this time. "I need you."

Bay closed her eyes. I need you too, she thought, but the words caught in her throat and stayed there, unsaid.

Allura looked between them. For a long moment, she said nothing, but then she exhaled, tension unwinding from her posture like a slowly drawn bowstring. "Fine. She can stay."

A grin spread across Atlantis's face. "We'll say she's my twin sister."

"No one will believe it," Allura replied, the protest automatic.

Bay glanced down at herself and nearly gasped at the sight of her lavender arms. She turned toward the small mirror above the dresser. Her black hair was the only thing that still looked familiar. The rest of her—purple-hued skin, a leaner frame, a more angular face—felt like a stranger. She imagined she looked like a younger version of Ceto.

"We got this," Atlantis said, squeezing Bay's hand. "Bay, do your thing."

Bay smiled, but the edges of it wavered. She took a steadying breath and closed her eyes. Warmth flared beneath her skin as a shimmer of heat rippled through the air. The wish magic was still there, humming faintly beneath the surface, but it felt weaker now—muted. She wasn't sure how much remained or how long it would hold.

The transformation came slower than it had before the separation. The pain was heavier, deeper, but still she let it happen. Her form shifted gradually, her features softened, and her skin darkened to a golden bronze. Her straight black hair lengthened into long, shining waves that brushed her shoulders.

When Bay opened her eyes, a sharp breath caught in her throat. Pain flared for just a moment, barely visible, but she felt it deep in her chest. The taste of copper lingered, sharp and unsettling. Her fingers trembled. She stood still for a heartbeat longer than she meant to, then forced herself upright, finding her balance. The smile she gave Atlantis was real, but it took effort to hold.

They didn't look like mirror images. Atlantis was taller and more athletic, her wild blonde curls framing bright blue eyes. Bay stood beside her with sleek black waves and eyes dark as onyx. And yet, together, they looked like sisters.

Bay could feel it, the magic humming low and quiet in her body. Weaker now. Distant. The transformation had taken something from her, though she couldn't say what. Only that it was gone, and she wasn't sure how much more she had left to give.

CHAPTER SIXTY-ONE

A Kingdom's Weight

The wind that swept through the high chamber carried salt and the scent of a storm still hours away. Pale curtains fluttered like jellyfish tendrils around the arched windows, and the late afternoon light was diffused into an opalescent shimmer. The chamber was carved from coral and moonstone, elegant and ancient, like something that had always existed. It smelled faintly of sandalwood and sea kelp.

Atlantis sat stiffly on a cushioned bench, her shoulders bare in a gown she hadn't chosen, her legs too long for her to feel graceful. Her reflection in the tall bronze mirror startled her. Her skin had color now, not just light. Rosy undertones and freckles marked a face that didn't belong to Bay. Her hair, a wild, luminous halo of golden coils, fell around her face like seafoam gilded by the sun.

Allura stood behind her, brushing it gently, silently. The Queen's movements were practiced, her grip never too hard or too soft. The silver comb gleamed in her fingers. It was a tender moment, one that helped fill the pit of missing memories. Yet, awkwardness clung to them both. Neither knew how to step into this new bond as mother and daughter, princess and heir, or student and tutor.

There was another force to navigate. Atlantis debated whether she was brave enough to share her resolve with her mother. "I'm not going," Atlantis said at last, her voice barely above a whisper.

Allura paused. The brush hovered mid-stroke. "You must."

"I'm not ready."

"You are the daughter of a queen. You were born ready."

Atlantis turned to face her in the mirror, her eyes stormy and uncertain. "I wasn't born, Mother. I was made. Weeks ago."

Allura said nothing. Her face remained unreadable, lips pressed into a thin, practiced line.

"I can barely walk without wobbling," Atlantis continued. "I have to concentrate just to keep my shape. If I get overwhelmed, I can't keep upright. I'm not ready."

"You don't have to be perfect. You just have to show them you're strong."

Atlantis turned away, eyes burning. "I'm not strong. I'm scared. And none of this, not the dress, the crown, or the throne, feels real to me. Not yet. And you won't even look me in the eye long enough to ask how I feel. You haven't told me why…"

The brush stilled in Allura's hand.

"You chose your kingdom," Atlantis finished quietly.

"I asked," the Queen said tightly. "Every healer, every scholar, every wise woman in the kingdom. I went to the Oracle of the Cold Trench. I even tried to barter with the Sea Witch."

Atlantis turned.

For the first time, Allura's voice trembled. "She laughed. Said no curse that old could be lifted. That I needed to accept my fate. Either kill my child or watch her soul be devoured forever. Every path I took, every scroll I read, every vision I begged for led me to the same truth. Only her daughter lives. Or both must die."

Silence settled in the chamber like mist.

"You still chose your kingdom," Atlantis whispered.

"I chose my duty," Allura said, a sudden sharpness to her tone. "Because a queen who puts a hopeless cause over an entire people condemns them all."

The words sliced through Atlantis's chest. "I understand why you saved the kingdom. It hurts, but I understand," she said. "I'm angry you never once asked what it felt like. What it's been like to be nothing for sixteen years. To not know I existed. To wake up and not even know how to hold a spoon. I'm angry you didn't even want to let me exist for those sixteen years. Couldn't you have tried to love us both like Dad did?"

Allura lowered the brush.

Atlantis's voice cracked as she added, "And Bay, you haven't even tried to thank her."

Allura's face hardened. "She is dangerous."

"She saved me. Don't you think that counts for something?"

"She didn't do it for you. She did it because she did not want to become what she was made to be. That doesn't make her safe."

Atlantis rose from the bench, unsteady but proud. Her form flickered briefly, a shimmer of uncertainty in her outline. She clenched her fists, and it solidified again.

"You think you're protecting the kingdom," she said. "But sometimes I wonder if you're just protecting yourself. From guilt. From grief. From ever having to admit that the daughter you were meant to have was buried alive inside someone you condemned."

Allura's hand gripped the brush so tightly the silver teeth bent. "I am a queen," she said, but this time it wasn't to Atlantis, it was to herself.

"And I'm a girl who's just trying to learn how to exist," Atlantis said softly. She turned and walked toward the door, each step steadier than the last.

Behind her, Allura didn't follow. She stood frozen in place, her eyes stinging as she looked down at the strands of golden hair tangled in the brush. Hair from a daughter she had never had the chance to raise, and perhaps never would.

CHAPTER SIXTY-TWO

Before the Curtain Rises

The ocean wind rattled the panes in Atlantis's bedroom windows, carrying the scent of salt and jasmine up from the courtyard gardens. The sun was beginning its slow descent beyond the horizon, casting golden-orange light through the curved glass, making the coral-inlaid walls glow like fire beneath her feet. Servants' footsteps echoed faintly in the distant hallways, and music drifted up from the lower ballroom, ceremonial and rehearsed, heavy with expectation.

Atlantis sat near the edge of her bed, her back straight, her palms flat against the silken quilt. Her formal gown, deep violet, with delicate pearl-threaded sleeves, hung over a mannequin in the corner. The sight of it made her stomach churn. She hadn't cried yet, but she felt like she might. The emotions were bottling up too tightly inside her, pressing against her ribs, tangling in her throat.

They expected her to go downstairs tonight. To present herself as the princess thought long dead, now reborn, to a nation. She was supposed to smile, to be radiant, to make the people believe. Yet she didn't even know how to walk in heels without wobbling.

She turned toward the arched mirror across the room. Her reflection was still unsettling. Her features were her own now, with round cheeks and golden curls, but the eyes were too bright, too stormy. They held questions she didn't know how to answer, even to herself.

A faint shimmer formed on the wall near the bookshelf. A secret door, woven by wish magic, peeled open with a whisper and Bay slipped in quietly, barefoot and cloaked in moonlight.

"How are you doing?" she asked, closing the passage behind her. Her voice was low and cautious, not probing, just interested.

Atlantis didn't answer. She stood up too fast, pacing toward the center of the room. "I can't believe it's already tonight," she muttered. Then louder, almost to the ceiling: "I don't want to go." She threw herself backward onto the bed with a practiced dramatic flair, arms sprawled, hair fanning around her head like a golden storm cloud.

Bay raised an eyebrow but didn't smile. She walked over and sat beside her, moving with quiet care. She didn't rush to speak. She didn't offer advice. She just sat there, still and present, listening. And for the first time, Atlantis felt truly seen.

Atlantis exhaled sharply. "I mean, I know I should do it," she said. "It makes sense. I should introduce myself to my people and show a united family to the kingdom. Lead the appearance of strength. I just didn't know how hard emotions were. How they change everything. I haven't felt them this strong before. It used to be easier. Right and wrong were just facts. Not...clouds."

She closed her eyes, frustrated. "Now everything's rolled in fog. I feel too much. All the time. Excitement. Dread. Guilt. Hope. They don't stay in their lanes. It's like standing in a current when you can't swim."

Bay glanced sideways. "But didn't you feel things before?"

Atlantis opened her eyes. "Not like this. Not all at once. Before, it was more like...suggestions. A splash of warmth toward you. A knowing. But now? I feel hot. My palms sweat. My stomach flips. I want to run away and hug everyone at the same time. It's madness."

She sat up too quickly and started hyperventilating. "Maybe there's something wrong with me."

Bay gently reached over and took her hand. "That's normal," she said with a soft laugh. "Overwhelming, yes. But normal. You're not broken—you're just alive. And, hey, you're getting the physical control part down. That was a dramatic bed fall. Pretty believable."

Atlantis let out a breath that fell somewhere between panic and a laugh, then lay back down. She grabbed a pillow and smacked Bay with it. Bay caught it easily, grinning, then lay beside her on the bed, close enough that their shoulders touched.

"You know I'm here for you," Bay said. "Whatever you decide. I support you."

Atlantis stared at the ceiling for a moment. "Well, my— Allura won't."

Bay's brow furrowed. "She's your mom, Atlantis. You don't have to feel guilty calling her that. Not in front of me."

Atlantis looked away; her voice quiet. "It just doesn't feel fair. You don't have anyone."

Bay squeezed her hand again, steady and warm.

Atlantis turned her head toward her, eyes glimmering with something close to awe. "I'll do it," she said softly. "I'll make an appearance."

Atlantis looked down, then added, "Mom said if I go through with it, we can start the trip to Avalon Cove tomorrow." Her voice lifted slightly, a hopeful thread weaving through the nerves. "I'm so excited to see them again. Catalina, Cyrus. I think... I think it's also because Dad's there. And she can't wait to see him."

Bay closed her eyes, her voice a whisper. "Yeah. Probably."

"It'll be different with him, Bay. You know Dad. He'll accept you."

Bay didn't answer. She just gave a soft smile and pulled Atlantis into a hug. But the way her arms tightened and the slight shake in her breath told Atlantis there was something heavy lingering behind it. A worry Bay wasn't saying out loud.

Atlantis rested her head on Bay's shoulder. She didn't press. She didn't need to. Whatever storm Bay was carrying inside her, this moment and this safety would hold it together. At least for now.

CHAPTER SIXTY-THREE

The Crown Between Us

The ship cut through the sea in silence, its sails swollen with breathless wind. The stars overhead shimmered like forgotten oaths, and the moon's reflection trembled on the surface, pale and fractured. Allura stood at the bow, her back to the crew, eyes fixed on the black horizon that held Avalon Cove.

Allura's fingers curled against the carved rail. The ocean mist kissed her cheeks, but it did not cool the ache behind her eyes. She had not slept. There had been too much to weigh. Trent had been right. He had begged for time, pleaded for the impossible, to save the child, to fight the curse. She had called him a fool, weak, driven by heart instead of reason. Yet he had found a way. Not a clean way. Not a painless way. But a way that let Atlantis live.

He had risked everything to give their daughter a future. While she… She had prepared the execution blade. Her throat tightened. When he could not get her to listen to reason he had run away with their child. He had said nothing, but his silence thundered like a roar. And she had responded: the *Socius Animae* bond that bound them, she severed. That tether that had once made them more than lovers. More than rulers. They had been two halves of the same current, soul-bound, life-extended. She had felt his breath as her own. His pain as a whisper against her skin.

Until she no longer could.

He must be aging as a human again. Now, as the ship glided toward the cove, she wondered if he would speak to her at all. Would he still see the Queen? Or only the executioner who had nearly slain their child? Would he see the woman he once loved, or the stranger who could no longer feel his heartbeat in her chest?

Allura pressed a hand to her sternum, as if the memory of that rhythm might return. It didn't. She turned her gaze toward the stern, where Atlantis was likely resting. The girl had cried after the ball, not where anyone could see, of course, but Allura had heard it through the door. The stifled sobs, the gasping breath. It had struck something old and aching inside her.

Atlantis didn't understand yet. She didn't understand that mermaids were shaped by pressure, by the weight of the sea, the demands of rule, and the crushing tide of history. Strength wasn't a choice. It was survival.

Humans taught their daughters to feel. To spill. To weep. But the ocean taught them to endure. And queens? Queens were forged in silence. She had not meant to be cruel. But she had to show her daughter how to carry the crown without letting it shatter her spine.

Still, there had been a moment at the end of the ball when Atlantis stood beside her, upright, radiant, stubborn as coral, and Allura had felt it. Pride. Bone-deep, breathtaking pride. She had wanted to reach out and touch her daughter's cheek. To whisper, *You are more than I ever dared hope for.* But she had only nodded once.

A queen's mask. Even now, she wore it. The guards on deck saw only her stillness. The crew heard only the crisp commands. No one saw the fracture. But, for just this moment, in the hush of the ocean, she let the mask slip and closed her eyes.

She was tired. Not of ruling, never that, but of losing. She had lost her mate. Lost years. Lost the chance to be a mother without sharp edges. She had gained a daughter, yes. But not without cost.

Still, she would not trade Atlantis for anything. She was proud. And if her daughter ever grew strong enough to hold both love and duty at once, stronger than Allura had been, perhaps that would be her greatest legacy.

The moonlight brushed her shoulder like a memory. Allura straightened. The coast was closer now. She could hear the gulls. She would meet Trent again soon. The sun was rising. They would be there by morning.

For better or worse, they would stand, not as lovers, not as enemies, but as two people bound by the one thing stronger than fate: a child worth fighting for.

CHAPTER SIXTY-FOUR

Return to Avalon Cove

The ship creaked as it pulled into Avalon Cove, its hull cutting through water that shimmered beneath the rising sun. Sea birds called overhead, and the town slowly came into view, with small, crooked buildings that still looked more like coral reef on land than a town. It was the same as when Bay had first seen it a few months earlier. But everything was different now.

Allura stood tall at the bow, her royal colors rippling in the wind, with Atlantis beside her, radiant and visibly tense. The Queen's guards flanked them in quiet formation, but their presence only made the locals more curious. Word had traveled fast: the Queen of the Pacific was returning, and she wasn't alone.

Bay watched from a few paces back, her hood pulled low. She didn't want to draw attention. She just wanted to feel the dock beneath her feet again. To feel anything that reminded her of before. She had thought coming back here would give her closure. It didn't. She was still untethered. Still wondering where she belonged.

"Allura and Atlantis are anxious to reunite with Trent," Bay heard someone say, and her heart jumped. She had forgotten how easily people talked about things they didn't understand.

She didn't want to be part of the fanfare. She didn't want to interfere with the reunion that was rightfully theirs.

Still, when she stepped off the boat and smelled the salted wood and distant bakery sugar, a smile touched her lips. This town had been the beginning of everything. And, somehow, even now, it felt like a kind of home.

She caught sight of the dock landlord, Sumner, now overdressed in a pressed vest and pinched cravat, bowing awkwardly before the royal procession.

Bay stepped forward. "Oh, we've met already," she said lightly.

The man squinted. "I don't believe I've had the pleasure, Your High—"

"Are you sure?" she asked, lips curling. "You gave me quite the welcome the first time. Rent speech and all." His jaw dropped in slow realization, but Bay just swept past him as Allura raised an eyebrow. Atlantis giggled.

The sight of the *Contessa* waiting at the dock made Bay's breath catch. She hadn't realized how much she missed its silhouette, with its worn rails and patched sails. The boat had carried her away from everything, and somehow back to it again.

She and Atlantis glanced at each other.

Then they ran.

Cyrus and Catalina were already descending the gangplank. Atlantis reached them first, flinging herself into Cyrus's arms. Her laughter rang out, wild and unguarded. For a heartbeat, he stood frozen, arms half-raised in surprise. Then he gave in and held her tight, as if catching a memory they thought was lost.

Bay slowed. Her legs moved forward, but her heart stalled in her chest. She watched Cyrus's face as he pulled back from Atlantis—something about him had changed. The guarded sarcasm was still there, but it was thinner now, worn at the edges. He looked... relieved.

Then Catalina reached her.

"Bay?" Catalina's voice cracked as she stared into her eyes, searching for confirmation, no doubt looking for the deep onyx color she remembered. She had guessed correctly.

Bay nodded, her throat thick. "Hey," she whispered. "I missed you."

They folded into each other like two parts of the same whole, clinging tightly. The kind of hug that rewrote the space between them. Bay breathed in the familiar scent of salt and sea and lavender soap. Catalina's hand pressed between her shoulder blades, steady and certain.

"I couldn't have done it without you," Bay said, voice raw.

Catalina pulled back just enough to look at her, brushing hair from her cheek. "You did more than I ever could."

Atlantis was next, throwing her arms around Catalina with a squeal. "I've been dying to hug you," she laughed.

Cyrus stepped forward, lingering a few feet away from Bay. He scratched the back of his neck and looked everywhere but at her.

"Thanks," Bay said quietly, eyes lowered.

"Well," he muttered, shrugging, "you couldn't have done it without me, newb."

Bay smiled at that. She looked up and gave him a playful punch on the arm.

"Guess not."

He laughed. Just once, but it was real.

Then a voice cut across the dock.

"Atlantis!" Allura called.

"Is that the Queen?" Catalina whispered.

"Yup," Atlantis said, her voice proud. "That's my mom."

She turned to the others. "We're going to go see my dad."

She hugged Catalina again, tighter this time, then turned to Bay.

"Come with us?"

Bay hesitated. Her fingers curled against her palm.

"No," she said softly. "You should do this... for your mom."

Out of habit, Bay reached for her necklace, then stopped. It was gone. Returned. It now hung around Atlantis's neck. A hollow pang echoed in her chest.

"You got this," Bay said gently. "I'll meet you back at the hotel."

"All right," Atlantis replied, her voice low. She let go reluctantly, her gaze lingering on Bay, Catalina, and Cyrus, as if trying to hold them all in her memory at once.

Bay stood on the dock, watching her go. And for the first time in a long time, she didn't feel alone.

Not really.

CHAPTER SIXTY-FIVE

The Ones Who Waited

T̸he sun dipped low behind the cliffs of Avalon Cove, casting long amber streaks across the cobbled streets as Bay walked between Cyrus and Catalina. The town glowed in the soft light, its crooked rooftops and coral-hued buildings tinged with gold. Everything looked smaller than she remembered, quieter and gentler, as if the Cove itself were holding its breath to welcome them home.

They had spent the day aboard the *Contessa*, with Bay recounting everything: the strange twists of her adventure, the shock of being separated from Atlantis, and the slow process of getting to know her as someone new, yet deeply familiar. It still felt surreal, even now.

Bay hadn't dared to enter the ocean. The curse might have been broken, but she wasn't ready to test what still lingered beneath the surface. The pull was gone. That endless, aching call no longer whispered to her from the deep. And yet, she wasn't sure if what replaced it was peace or simply emptiness.

As evening fell, they left the docks behind, their footsteps echoing softly on the uneven stones. They made their way uphill toward the warm, flickering lights of the Sweet Cream Bakery. The scent of sugar and sea salt floated through the air, and shop windows gleamed with reflections of passing gulls and the last light of the setting sun.

The sea breeze picked up, cool and briny, tugging playfully at Bay's hair. She didn't stop it this time. She didn't pull her hood up or smooth it down. For the first time in what felt like forever, she let the wind touch her. No disguises. No spells. No fear of being recognized. She was just herself, walking in the open, between two people who had waited for her to come back.

A quiet smile pulled at her lips. She didn't need to hide anymore.

Inside, the scent of fresh dough and sugar wrapped around them like an embrace. They slid into a booth by the window, where condensation quickly fogged the glass. Plates began to stack with warm pastries sticky with fruit and buttery rolls drizzled with sea salt and honey.

Catalina ordered three rounds of pastries, lifting a brow when the server glanced at Bay and Cyrus. "It's all for me," she said seriously. Then cracked a grin.

They laughed. Loudly. The kind of laughter that curled into your ribs and lingered. The kind that said we made it. And for a while, they just sat there, warm and full, letting the moment settle between them.

When they stepped back into the night, the streets were quieter. The cove had stilled, the way it always did when the tide was calm and listening.

"Where are you staying?" Catalina asked as they walked.

"The Grand," Bay said. "With Atlantis."

Cyrus shifted beside her. "You can stay on the *Contessa* if you want."

Bay smiled. "Thanks. But I promised her I'd come back."

Cyrus glanced sideways at Catalina. "Don't you need to meet a customer?"

"What customer?" Catalina asked, far too innocently.

Cat, go! Cyrus said through their link.

Bay arched a brow. "Subtle," she muttered.

"Oh—right!" Catalina said brightly, clearly not fooling anyone. "Well. See you tomorrow!" She gave Bay a quick hug and all but jogged down the path.

Bay turned to Cyrus, amused. "You two really need to work on your coordination."

"We try," he said with a shrug.

Silence crept in between them, softer than awkward. His hand brushed hers.

"I didn't know what I would've done if you hadn't come back," he said.

Bay looked up, her heart thudding in her chest. "I missed you."

He laughed quietly. "You were the only thing I thought about."

Then his hand lifted, hesitant at first, and came to rest at the back of her neck. His thumb brushed her jaw, drifting to the corner of her mouth. Just enough to feel her breath. His fingers lingered a second longer than they needed to. Bay didn't move. She couldn't.

"Your eyes..." he whispered.

"I know," she said. "You were right. They were a giveaway."

He tilted her chin up. "They're endless."

Then he kissed her.

It was new, but it felt like something she'd been waiting for. Soft. Sure. A kiss that didn't ask her to be anything but herself. It didn't sweep her away; it brought her home. It was real.

When they pulled apart, Bay was still smiling. "If you still call me a newb, I'm leaving."

Cyrus grinned. "Noted."

From the hotel steps, a voice rang out. "You're back!"

Atlantis jogged toward them, her golden hair catching the moonlight. Cyrus stepped back quickly. Bay wiped her smile away, but not fast enough.

"Hey, Cyrus!" Atlantis chirped.

"Hi, Atlantis."

"Want to come in?" she asked.

"Uh, no. I was just saying goodbye to Bay. Gotta help Catalina with the boat."

"Well… we'll see you tomorrow?"

"Yeah. Definitely."

She hugged him. Bay couldn't help but notice that Atlantis lingered just a second longer than expected. Then she turned to Bay, her eyes bright. "Come on. I want to tell you everything."

Bay gave Cyrus a small wave and followed Atlantis inside. The hotel door closed behind them.

Cyrus stood there for a moment, alone on the quiet street. Then he smiled.

CHAPTER SIXTY-SIX

Where the Tide Rests

The Grand Hotel smelled like salt and polished wood. Bay walked its quiet halls alone, trailing her fingers along the carved trim. Her shoes made almost no sound on the thick coral-patterned rugs. The excitement of the day was fading now, replaced by a nervous energy she couldn't quite name.

What do you think... she started to ask, instinctively reaching inward.

But the space where Atlantis used to stir was quiet.

Bay blinked, her hand drifting to the place where her necklace used to rest. *Right*, she reminded herself. *They're not here.* Atlantis had gone to check in with Allura. Bay had promised she'd wait in their room.

Her steps slowed as she reached the door. Part of her didn't want to go in yet. Not because she was afraid, but because she wanted to hold the feeling from earlier just a little longer.

Catalina's arms wrapped around her like a promise. That laughter at the bakery, so normal, so unbreakable. Bay had missed her more than she'd let herself admit. It wasn't just a friendship; it was a bond soldered by everything they'd almost lost.

And Cyrus. That kiss.

Her hand touched her lips, almost unconsciously.

It hadn't been dramatic. It didn't need to be. It was grounding, steady. Like a door she hadn't known was locked had quietly opened. He had seen her, every version of her, and kissed her anyway.

Her chest ached, not with pain, but something close to longing. Even in all this comfort, a part of her still grieved. The small family she had grown up with had never truly been hers.

She exhaled and reached for the handle.

Quietly, she opened the door, expecting stillness. Instead, someone was there.

Trent. He rose from the edge of the bed, slowly, as though afraid to startle her.

"Oh. Sorry," Bay said, heart thudding. "Are you looking for Atlantis?"

"No," he said softly. "I was looking for you."

Bay froze.

"I was so worried about you," he said.

"You were?" Her voice was barely a whisper.

"Of course I was."

"But I'm not your daughter," Bay said, her voice breaking as tears streamed down her cheeks. The ones she had fought so hard to hold back were falling now, unchecked.

Trent didn't hesitate. He pulled her into a hug. "I thought I lost you," he whispered.

When he pulled back, he gently wiped tears from her face.

"You saved my life," she said, her voice shaking. "Allura wanted to kill me, and you took me in. You raised me."

"I knew there had to be a way," Trent said softly. "We just needed some time and a little luck. I hoped my love would be strong enough for my daughter to feel it—strong enough to encourage her to fight, to know love at least once. But then… I started to care about you too. I didn't know when the transition had happened, or even if it had. You were changing. And when you asked me to start calling you Bay… I knew."

Bay stared at him, lips parted.

"I could tell you weren't evil," he continued. "And you made it so easy to love you. I wasn't sure what I was getting myself into. I didn't know what you would be like. But there you were. A little girl who needed someone. Who needed her dad."

"That must have been so hard," Bay whispered.

"I was shocked by how natural it felt," he admitted, his voice softening as he took her hands in his. "You were just a child who needed me. And I needed you too."

Bay's voice trembled. "You're still my dad?"

"Always, Bay," he said. "You will always be my girl. One of them." He smiled. "And I'm so proud of you. For what you did. You saved your sister. You gave me back my family. You are incredible."

He pulled her close again, and this time she hugged him back—hard.

"Allura doesn't think so," Bay said quietly as she pulled away.

"Give her time. She's stubborn, but she has a good heart. She just needs to see you the way Atlantis and I do."

Bay turned at the sound of soft footsteps. Atlantis stood in the doorway, smiling through her own tears.

Bay motioned for her to come closer.

And when she did, the sisters wrapped each other in a long, quiet hug. It wasn't perfect. There were still questions, still things unsaid. But it was a beginning.

And as Bay held onto them, feeling Trent's warmth and Atlantis's arms around her, she considered something else Allura's hatred had once meant death. Now, it only meant distance.

That, at least, was progress.

Somewhere beyond the room, the tide whispered against the docks, the sea calm and still. But Bay knew better than to trust stillness. It never lasted. The ocean always shifted eventually.

She didn't know what the future held. She didn't know what it meant to be what she was now. Or what might still be growing inside her. But in that moment, in that room, she felt something she had never truly felt before.

She felt whole.

If the ocean came calling again, if the Sea Witch's shadow returned or the tide began to pull at her blood, she would face it. Not with fear, but with everything she had found. And with everything she refused to lose again.

She looked through the windowpane from between her loved ones' arms, staring out at the still water. The tide didn't rise. It breathed.

Acknowledgments

To Erik, my muse—thank you for your unwavering support and for enduring the clack of keys and the glow of the laptop late into the night. Thank you for calling me back from those far-off worlds and reminding me I was missed, too.

To my mom and Art, whose creative spirits filled our home with inspiration: watching you both dive into your passions taught me to believe in the beauty of ideas and the joy of bringing them to life. Dad, thank you for instilling in me a love of reading and storytelling from such a young age.

To my editors, Jacqueline, who nurtured my writing even in childhood, your thoughtful edits gave this story wings. Nis, your gift for pulling threads is nothing short of magical. You have a way of unraveling tangled words to reveal the story's true heart. Staci, thank you for not laughing at my earliest draft and instead offering constructive, kind guidance that taught me so much.

Sara and Sue, thank you for showing me that family isn't only what you're born into sometimes it's the people who make you feel most at home.

To my son, Miles, thank you for every nighttime wake-up that gifted me quiet hours to write. You've shaped this book in your own unexpected and beautiful way.

To my siblings, the whole wonderful, sprawling lot of you, thank you. Each lesson, each emotion, each storm we've weathered and wave we've ridden together has shaped me. Like the tides, you've helped me grow, drift, and find new horizons.

Riana, thank you for reading this story when it was still a whisper across a restless sea. Kris, thank you for every book you placed in my hands, each one launching me deeper into a love of fantasy. Kelly, your fearless approach to life taught me that true adventure begins the moment you leave the safety of the shore. Gibran, your bold spirit was a lighthouse in moments I needed courage most. You toughened me just right. Sara, thank you for letting me practice my (smothering) mothering skills and for meeting them with such patience and light.

To Jenny, whose artwork moves like tides, wild, stirring, and soulful. To James, whose laughter breaks through any stormy day. Faith, the perfect endnote in our family's song, thank you for your fierce honesty and heart. Hunter, your quiet nature is a steady current I'm grateful to know. Paul, your thoughtful silence carries the depth of stories untold. Tony, your violin drifts like a sea breeze, your music casting its own spell. And Friday, thank you for casting such a wide net. By sharing your dreams and passions, you've inspired me to build my own.

To each of you, my first ocean of inspiration, I am endlessly grateful.

About the Author

Freya Aguiar grew up surrounded by the sun, sand, and stories of Southern California, where her love for the ocean and fantasy adventures first took root.

Today, she lives in the beautiful Pacific Northwest with her husband, their three wonderful children, and plenty of daydreams yet to explore.

When she's not writing or reading, Freya enjoys hiking forest trails, drawing new worlds, and most of all, spending time as a proud mom.

Her stories are filled with magic, heart, and the quiet courage of those who dare to chase the tides of destiny.

Water Wishes: Book Two Coming Soon

The Pacific Kingdom is on the edge of unraveling. Rumors whisper through coral halls, secrets bubble to the surface, and the Sea Queens are watching.

Atlantis is trying to become the heir her people expect. She is learning how to lead, how to fight, and how to feel for the first time. But every time she opens her mouth, she is reminded that she was never meant to stand alone.

Bay is losing control. Her power is growing wild, her instincts sharper, and her place in the palace more dangerous by the day. When love complicates loyalty and the past refuses to stay buried, Bay must decide who she is becoming, and what she's willing to lose to protect them all.

Two sisters once shared a mind. Now, the kingdom may not survive what happens when they each choose their own path.